The clouds had moved over us, dark and threatening, and when we were halfway down the hill there came a sharp crack and rumble of thunder, though I hadn't seen a lightning flash.

I started the car and we sat waiting, and waiting.

"Damn," said Grace, climbing out and starting purposefully up the slope once more. I got out and watched her go, then, moved by some obscurely troubled impulse, went after her. I was almost to the terrace when I heard her cry, a high, keening sound, like the howl of a dog. I broke into a run, burst out onto the terrace, and followed the sound to my left.

There was a smell in the air, a gunpowder, firecracker smell. I struggled down the narrow rock alley, now inexplicably littered with stones, and came upon her where she crouched just outside the little niche the privy was in. Had been in. Now there was nothing there but a pile of stones and air thick with the smell of explosives. Of brother Ron there was no sign, no sign at all.

By A. J. Orde
Published by Fawcett Books:

DEATH AND THE DOGWALKER
DEATH FOR OLD TIMES' SAKE
A LITTLE NEIGHBORHOOD MURDER
DEAD ON SUNDAY
A LONG TIME DEAD

A LONG TIME DEAD

A. J. Orde

FAWCETT CREST • NEW YORK

A Fawcett Crest Book
Published by Ballantine Books
Copyright © 1995 by A. J. Orde

Library of Congress Catalog Card Number: 95-90027

ISBN 0-449-22359-0

Manufactured in the United States of America

First Edition: June 1995

10 9 8 7 6 5 4 3 2 1

A LONG TIME DEAD

one

I'D BEEN IN New Mexico, trying to find out who murdered the brother of an old friend of mine. Finding out, I should say, and wishing I hadn't.

The net result of the trip, so far as my personal life was concerned, was that I came back to Denver with the firm resolution to stop drifting, which I'd been doing a lot of lately, and get on with a life. Part of the life would be to resolve the on-again, off-again relationship Grace and I had settled into. We had to stop dithering over it. Our tentative this and tentative that, so I told myself between Santa Fe and Taos, between Taos and San Luis, between San Luis and Walsenberg, et al, had gone on long enough. We either did or we didn't. She either did or she didn't, and if she didn't, then time I moved on and . . . and something.

I shied away from the thought that she might call my bluff—if it was a bluff. When I summoned up the image of doing without her, unpleasant things happened to me. I choked. My stomach churned. I got a sick, unbalanced feeling somewhere behind the eyes. If that was just imagining, what would the reality be like? And that dilemma, of course, was just what had been stopping me for the last year or so. She couldn't quite bring herself to say yes, let's get married. I couldn't come any-

where near bringing myself to saying let's get married
or else. Still, we couldn't go on as we were, with her biological clock ticking toward nonreproductive midnight
and mine plodding toward the early elderlies. Well ...
later middle age.

I explained some of this to my assistant, Mark, first
thing Monday morning, over coffee, being both pontif-
ical and ponderous about it. I'd found myself doing that
a lot lately, sounding like a duffer, a gaffer, an old coot.
Mark was kind enough not to mention that fact as he
nodded understandingly.

"I think she's a little frightened of taking the step, Jason. She likes her work. She enjoys you. She does want
children, the way some women do want children, not as
a passion or justification, but as an experience. Not that
she wouldn't love them, she would, but she's not obsessed."

True. Grace was not obsessed by anything much. Not
money, not fame, not security. Her younger brother,
Ron, was probably an obsession with her. I had thought
so on occasion. And food, maybe. She had an enormous
appetite for food. Other than that, she usually seemed to
be a completely-in-control and self-sufficient person.
Where I fit in, I wasn't at all sure.

At any rate, on the seven-hour drive from northern
New Mexico, I'd resolved firmly that things had to be
brought to some kind of conclusion: marriage or else,
and I sat at my desk that morning, twiddling a pen and
looking into the distance as I rehearsed the speech I
would make that night, when Grace got home from the
cop shop. Grace is a plainclothes policeperson. She prefers "cop," actually.

"We've got two new clients," Mark announced,
breaking in on my reverie. "One of them needs to see

you today. Her name is Valerie French. She's about to be married, and she needs your help."

I found that ironic. "To get married?"

"I gather there are difficulties. She needs to see you."

I grunted. "This afternoon."

He trotted off to call Valerie French, and I set my musing aside in favor of clearing up the few odds and ends of Jason Lynx Interiors business that Mark hadn't taken care of in my absence, answering letters, completing files. Mark popped his head in to say the French woman would be over about one, so I neatened up my desk and put the messy piles of catalogs on the shelves, making ready for a client.

She arrived as though blown by the wind, hair tumbled, blouse partly untucked, skirt hitched a bit to one side as though she'd tugged at it impatiently. She dropped her purse to the floor, where it landed with a clunk, and dropped herself into the chair across from me. My first thought was that she was incredibly young, but then I noticed the tiny lines around the eyes, across the brow. She was thirtyish. She was also gorgeous, as a full-blown rose is gorgeous, in a totally uncontrolled way, as though she might start dropping petals on the carpet at any moment. She smelled wonderful, of no definable scent, exuding an air of freshness and delight. I grinned at her, caught myself grinning, and adopted a more sober manner.

I asked her what we could do for her.

She looked vaguely and uncomfortably toward the open door. I got up and closed it.

"I got your name from a friend of a friend," she said. "Somebody you did something for once. You helped him out of a dreadful mess."

"Who was this someone?"

She mentioned a name. I had helped him out of a dreadful mess. I nodded.

"I'm engaged to be married," she said, almost in a whisper. "To Espy Gryphon." She paused, waiting for comment.

"Is that the banking family?" I asked. "He's the only son, I believe."

She twisted her hands together. "We're terribly in love. We want to get married and have babies and do the whole thing, you know."

I frowned. "I'm not a premarital counselor."

"I know. I know just what you are. Oh, I don't mean that. I mean, I know just what you can do. You see, Espy's parents don't want him to marry me. He's two years younger than I am, and to hear them tell it, that makes me middle-aged. They want him to pick some girl just out of college, preferably an eastern college. From a moneyed family, of course."

I shook my head. "I still don't see. . . ."

"I'll tell you. So, Espy wants me to invite his parents to my place for dinner so they can get to know me better. He doesn't want it to be at their place, because he thinks I'd be at a disadvantage on their turf. That's how he says it. Anyhow, in a weak moment, I agreed. I told him I'd need to fix the place up a little first, so he gave me an engagement present." She heaved the purse into her lap and searched through it like a small dog digging for a bone. Eventually she found what she wanted, a slip of paper folded into quarters, slightly messed up with makeup stains. She handed it to me, and I unfolded it. It was a check for twenty thousand dollars.

"Will it be enough, do you think? I have a little of my own, but it won't add much."

"Enough for what?" I asked, trying to make sense of all this.

"Enough to redo my place, make it look as though I'm a fit mate for Espy. That I have taste. You know."

I gave her a long, level look. She blushed, bright red. "I know I don't," she cried. "I'm a biologist, not a fashion model. I don't even know what colors go together!"

I tapped my teeth with a pencil, thinking. "How big is your place?"

"It's just an apartment. Living room, dining area, kitchen, bedroom, bath. There's an extra room I use for an office."

"How is it furnished?"

She blushed again. "One of my friends says it's early Salvation Army. She meant it to be a joke, but it's almost true. It's just stuff I've picked up. None of it really fits together."

I liked her, her blushes, her honesty, her openness. Her looks, her smell. We talked. I asked her how long she could put off the putative in-laws, and she thought a couple of weeks. I told her I had to see the situation before deciding to take the job. She insisted on leaving the check with me. I told her I'd come see the apartment today. She flushed yet again and asked me to make it early the following week. She needed to straighten up first.

We left it at that. I told Mark about it when I gave him the check to put in the safe; we certainly wouldn't cash it until we'd decided what we were going to do. When he saw the signature on the check, his face changed, his mouth turned grim.

"She's beautiful," he said. "But very untidy."

"She is. Someone should take her in hand," I replied, wondering what was going on with Mark.

"Do you have itchy fingers? Does it occur to you that the Gryphons, son and parents, may be intending this as a test?"

The thought hadn't crossed my mind.

"You think Mom and Dad put him up to it? A conspiracy?"

"They may have convinced him he should see how she would spend money, if she had it."

An interesting idea. Mark, who comes from a very moneyed family, would know better than I what the class is capable of. He didn't pursue the question any further, nor did I. He had told me we had two new clients, but I thought I'd wait until he was in a better mood before asking who the second one was.

At about five o'clock, I stopped pretending to work and phoned Grace, knowing she'd be off duty and home. She answered the phone in a strange, wounded voice that was totally unlike her usual self.

Before I had a chance to tell her I was coming over for a serious talk, she said, "Jason, my idiot brother is on his way back to Denver." Then she began sobbing. I could guess why. There would be only a few reasons for Ron Willis to return to Denver from San Francisco: he was in trouble with the law; he was in some other kind of dangerous trouble; he was ill. If he was ill, there would be only one logical illness.

I had seen but never really met Ron, though Grace had told me about him—enough to make me dislike him. It wasn't that he was gay. Mark, my assistant, is gay, and that's fine with me. It wasn't that he took advantage of Grace. Younger siblings do that kind of thing and one either tolerates it or one doesn't. What annoyed me was his complete fecklessness, his total irresponsibility, as reported by Grace. He repeatedly got himself into trouble through sheer unwillingness to think things through, and this inevitably injured Grace, who always, despite all I could say to the contrary, blamed herself.

"What's the matter with him?" I asked her, already knowing the answer.

"He's sick," she whimpered. "I knew he'd get it sooner or later, Jason, I just knew it."

"AIDS," I said.

She wept. I murmured comforting words and told her I'd be over as soon as I could get there, though I did stop en route and pick up some deli odds and ends. From long experience with Grace, I knew the chances of her having food in the house were small. Food vanishes from her vicinity as though beamed up by extraterrestrials. Though she might not feel like eating, she would need to, for she hasn't an extra ounce to get by on between meals. Unlike me. I have about six or eight comfortable pounds pushing at my belt buckle. Enough that I have to suck it in before admiring the rest of myself in the full-length mirror on the bathroom door.

Grace's back door was open—a sure sign that she was seriously upset. Grace's experience as a cop makes her careful, as a normal rule. She usually locks up tight and demands to know who it is before opening doors. I locked the door behind me, dumped the stuff in the kitchen, and went looking for her. She was in the bathroom, washing her face in cold water, still crying.

"Oh, Jason," she said. "He's so . . . so stupid."

I agreed that he was stupid. If Grace could be believed, there wasn't a mean cell in the entire Ron organism, but the creature as a whole was barely functional. He was a floater. A jellyfish. One who went wherever the current took him. A bit of a sensualist. Rather vain. Fond of nice clothes (pretty clothes, Grace had said, blushing). With all the emotional stability of the average fifteen-year-old groupie at a rock concert. He supported himself, when he didn't get Grace to do it, by dishwashing, envelope stuffing, or any one of a host of other low-paying, repetitive jobs that could be done, more or less, by someone barely educated and partly stoned.

"The worst of it is, he's smart," she'd told me. "He got good grades in school. But by the time he graduated high school, he was in with this weird crowd."

"Grace, didn't he buy into some business out there in California?" I asked her both to get her talking and because I recalled buying some of Grace's grandma's furniture so she could send him the money.

"That's just what he told me," she murmured. "I think it was all a lie. I think he owed money to someone. For drugs, maybe."

"Gambling?"

"No. Ron was never into that much. He couldn't concentrate long enough to gamble. A few quarters in a slot machine was always his limit. But he could have bought drugs from someone and maybe not paid them. Or, more likely, he got in the middle, the way he always does." She put her head on my shoulder and wept. "Oh, Jason. If Mother were still alive, she'd be so sorrowful. She loved him so. It's such a lousy thing."

It was a lousy thing. Nothing I could say would make it any easier. So I said little, fed her the deli stuff I'd brought, sat on the couch with her, cuddling her while she cried. Eventually, she fell asleep, worn-out from her usual hard day plus the emotional wear and tear. I tucked a blanket around her and went on home. There was a message on the machine to call Mark.

"What was it?" he asked. "With Grace's brother?"

"He has AIDS," I told him.

"AIDS? Or just HIV?"

"The full-blown thing, Mark. And, of course, no medical insurance of any kind."

"Damn," he said. "That poor kid!"

"Grace? Or her brother?"

"Both, actually, though I wouldn't call Grace a kid. She's as adult as they come. No, I meant him. He's probably a type, you know—the gay equivalent of a chorus girl. The pretty thing with good legs who doesn't have one brain in her lovely head. The one who's terribly surprised when she ends up pregnant. You know the type."

"Well, actually, Mark, I haven't had the pleasure. I know the stereotype, if that's what you mean."

"That's exactly what I mean. He's probably girlish. As opposed to womanly. Giggly and silly and totally self-centered. Stuck forever in emotional adolescence."

It was what I'd been thinking. "I'm afraid you may be right."

"So what's he going to do?"

"He claims to be unable to work. He can't keep his mind on anything enough to work, so he tells Grace. He's coming back here so she can take care of him."

"You didn't ask her about . . . you know?" Mark avoided the word "marriage" whenever possible. A couple of years ago Mark's longtime relationship had been ended by his lover's going back into the closet and marrying, for family's sake. Though Mark had since found someone else, it still rankled.

"It hardly seemed the time to mention it," I replied.

"Not really." A long pause. "If I can be any help, let me know, Jason. He might listen to me where he wouldn't to either of you."

I thanked him and hung up. He was right, so far as it went. Ron might listen to Mark where he wouldn't listen to me, but it was a little late for listening to do any good. I spent half a minute cursing at things in general, enough to bring the animals to the door of my bedroom to see what was going on. Schnitz wandered back and forth under Bela's chin, his tail brushing the big dog's nose. Bela feinted in the cat's direction; the cat hissed and batted at him; Bela grinned.

"You two clowns," I said. "Time for dinner."

I'd had enough to eat at Grace's, but I made a short pot of coffee and drank two cups of it to keep the animals company, meantime fretting about the timetable of coming events. Once people had AIDS, how long did it go on? And, if it was some time, should I push Grace on the marriage question? Should I even mention it? On the one hand, it might be good for Grace to have other real family, me, to be interested in. One of the reasons she wanted to marry was to have children, and if I didn't pursue the question now, it might end up being too late. On the other hand, given Ron's situation, she might feel she didn't have the energy to spare for marriage, much less children. Anything I did or said might seem unfeeling. Even thinking about it seemed unfeeling!

No way to know or decide in advance. The only thing I could do was wait to see what happened and try to figure out how she felt about it.

Tuesday morning, fate took a hand in the guise of a large, strong-jawed woman whom I had known for a year or so: Amelia Wirtz, friend of Mark's family and mine, attorney-at-law, well-to-do, sure of herself, but nonetheless seeking assistance for which, she said, she would pay extremely well.

"I am planning my retirement," she said, after shutting the door in Mark's curious face and plumping herself down in the chair across from me. "From the practice of law, that is. However, I do not want to retire from the practice of life. I have made a good deal of money in my career, and my father left me more than any human being needs. Since I have not kit nor kinder, I see it as time to invest in the future of our world or to buy myself into heaven, one or both."

"What do you have in mind, Amelia?"

"I'm thinking of starting a think tank. An institute."

"For what purpose?"

"For the study of environmental law."

I was confused. "Why?"

She settled herself, looked me straight in the eye, and gave me an obviously well-rehearsed speech:

"Because I am concerned at what is happening to the world. Because most of our laws were originally formulated to foster exploitation in a frontier society. We desired to encourage settlement, development, or business. Even today, any effort to control exploitation of the environment is castigated on the basis that it costs jobs. We can't charge ranchers higher grazing fees, it'll cost jobs. We can't stop cutting down trees, it'll cost jobs. We can't stop polluting the earth, it'll cost jobs. The birth of a hundred thousand more babies anywhere in the world takes precedence over any attempt to save the earth itself. Actually, you and I both know that the world cannot support and provide work for an infinitely increasing human population. That is truth which, though evident to virtually everyone, has not yet been built into law, and every time we apply old laws to the new situation, we make things worse.

"I'm interested in asking the question how can the

law be structured to foster reduced human population and an improved environment? I want to start an institute to consider the matter."

I thought it likely she had this prologue written down somewhere, perhaps as the introduction to a prospectus. "Ambitious," I murmured. "Expensive."

"Very. I visualize a place on some property I own up above Dumont, toward the Arapahoe National Forest. I've had it for years. I've gone camping up there for the last thirty-some-odd years, whenever the weather's good and I've had the time. I want to build a place where from twenty to fifty people can gather and live for some days or weeks at a time. A place designed to take advantage of recent and impending communications breakthroughs. Computer links to libraries around the world. A resident staff to attend to the care and feeding of the participants. Perhaps we'll focus on lawyer-legislators, those few who think with their minds instead of their wallets. I want a place to which it will be an honor to be invited and a privilege to attend. I want an invitation to say something to the world at large. Something like, 'This person has been asked to be here because this person is incorruptible.' "

"You want an architect," I said. "And an archangel."

She laughed. "I don't know about the archangel. Of course we'll need an architect, but I also want someone who is accustomed to thinking in terms of creature comforts. Architects sometimes get so carried away by their vision they forget human attributes. They build monuments, not habitats. This place is to be special, Jason. I want to hire you to help make it that way."

I gulped, thinking furiously. "It will depend on your architect, Amelia. Some people might not want to work with me. They might question my interest or ability.

God knows I'm no expert in . . ." In anything she had in mind. I couldn't imagine why she'd come to me!

"I want you to pick the architect," she said. "Find someone you will be able to work with."

"Why me?" I asked, baffled. "Why not someone with more experience. More background."

"I've decided on you. My reasons are personal ones. You have no real reason to refuse. Mark virtually runs this place with little or no help from you. If the truth be known, it bores you. I knew that when you did the job for our law firm, Jason. I could see it all over you. A man going through the motions. Doing a thing not at all shabbily, but without any real enthusiasm. And then there was the matter of my old furniture."

I flushed uncomfortably and she gave me a foxy grin. Shortly after we'd finished the law-firm job, Amelia, a longtime widow, had decided to move from the large house she had lived in since her father's death to a smaller house, one easier to maintain. She'd asked me to appraise some of the pieces she wanted to sell, which I'd done, then she'd taken me upstairs, to the former servants' quarters, and asked if the furnishings in there were worth anything. Most of them were missing parts, many had been overpainted, but there were a few pieces that would probably restore well, and I'd offered her five thousand for the lot, which she accepted.

The pieces were delivered to the shop, and as we were unloading them I saw a maker's mark on the bottom of a painted desk-bookcase. Later that day I had shamefacedly called Amelia to tell her the piece was worth five times what I'd offered, even in its present condition, and worth ten times that when I got around to restoring it.

She'd laughed. "Found me an honest man and didn't

even need a lantern!" We'd agreed to split the proceeds when and if I sold the pieces.

Now, shaking my head, I asked, "Why in God's name were those pieces painted, Amelia? Who would have done such a thing?"

"I haven't any idea. I sort of remember that the little desk thingy was Mother's, but maybe it belonged to Father. He left the pieces to Uncle Maddox, but Uncle didn't want them. Have you done anything with them yet?"

I shook my head.

"See." She poked a finger at me. "You're just going through the motions. You need more challenge."

She uttered a few more simultaneously flattering and deflating words and then left me sitting there with both my mouth and the door to my cerebral attic open. She hadn't told me not to tell Mark, so I told Mark.

"My Lord," he murmured. "Now if that isn't something."

"Is she wealthy enough?" I asked. "Something like this costs real money, Mark. Millions."

"Oh, she has that. She's not ostentatious about it. Most of the income goes to charity and education."

"Income from what?"

"The Janet Epstein Foundation."

My jaw dropped yet again. Almost every time I watched public television, I saw that name among the donors who supported nature and conservation programming. "I had no idea."

"As I say, she doesn't talk about it a lot. Most of it was her daddy's and granddaddy's money. Old Man Wirtz and son Hector were into ranching, mining, and timber. If you find an overgrazed slope, an eroded mountain, or an abandoned mine leaching poison into a

stream on the front range of the Rockies, likely
Amelia's grandfather or father had a hand in it."

"Real robber barons?"

"People who worked for Hector called him the 'Lord
High Executioner.' Anybody made a mistake that cost
him money . . ." He made a graphic, throat-slitting
motion. "Amelia has said publicly that she's making
restitution for the family, using the money as she is."

"Who's the Janet Epstein?"

"That was Amelia's mother's maiden name. According to Amelia, her mother used to tell her father he was
wrong about certain things: the slave wages he paid, the
environmental damage he did, in addition to a lot of
less impersonal baggage. He evidently abused her for
disagreeing with him, so now daughter gets even by
naming the fund after Mama and keeping his name out
of it."

"I'd have thought she'd have had her name changed."

He shrugged. "There are other family members she
has no quarrel with, so far as I know. She even excuses
her father from time to time. Back at the turn of the
century and well into this one, exploiters didn't realize
what they were doing to the environment."

"Evidently she doesn't feel the foundation is accom-
plishing what she wants to accomplish. I wonder just
how effective this new idea of hers may be."

He shrugged. "Quite frankly, it sounds a little simplistic. Too simplistic for Amelia. If I know her as well
as I think I do, there'll be a few cards up her sleeve
she's not talking about."

I spent the rest of the morning jotting down ideas and
questions. The place would need guest quarters, of
course. A dining room. A kitchen. Staff quarters.
Meeting rooms. I dug some maps out of the desk in my

living room and found one of the Arapahoe National Forest. Dumont was on the highway west of Idaho Springs. North of the highway was an extensive area printed in pea green: national forest covering mile after square mile, north, west, and south. Just north of Dumont, the green was fractured with pointy areas of white, branching crystals of private land growing into the green, all of them decorated with the crossed pickaxes used to denote mines. From recent newspaper reports, I knew the whole system of mining patents was up for reevaluation. In the past, miners had been allowed to buy up public land for a couple of dollars an acre, take out all the minerals, then leave the area polluted with mine tailings and dangerous with abandoned shafts. Perhaps this location figured in Amelia's plans. One way to make people aware of the destruction of nature was to set them down in the middle of a devastation. Or perhaps, I told myself, on the border between nature and the devastation, so they could see both and, presumably, make an enlightened choice.

It wasn't an area where one would be likely to find local people qualified as chefs or maintenance people or cleaners. Staff members would probably have to be recruited from the Denver area and they'd have to live in. How many staff would it take to care for fifty guests? Fifty beds to be made daily, fifty rooms to clean, plus common areas. I'd have to call a hotel manager and find out just what that involved. Breakfast, lunch, and dinner would imply two shifts of cooks and waiters. Would people drive there? Would cars need to be garaged? If not, would there be institute-owned buses or vans? With drivers? What about a mechanic? What about heating, ventilating, air-conditioning? Sewage? Water!

If this place was to focus on the environment, each of these questions should be answered in an environmentally sound way. That, in and of itself, might prove a lengthy and troublesome matter. Amelia already owned the land, so one would have to work with that. First off, I'd have to see the place. Then I'd worry about an architect.

None of my concerns answered the fundamental question. If she built the place and think-tanked it, would it really do any good? I tried to remember any committee effort that had changed the course of human events. The Club of Rome report on population and environmental degradation. Largely ignored. Various governmental and quasi-governmental reports on whether gays ought to be in the military. Largely ignored. Reports on waste in government. Totally ignored. On the other hand, works by single individuals had sometimes changed things. Darwin's *Origin of Species*. Rachel Carson's *Silent Spring*. Millett's *Sexual Politics*. Friedan's *Feminine Mystique*. (Grace had told me to read those two.)

Which brought my mind guiltily back to Grace. I hadn't thought about her for several hours, not her or Ron. Though I was ashamed of myself, it was still slightly exhilarating to have been totally interested in something else for a while. It had been some time since I'd felt real enthusiasm for anything besides Grace herself.

I phoned her about suppertime. Ron had arrived during the afternoon and was there with her. She was trying hard not to be emotional, though her voice betrayed her. "Could you come over?" she asked, in the tone of a child asking for one more drink before bedtime, wheedling, not quite hopeful. I told her I'd be there as soon as I'd fed the animals. Then I took my time about that, trying to decide what manner to adopt vis-à-vis Ron. Fatherly wouldn't do. I wasn't quite old enough for that, besides which he'd resent it. Avuncular wouldn't work. Brother-in-law it would have to be, even though I wasn't, yet.

Like so many things you spend time worrying over and deciding about, I could have spared myself the trouble. Ron was mad at the world, and so far as he was concerned, Grace and I were part of the world he was mad at. It was our responsibility to take care of him and make everything all right.

"I suppose she's told you," he greeted me at the door with something between a sneer and a whine. "She seems to be telling everybody she knows!" He was as tall as I, but slimmer, with curly dark hair, huge eyes, and a sensual mouth disfigured by his petulance.

"I have told one person," Grace said firmly, pushing herself between her brother and me. "I've told Jason, of course. It's not exactly a secret, Ron. It's not something we can keep from the world."

"Oh, no," he jeered. "The world's just waiting to know what happened to Ron Willis. That's very much on the world's mind!"

He made me furious. AIDS or no AIDS, he had no reason to speak to Grace like that. I said so, vehemently, and he turned very pale and shut up. Grace gave me a not-quite-reproachful glance, sort of a half thank-you, half Jason-how-could-you-slap-the-baby?

I decided while I had his attention, I needed to make the most of it. "You've come back here uninvited, Ron. You're expecting Grace to provide for you. I care a great deal for Grace, so I intend to make that as finan-

cially painless for her as possible. I want you to come
to work for me, tomorrow."

"I can't work!" he cried. "And why shouldn't I come
back here. Gracie owed me something. She got Grandma's house. She got all Grandma's stuff—"

"She got half," I said firmly. "You got the other half.
I know, because I advanced Grace the money she sent
you—"

"But it's worth more than that now!" he cried.

I wanted to hit him. "It's worth more because Grace
has put hours and hours of effort and much of her own
salary into it! You didn't help. You've got none of that
coming. So get off it."

He made a face, tears welling in his eyes, and stalked
off toward the bathroom, slamming the door behind
him.

"What are you hiring him to do?" Grace asked in a
horrified whisper. "You're crazy, Jason. He's never held
a job in his life more than a month or two. He always
quits or does something to get fired."

"I don't know," I admitted. "There's a certain amount
of routine stuff at the shop he could probably do.
Dusting, sweeping, washing windows, none of it very
heavy. He doesn't look up to anything heavy, does he?"
He looked dreadful. Very thin, very pale, those huge
eyes made even larger by the dark circles around them.

"There's only one good thing about all this," she said,
wiping her cheeks on her sleeve. "I've always carried
him on my health insurance."

"You have? I didn't know that."

"Well, I always worried about him, you know. Like it
was inevitable. He's been on my coverage for almost
eight years, but I've never made a claim. That's long
enough that they can't exclude him on the basis of a

preexistent condition. So at least hospitalization and doctors will be mostly paid for."

"Gracie." I held her tight. "You're such a revelation, sometimes. Such a thoughtful, practical little person under all that gorgeousness."

"Me? Gorgeous?" She managed a tiny smile, looking more like the little match girl than anything. For the first time I noticed the resemblance between her and Ron. It was in the way the eyes were set, and the cheekbones. It was in that vulnerable softness at the corners of the mouth. Haggard as he was, he still looked a lot like her. I hadn't felt much pity for him until that moment, until I thought of them as somehow joined, part of something.

"You can't keep him here with you," I said, looking around the living room. There was only one small bedroom, a kitchen, and bath in addition to the room we were in. Grace had converted the rest of the big old Victorian house into three apartments. "There isn't room here, Grace."

She whispered, "My tenant upstairs in the front apartment is leaving the end of this week. He has a new job in Seattle. I thought maybe you'd help me get together a few odds and ends of furniture, and Ron can live up there."

"No problem. Just give me a list."

"That's easy. Bed, dresser, a couple of lamps, maybe a chair or two. I've got extra linens and towels and a few kitchen things. He's not much of a cook."

"Can you manage without the income from the apartment?"

"Easier than I could manage with him living down here with me. Not if it's like last time he visited. He had people in and out all the time, squabbling, screeching at each other. All the people Ron picks up seem to be so loud."

"I heard that," Ron said, emerging from the bathroom. "If you don't like my friends—"

"I don't," she said firmly. "Which is unimportant, Ron. You don't like my friends, and I don't like yours. You don't like my job, and I don't like yours. Let's leave it at that. That's why I'm giving you a place to live, so you can have whatever friends you like."

He fumed, wordlessly, hand on hip, hip canted out, lips pursed. Jack Benny, I thought, irrelevantly. He stood like Jack Benny. He had that same prissy attitude. I was ready for it when he jerked his head a little and said, "Well," in that familiar tone of disgusted pique.

"It's agreed, then," I said. "You're working for me."

He pouted. "I told you, I can't work."

"You can work. Nothing heavy. But you have to contribute something toward your care, Ron. You can't expect Grace to do it all."

"It's not fair," he whined. "She's not sick."

"You'd prefer it if she were, I suppose!" I snarled.

"She could be. She gives blood. That's how I got it." His tone was self-righteous. "They infected me at the blood bank."

"They wouldn't take your blood," she said wearily. "Don't lie to us."

"They did take it!" he asserted. "Of course, it was a long time ago."

"In California?"

"Here!" he said. "I gave blood here."

I, too, had given blood a time or two. "There's no way you could have been infected like that, Ron. They use disposable needles. It couldn't have happened."

"Well, it did," he said stubbornly. "I guess I should know."

I threw a covert look in Grace's direction. She looked worn-out. "Grace and I have a dinner date," I said. "I'm sure you can find something in the kitchen, Ron. Grace and I are meeting some people."

She was surprised, but she recovered quickly. "There's some deli salad and sandwich stuff in the refrigerator," she said. "I'll just put on a jacket. . . ."

She departed, leaving Ron and me awkwardly in the same room as we tried to pretend there were several miles between us. He steamed for a moment, then flounced his way into the kitchen, where I heard the refrigerator door and then water running, both accompanied by a plaintive mutter. Grace returned. She and I fled.

"I'm not sure I'll be able to do it," she said, when we were under way. "I get so mad at him I want to hit him. Then I feel so awful, I want to cry."

"Does he believe that infection-at-the-blood-bank story?"

"I'm hardly ever able to figure out what Ron really believes," she said wearily. "He always seems to believe pretty much whatever he likes. He's going to strike it rich, he's going to discover a sunken treasure, he's going to get this really great job, he's going to learn the meaning of life, he's going to get into the movies. I've heard all those at one time or another, usually offered as an excuse for doing something dumb."

"Like?"

"Oh, last time he was home, you remember, Jason. That . . . that winter." She was being delicate, trying not to remind me too specifically of that winter. I nodded, telling her to go on.

"He was broke, as usual. I gave him some money, but it wasn't enough. So, he shoplifted an outfit."

"An outfit?"

"Shiny blue, polyester, I think. Silk, maybe? Trousers and shirt with full sleeves. He wore it open-necked with this brocade vest. He moussed his hair. He wore mascara and lip gloss. When he was ready to go out, he looked like the last act of *Chorus Line*."

"And the excuse for stealing?"

"There was going to be a movie producer at the party he was going to. He had to dress right to attract attention."

"What did you do?"

"I found the tags in the wastebasket, the ones he'd cut off the clothes. I went to the store and told them I had a mentally defective relative who had ripped them off, and I paid for the clothes."

"The merchant was willing to do that?"

"Maybe I used my badge a little."

"Oh, Grace. That couldn't have been easy."

"Easier than seeing him in jail. I keep remembering him the way he was when we were kids. He was fun. When we went to our uncle's place, he was full of made-up stories and wonderful imaginative ideas. We used to play adventure. I'd use my dolls for the characters, and he'd make costumes for them, to fit the parts. He'd make scenery, as though it were a play. He was wonderful with his hands. Even when he was tiny, he could build anything! I don't know what changed him. What made him suddenly so foolish. I loved him."

"You still do."

"I know. But this isn't the same kind of love. This is a very sad kind of love, Jason Lynx."

Later I told Mark what she'd said, and he nodded,

grimacing. "I know what she means. Some gays ... some gays can't deal with the dichotomy between the roles they envision for themselves as kids and the role they get pushed into when they're older. I mean, we have no heroic tradition. The Ancient Greeks, yes, they could be homophile and heroic. But our culture separates the two. You can be a wife beater and be heroic, an all-right guy, a good old boy. You can be a child abuser or a racist pig or a naval pilot roughing up women at a Talehook convention, and you can still be heroic. But you can't be gay. There was that guy a few weeks ago, found himself in a hostage situation, jumped the gunman, saved several lives, including his own. People said, don't make him a hero."

"He was in drag," I said, remembering the TV accounts.

"Right. He was in drag. So he couldn't be a hero. That's what's really behind the whole gays-in-the-military bit. Society can accept gay cooks, gay stewards, gay quartermasters, gay medics, but we can't accept gay heroes. If a gay can be a hero, then that puts the lie to Pat Robertson and Jessie Helms and the whole religious right. Never let a gay be a hero. That's rule one."

He sounded embittered, something Mark rarely was anymore, enough to make we wonder what painful event he was remembering. Probably some confrontation with his father, who was, by all accounts, a good old boy of the most unregenerate type, albeit somewhat aristocratic. He wouldn't say good old boy, of course. He would call himself a man among men.

"So, you've hired him to work here?" Mark asked.

I grimaced apologetically at him. "Make a list of stuff that needs doing. Light stuff. I'll tell Eugenia. She'll have a fit."

Which she did. Eugenia Lowe was unbending about almost everything. She didn't mind Ron's being gay, but she did mind his being incompetent. She knew he was incompetent because I'd fumed about him a time or two in her hearing.

"Eugenia, I'll pay him personally. It won't go on the overhead." Both Eugenia and Mark got a share of the profits every year, so it wouldn't be fair for me to increase the overhead for purely personal reasons. "I'm doing it for Grace." Eugenia approved of Grace. "If it gets to be too much, we'll quit, but just for a time . . ."

She made a face, but she agreed, just for a time. He could vacuum the showrooms. He could wash the windows.

I'd told Grace to bring him over, and they showed up on her lunch hour on Wednesday. He looked a little better than he had the evening before, though still sulky and whiny. Eugenia showed him where the cleaning things were and told me to get lost. She'd supervise the matter, thank you very much. Recurrently through the afternoon I heard her voice raised and thought I'd hear Ron storming out at any moment. Along about four, however, when I offered to drive Ron home, he seemed more relaxed, less self-engaged than he had been earlier.

"I didn't know you had furniture and stuff," he said. "I thought it was, you know, just decorator stuff. Wallpaper. Things like that."

"We deal in antiques," I told him. "The so-called decor is sort of ancillary."

"You've got this inlay table—"

"Marquetry," I said.

"Is that what you call it? Marquetry. Flowers and

fruit and stuff, all shaded so it almost looks real. I counted at least fifteen colors of wood in that."

"At least," I agreed, totally surprised. "Plus mother-of-pearl."

"What is that, mother-of-pearl?"

"The inner shell of pearl oysters, or abalone, or mussels."

"I wondered why it was cut so little. Because the shell curves, right?"

Again I was surprised. "Right. Small pieces, so they're flat."

"And what's the black wood?"

"Ebony. Like piano keys. The trees are found in Asia and Africa. Or sometimes bog oak or jacaranda. They're black, too."

"They have jacaranda in California. What's bog oak?"

"Oakwood that's been buried in a bog for a long, long time. The moisture is acid, from the peat. It colors the wood without rotting it."

"And the table's old, right?"

"A couple of hundred years."

"How do they do that? Set it in that way?"

I spent the remainder of the drive to Grace's talking about marquetry, the woods that were used, how and why veneering was done. He took it all in, with a sort of quiet relaxation. I realized, as we approached Grace's, that for the moment he'd forgotten he was ill.

"Those curly-looking woods, they're where the tree isn't straight?"

"That's what a burr or burl is," I said. "If the top of a tree is cut off, pollarded, the trunk thickens and sprouts lots of branches. The wood in the thickening isn't straight, the grain twists and turns on itself, making patterns. Burls are found on trunks and branches, too. They're like warts on a tree, but they're never very large."

"So the only way there's enough to see how pretty it is, is if it's cut real thin and used to veneer something else, right?"

I told him right, pleased to hear the eagerness in his voice. "Where a tree forks, there are flame-shaped patterns. Those are used, too."

When we drove up in front of Grace's, he asked, almost hospitably, if I was coming in. I thanked him and said no, I had a few things to do. Grace had already told me she was working late at something or other, and I'd planned to pick up some decent hiking shoes at Cherry Creek Mall. I wanted to drive up to Dumont to see the site of the planned institute, but my old boots, after some fifteen years of occasional abuse, had lost the will to live. The third place I tried had a pair that felt like they wouldn't give me blisters, and they were under two hundred dollars. I figured that was all right for another fifteen years' peace of mind regarding footwear. Since I was in the area, I dropped up to Little Saigon for supper. The place wasn't crowded. I had a table by the window, looking down on the street. Quiet midweek, summer evening; flavor combinations I wasn't used to: mint and cilantro. Peppery shrimp.

I got home about eight. The animals were hungry and annoyed at me. Usually, if I'm going to be away, I feed them first. The phone rang while I was getting out their kibble.

"What did you do to him?" Grace asked.

"To Ron?"

"He's very quiet. Sort of peaceful. He actually made a joke at supper."

I confessed I didn't know, and then told her about our conversation in the car. "Maybe he just saw something that interested him," I said. "Maybe he hasn't been interested in anything lately."

"That's the truth," she said vehemently. "It's the kind of thing he used to be interested in, when he was just a boy. Well, whatever it was, I hope it goes on."

It went on the next day. Eugenia came up to tell me that Ron was a demon with the lemon oil. "Some of those pieces are cleaner than they have ever been," she said in a hushed voice. "If you have no objections, I'm going to try him with the stripper on those pieces you brought in from Amelia Wirtz."

I had no objection. Working with stripper is not difficult, merely time-consuming and boring. One brushes on the stripper, one waits, then one gently scrapes off the bubbling paint or varnish, then one brushes on more stripper and does it again. And again. And again. Eventually, if done carefully, the wood comes out unscarred and perfectly clean. When I went to offer Ron a ride home at about five, I found him working with total absorption, stripping one of the lower doors of the desk-bookcase. It was a nineteenth-century rosewood piece, lined in satinwood, with brass detailing.

"Can I just finish this?" he wanted to know as he moved a narrow bladed putty knife along the curve of a quatrefoil panel. "I've almost got this door, and I'm dying to see it with the paint off. I want to work some more on that little what-you-call-it tomorrow. . . ." He gestured over his shoulder at a little rolling desk with drawers down the sides and a fretted gallery at the top. He'd already applied stripper to the sides, where the drawers were.

"It's called a davenport."

"I thought a davenport was a sofa."

"It's also a little desk. Supposedly the first one was made for a Captain Davenport, back in the seventeen hundreds. I think the sofa started out as a divan-à-porter, that is, moveable bed, and became davenport later."

"Do you have a book I could borrow? About, you know, this stuff."

I fetched him a couple of books and told him to be sure the front door was locked behind him when he left. It was hours later that I heard him leaving and looked out the window to see him strolling down the street, books under his arm, hands in pockets, kicking at pebbles.

Friday dawned bright and not too hot. A good day for mountain looking. I called Amelia, got directions to the place, wrote them down, read them back to her, then put Bela in the car, drove south to Sixth Avenue and west on Sixth to where it joined I-70. That took me west through Mt. Vernon Canyon, past Genesee Park, and over that breathtaking rise where the whole rugged line of the continental divide suddenly appears like a blue backdrop against the lighter sky. Past Idaho Springs, striped with the roadbeds of old railroad spurs leading to defunct mines, dilapidated loading towers, broken and sagging conveyors, then climbing northwest through forty or so square miles of Bureau of Land Managment territory crosshatched with private mining claims. Though Amelia's land lay north of Dumont, she'd told me her preferred route was to turn off at Interchange 238, before Dumont, and take the mostly paved Fall River Road northwest up the canyon, toward Alice. About a mile and a half before Alice, a dirt road cut back to the southeast, and this led to Amelia's land, downhill. She'd given me landmarks and told me her property was marked by stripes of blue paint on roadside rocks.

"It's an old mining patent," she said. "Actually, it's about five of them. I bought the first one years ago, when I was just a girl, then added to it as the others became vacant. I've got almost a hundred acres."

I missed the turn the first time around, went all the way to Alice, turned around, and came back. This time I saw it, leading downward among the trees. The car bucked and growled. I crawled along, thinking I should have rented a four-wheel-drive or borrowed Amelia's. She'd offered, but I'd foolishly turned her down. The blue-striped stones suddenly appeared on my left. I pulled off, into a clearing, and climbed out of the car, Bela right behind me. He set off immediately to explore the vicinity, and I, seeing light among the trees to the east, trudged up the slope in that direction. Bela marked a few trees, then galloped up beside me, and together we came through the trees into the air.

We stood on a wide rock shelf pierced by a few small, twisted trees, commanding a view that seemed to go all the way east to the prairies. At either end of the shelf were pillars of standing stone, like surrealist chessmen, intricately wind-carved. The wall plunged before us, and below, in the canyon I'd driven through half an hour before, were spread the bare squat cones of mine tailings and the metallic glitter of settling ponds, bright copper red and ocher and vile yellowish green. Among these, the falling silver of the river wound its way toward a junction with Clear Creek, the stream for which the county was named.

"And not so very clear," Amelia had muttered at me. "If those tailing ponds aren't cleaned up!"

I stretched and yodeled, listening for the somewhat discordant echo. Bela looked startled. Yodeling wasn't a usual thing with me. The place seemed to call for it. Either that or alpenhorns. Standing there, I could visualize the institute, not in any detail, but in essence. This rock shelf should be a terrace, outside the meeting rooms and dining room. It would catch the morning sun. If the building were two stories high, with a porch on the other side, one could see the sunset from the upper story, over the tops of the trees on the slope behind me. The quarters for guests and staff should be down that hill, somewhat sheltered in the trees, connected to this exposed aerie by covered walkways.

Water would be the problem. Fall River was in the canyon before me, a long way down. I'd seen no stream in the smaller valley behind me. I grabbed a convenient tree trunk and leaned out, trying to see down the rock wall. There, to my left and some sixty or seventy feet below, silver spurted from the rock face and fell plashingly into the trees.

"Well, well."

Bela wagged, agreeing with whatever I was saying as we walked north along the shelf, me leaning out every now and then, trying to get immediately above that spurting fountain. The way was closed by pillars of stone with narrow spaces among them. We wound our way through, coming to a blind pocket among the stones, a kind of three-sided chimney. There, perched across two handy protrusions, was a seat, a wide, thick plank with a hole cut in it. A one-holer, a privy. In a crevice to one side was a coffee can, tightly closed with a plastic lid. No surprise. Toilet paper. Amelia, or someone, had built a handy toilet. I tipped up the plank. The opening was about three feet across and went straight down. One would definitely want a stout seat between one's bottom and all that descending darkness!

I still wanted to get above that spring, but there seemed to be no way to it. Out of the blind pocket, we squirmed between rocks, around others, backing and trying again, each time ending back at the privy shaft. Finally, after about ten minutes of frustration, I noticed faded blue paint spots on some of the stones, low down, quite purposeful. "It's a connect-the-dots," I explained to Bela. Which I then proceeded to do, coming out shortly onto a tiny shelf, no bigger than a bathroom floor, most of the area taken up by a stout six-by-six lid or door made of thick, grayed boards bolted to cross-pieces. It was not fastened to anything, so far as I could see, and when I shifted it, it exposed a roughly triangular shaft with light wavering on the surface of water a long way down. A quick look over the edge confirmed that I was seeing the source of the fall that spurted from the rock face. Since the water was not merely flowing, but spurting, it was obviously under some pressure. The light on the water came from a fissure in the cliff face that ran from where I stood down to the water level. There was a reservoir down there, quite a deep one, despite the spring meltoff having ended months ago. If Amelia had been coming here for thirty-some-odd years, she would know whether it was a steady, year-round water source, possibly with enough flow to supply the institute she envisioned. I found it interesting that she hadn't told me about the spring. Maybe letting me find it for myself was part of her strategy for getting me interested.

Bela and I returned through the rock alley to the shelf, where I climbed a rock and stared off to the north. The land seemed to rise without interruption to the limit of vision at the continental divide. No doubt the spring flowed from that high, usually snowcapped area through faults in the stone to emerge here weeks or months later and thousands of feet below.

Amelia had said she'd camped out here for years. I went looking for evidence—a circle of blackened stones, a place where a tent might have been, and found absolutely nothing. I'd have missed it completely if not for Bela, who had disappeared among the rocks at the south end of what I was already thinking of as the terrace. When he didn't reappear, I called him. He barked, his don't-bother-me-I'm-smelling-something bark. I followed the bark, around two wind-carved pillars, between two others, and there was a narrow cave with a tall slit of a window out onto the southern sky. The floor area was about five feet across, twelve feet deep, and sandy. A circle of stones by the window slit made a fireplace. On a rocky shelf at the back was a stash of dry wood and a tin trunk containing a tightly rolled sleeping bag, and some odds and ends I didn't bother to inventory. From the looks of the place, it was an ideal campsite: dry, protected from either rain or snow, and so hidden that nobody had bothered it.

Bela was curled up on the sandy floor, contentedly thumping his tail as though to say, hey, this is a good place. I agreed heartily. It was a good place, the kind of good place I'd always dreamed of as a kid. Secret, hidden, high; a nest from which a person could look down on the world without fear. A place no one could find. Not in any sense a king-of-the-castle kind of place, which one would have to defend against interlopers. Not a cockcrow kind of place where one stood, as on a high fence or a roof shouting, hey, look at me. No. This was a secret place of one's very own, never shared with anyone or, at most, with one person only.

And so it had obviously been for Amelia. Until now. Now she was willing to make something else of it. I wondered what her real plans were, if, as Mark said, she had ones she hadn't told me about.

It was midafternoon when I returned to town, stopping at the federal center to pick up some Forest Service topological maps of the area I'd just seen. When I spread them out on my desk, they confirmed what I'd already supposed. The land to the north and west of Amelia's site did slope up to the continental divide. The site itself was around nine thousand feet up. Not as high as Leadville, but almost. High enough that one would need to make certain provisions for the health of flat-lander participants. High enough that one would have to make provisions for access in winter. The Silverlake ski area was above Alice, so that road would be maintained in winter.

A tentative voice from behind me said, "Jason?"

"Yes?" It was Ron, looking different.

"Grace asked me to invite you to dinner tonight."

"Why, ah, sure, Ron. I'd love to."

"What are you doing?" he asked curiously.

"A client, Amelia Wirtz, wants me to help design a mountain place," I said, oversimplifying. "I've just been up to look at the site." I put my finger on the map and showed him the place I'd outlined with red pencil. "There."

"I love the mountains," he said. There was something eager in his tone, not at all self-pitying, but simply desirous. "I haven't been in the mountains in years."

"Let me tell you about this place," I said, full of enthusiasm as I described it to him, the way the shelf looked out over that enormous vista, the cave, even the potty shaft.

"Amelia Wirtz set herself up in some comfort," I concluded.

"Wirtz?" he asked curiously. "The person who owned the furniture I've been working on?"

"Her father."

"It sounds ... really interesting." He leaned over the map, focusing on the area, putting his finger on it.

"You're getting paint on the map," I complained.

"Sorry." He wiped at it, succeeding only in smudging it, his face full of such concentrated concern it made me ashamed of myself.

"Next time I go up, I'll take you along," I said without thought.

"Will you! I'd like that." He traced the red penciling on the map once more, gave me a strangely haunting smile, and was gone. I looked after him, my mouth open. A few moments later I went down to ask Eugenia what he'd been doing.

"I don't know what I did without him," she murmured in my ear. "I've never seen anyone as good with wood, Jason. He's been working on those old pieces in the basement for two days now, and he's wonderful at it. He's got that larger piece so clean you'd swear it was new."

That evening I gathered up the Forest Service maps to show Grace, offering Ron a ride when I encountered him downstairs. On the way I told him what Eugenia had said about his doing a good job. He didn't reply, just ducked his head and flushed, maybe with pleasure, maybe with embarrassment. Later, while Grace and I were in the kitchen together and he was in the bathroom, I told her what Eugenia had said. "More of the change you mentioned before?" I asked her.

"I think it's more like he's given up," she whispered to me, tears under her eyes. "He said something like that last night. He said he didn't need to fight anybody anymore. He didn't need to worry about being anything anymore. He's going to die, so he can just take whatever pleasure he can find. He doesn't have to keep trying to be something he isn't. All he has to do is live each day. It broke my heart. It was as if he'd . . . oh, I don't know, Jason. Do you believe in religious experiences?"

"Sure. That is, I believe people have experiences of enlightenment that they call religious. New connections that occur to people. Inspiration. Agnostic that I am, even I've experienced that."

"Of course you have. And so have I. But . . . the way Ron's been for so many years, I wouldn't have thought he could, do you know what I mean? He seemed shut off from all that."

"Maybe he'd only shut himself off. Maybe he'd told himself if he couldn't be what other people expected, he wouldn't be anything, and then he spent years proving it. Now he doesn't need to prove anything, he can just be."

"Well, whatever he's being, he's a whole lot more peaceful at it than he used to be. Shhh."

Ron joined us in the kitchen; I spread out a couple of maps and became eloquent about the Wirtz land, repeating more or less what I'd told Ron. We agreed to take a picnic lunch and drive up to the place on Sunday. I repeated the invitation for Ron to come along. We had supper. Ron ate very little but seemed to enjoy what he did eat. Afterward Grace came back to my place with me, though she didn't stay. About midnight she told me she really thought she ought to be home. I told her to take my car, have Ron bring it back in the morning.

"And the maps," I murmured, already half-asleep. "I left them on your kitchen counter. Ask him to bring them."

Which he did, putting the folded stack on my desk the following morning. He looked tired. I asked him if he hadn't slept well.

"Yeah, well," he said with the sneer I hadn't seen for a while. "Some friends of mine came over and they didn't leave till old sis came home. She threw them out."

I said mildly, "She probably just needed to get some sleep, Ron. When the tenant upstairs moves, you'll have a place of your own to entertain friends in." I asked him if he wanted to work half the day, which is all we do on Saturday, and he said he would. The conversation had reminded me of my promise to acquire some furniture for Ron's apartment. Mark was hovering, so I told him what was needed and asked him to check the odds and ends we'd stored in an old building off Sixteenth we use for a warehouse. As a building, it's derelict, but as a storage place for nothing very valuable, it isn't bad. The roof and walls are tight and there's adequate light. What more can you ask? It's the place we put furniture that comes out of places we redo, when the owners don't want the trouble of disposing of it. Mostly, the stuff is valueless, and I've threatened more than once to have a warehouse giveaway and clean the place out. Only fear of the liability has prevented me. A colleague of mine in a similar situation offered the contents of a warehouse free, to people from a low-income housing project, and he got sued because a stupid woman pulled a rickety armoire over on her foot. It cost him more to settle the stupid suit than it would have to have burned the contents of the warehouse. Niceness, so I've come to learn, doesn't pay.

At any rate, Mark came back with a list of things we had available, then called the local trucker who does most of our cartage for us and arranged for the stuff to be moved on Monday, by which time, so Grace said, her tenant would be out.

I called Amelia's home number and left a message on her machine telling her I'd seen her property and wanted to talk about it.

Grace and Ron and I went out to dinner Saturday night. I took them home early because Grace said they needed Sunday morning to clean the apartment Ron was to occupy. Over my Sunday-morning coffee, a picture of Amelia Wirtz smiled at me from page three of the paper, with an announcement that she was going to build an institute for environmental law. Whoop-de-do. My name was not mentioned, for which I was extremely grateful. The site, however, was sufficiently well located in the text that anyone really interested in finding it could do so. I didn't consider this quite prudent, but it was Amelia's property, not mine.

I spent the midmorning in sloth, which palled by noon, so I put on my woods-walking clothes and went over to Grace's, figuring she and Ron would be finished with the cleaning and we'd pick up some deli stuff on the way. I found Grace alone, just finishing the job. Her tenant had been a neat sort, so she said, and there hadn't been as much to do as she'd thought.

"Where's Ron?" I asked.

"Out," she said, grim-lipped. "Someone came by again last night after we got home. Some . . . acquaintance of his. They got into an argument, and Ron went off with him. I haven't seen him since."

"Who?" I asked. "What?"

"Oh, Jason, I don't know. I got the impression it was somebody he'd known in California, or a friend of somebody he'd known in California. I didn't want to get involved! I know that sounds awful, but I didn't! I used to try to get Ron out of trouble all the time, you know I did! It never worked. I usually just made matters worse."

"Let's forget it and have our picnic," I suggested, just to sidetrack her. "If Ron isn't here, we'll go without him."

She looked down at herself with a little moue of distaste. "I won't go anywhere like this. Give me a few minutes to change."

I waited while she showered and changed into clean jeans and a flannel shirt. As we were heading out the door a flashy blue car drove up and Ron got out of the backseat. A burly, unpleasant-looking individual leaned out the driver's window and yelled something about not forgetting Monday, then the car sped off, scarcely giving Ron time to get clear. He came up the walk toward us, head hanging, then looked up, saw us, tried a weak grin. He looked like hell, his shirt dirty and wrinkled, his hair disheveled, a nasty bruise on one cheek.

"Sorry," he said to Grace. "I was going to help you, wasn't I."

"I did it by myself," she said crisply. "Yes, you were going to help. What was that all about?"

"This guy." He shrugged. "He knows a friend of mine in San Francisco. And this friend of mine owes him money, so he wants me to call him and explain things. So I went over to his place, and spent most of the night making phone calls."

"Did you get it straightened out?" I asked, looking pointedly at his cheek.

He gave me that oddly haunted smile, fingering the bruise. "Yeah. I did." Then his eyes slid away.

I had the strong suspicion that the so-called friend was Ron himself, or at the very least that he was somehow involved in the debt.

"How much money?" I asked, as casually as I could manage.

"A lot," he said simply. He gave me a puppy look, one that said please, talk about something else.

I bit my tongue. "Grace and I are just leaving for our picnic," I told him. "Are you coming along?"

"Right," he said, suddenly eager. "Give me a minute. I don't want to miss that."

"Hurry," Grace said. "It's a long drive."

He started for the house. Grace stopped him and gave him the key, then we waited. It was only a few moments before he reemerged in a clean shirt and with his hair combed.

I was surprised he was coming with us, tired as he looked. Maybe he just didn't want to be alone. We stopped at a deli on Colfax for sandwiches and soft drinks and cartons of salad stuff, then out Sixth Avenue, repeating my trip of two days before. There was little conversation en route. Once we left the city, it took about an hour to get there, less than formerly, as this time I knew where we were going and spotted the backtrack road on the first try. We took the food and a blanket up to the "terrace" and spread it out there. I showed Grace and Ron the privy shaft and then the cave. It was just as when Bela and I had seen it first.

Grace peered around at it like some furry creature deciding to take up residence, and Ron ran a stroking finger across the tin trunk. They obviously felt, as I had, the attraction of the place.

When we'd eaten, Grace suggested we go mushrooming, an idea to which, again to my surprise, Ron acquiesced. The nearest easily walkable ground I remembered seeing was back down the road a way, on the west side, among the trees. We left all the picnic stuff, drove about three quarters of a mile north, and parked the car in a grove from which we found a network of game trails running north and south. Grace used to go mushrooming while summering with relatives in Minnesota, and she's dragged me along on a few forays. It's Grace's theory that it's better not to take a bag or knife along when mushrooming so as not to alarm the mushrooms, who would hide if they knew she was coming. True to form, as we had nothing to carry them in, we found them by the dozens, big fat boletes, the good ones with the dark caps and thick stems. I took off my jacket, and we made a backpack of it, which got rapidly filled as Grace and I wandered farther northward, really not looking very hard. Since *Boletus edulis* are monumental fungi, fully eight to ten inches across, of a particularly showy maroon color, they rather leap to the eye. We found them without ever losing sight of the road to our right. I heard an occasional car, saw an occasional flash of reflected light, bright red, light gold, metallic blue. Once in a while we yelled, just to be sure Ron was within hailing distance.

After half an hour or so it started to cloud up, with a distant mutter of thunder, so we turned back to the car, stopping only for the most interesting things we hadn't seen on the way out. Ron was at the car, waiting for us.

I dumped the mushrooms into the trunk, enough of them to keep us busy for several hours cleaning and slicing them, either to dry or to parboil and freeze. Then we drove back to Amelia's site and went up the hill to clean up after ourselves. Something had been at the food. Some of the containers were scattered. Ron commented on it, and I said a squirrel, most likely. We carefully policed the rock shelf, gathering up everything. Ron excused himself to use Amelia's privy, as Grace and I started down the hill with the stuff. The clouds had moved over us, dark and threatening, and when we were halfway down the hill there came a sharp crack and rumble of thunder, though I hadn't seen a lightning flash.

I started the car and we sat waiting, and waiting.

"Damn," said Grace, climbing out and starting purposefully up the slope once more. I got out and watched her go, then, moved by some obscurely troubled impulse, went after her. I was almost to the terrace when I heard her cry, a high, keening sound, like the howl of a dog. I broke into a run, burst out on the terrace, and followed the sound to my left.

There was a smell in the air, a gunpowder, firecracker smell. I struggled down the narrow rock alley, now inexplicably littered with stones, and came upon her where she crouched just outside the little niche the privy was in. Had been in. Now there was nothing there but a pile of stones and air thick with the smell of explosives. Of brother Ron there was no sign, no sign at all.

We called the Clear Creek County Sheriff's Office from a phone in Alice. They would come from Idaho Springs, and they told us to meet them at the turnoff.

We drove over there and waited, Grace gulping, then sobbing, then gulping again, trying desperately to think and behave like a cop and not succeeding at all. When the sheriff's car arrived, we led them to the site, and I told Grace to stay where she was while I took them up there. I took them through the rock and we stopped at the fall.

"You say there's a privy in there, under that?"

"Not a building. Just a hole in the rock with a seat over it. The woman who owns this land probably built it for when she camps here."

"So, how'd you know it was here?"

I took them back out, showed them the cave, told them I'd been hired by the owner, explained how I'd been exploring the site when I'd found the thing.

"So what were you doin' up here today?" demanded the larger of the two men.

"Just having a picnic, taking another look at the place. And we went mushroom hunting for a while."

I had to show them the picnic stuff, and the mushrooms, and Grace had to explain about Ron, then the larger deputy pulled me to one side.

"You think he's under that pile of rock."

"I don't know where else he could be."

"You think somebody what? Set dynamite there?"

I'd been thinking about little else for the last half hour. "Earlier in the day I went back there to pee," I said. "It seemed politer than simply letting fly over the edge. Besides, the wind was in the wrong direction."

I hadn't meant to be funny, but he grinned, nonetheless. "No," I protested. "I thought about it as soon as we knew what had happened. Why he got . . . hurt and I didn't. I didn't see a damned thing. I suppose there could have been a fuse leading off somewhere among the rocks, but I didn't see it. And it was when Grace and I were headed downhill that we heard it."

"You heard it?"

"I heard what I thought was thunder, but it had to be the explosion."

Above us the sky muttered, and the deputy looked up thoughtfully. "So you thought it was thunder, you didn't go looking until how much later?"

"I don't know. Ten minutes maybe. Five. We went down to the car, we sorted out the trash from the leftovers, we put the trash in a garbage bag, we put everything in the trunk. We admired our mushroom harvest. We sat in the car awhile, until Grace got impatient, then she came up here looking for him."

"Anybody out to get him?"

"Him? Or me? Or even Grace? I don't know it was meant for him, or even meant for anybody."

"Guess that's right. We don't know for sure how the damned thing was set off."

He spent some time on the radio. We stuck around, Grace curled up on the rear seat of the car shuddering, me ambling around, trying to stay out of the way. A rescue truck showed up. Three cars full of volunteers showed up. People conferred, went up the hill, came back down again. A while later, someone showed up with a portable compressor and a jackhammer. There were plenty of hard-rock miners around. Everyone involved seemed to be thoroughly familiar with the equipment. An incessant hammering echoed off some precipice to the north and came back at us from that direction.

"What are they doing?" Grace begged.

I'd gone into a remote mental place, not thinking much. I almost said, "A disinterment," but caught myself in time. "Removing the rock. So they can find out what happened."

"We know what happened," she cried.

"Grace. Think like a cop. You haven't any idea what happened, nor have I. Was there a fuse, a timer, or was it an old stick of dynamite left over from mining days? Was there a trigger, a remote control? Why Ron? Why not me? You don't know."

"No," she said. "I don't know. But there was the blue car."

"What blue car?"

"The one that left him off this morning. That flashy blue. There was a car on the road here, that same blue."

"There are probably ten thousand cars that same blue."

"I know." She wept.

We waited. The day crawled into evening and turned livid. Someone took lamps up the hill from the rescue truck. Everyone was busy but us. The noise had diminished. Evidently they'd broken up and carried away the bigger rocks. Either that or the sheriff's men had made them slow down so as not to destroy evidence.

Someone came galloping down the hill and got onto the radio. I heard only a few words, but they weren't words I'd expected. He wanted an ambulance.

I patted Grace and went over to him, catching him as he was about to take off up the hill again. "What?" I demanded. "What happened?"

"We think maybe he's alive down there," he said. "We can hear something moving around."

"You've got the shaft uncovered?"

"Right. We've dropped a line. It's about fifty feet down. Rodger Campton's going down to see. He's the smallest one of us. How big was the guy?"

"My height. Very thin, though."

"Maybe he just dropped down there and wasn't hit. Fifty feet though, jeez, that's a long way onto rock."

I didn't tell Grace. No point in her grieving twice. If he was alive, then he was alive, but if he wasn't, nothing had changed.

It got darker. The ambulance arrived, slowly, without fanfare. The medics went up the hill.

"Go," Grace said. "Go see what's happening."

"I don't want to leave you alone."

"It doesn't matter, Jason. Please, go see what's happening."

I trudged up after the medics. The terrace was littered with piles of broken stone. There was no room for me in the stone alley where the men were jammed on top of one another, but I could climb to a place roughly above where they were working. They had a light down the hole. It shone up, weirdly, lighting faces from below, making skulls of them. Someone was being lowered. He wore gloves and a face mask, which somehow surprised me. Evidently it wasn't his first time down for he was covered with rock dust.

Rope was played out slowly. Instructions were shouted. A man moved, and I saw another line disappearing into the hole. Evidently the rescuer was going to attach it to Ron's body. Assuming there was a body. Then they began to haul the rope up, hand over hand. Someone reached down and eased the limp burden through the hole in the rock. I couldn't see the face, but it wore the clothing Ron had worn, and who else would it be? Whoever it was went into a body bag, then someone else went down the shaft. What now?

The line was lowered again. The rescuer was still down below. Again the line was withdrawn, this time quicker. What came out of the hole was a canvas sack, followed almost immediately by the rescuer.

I climbed down. The deputy came out from among the stones, saw me, and ambled over, lighting a cigarette as he came.

"Helluva thing," he said conversationally.

"What?" I demanded.

"Young fella was down there, all right. Dead. What we heard moving was bats. Man got down there, here's the one dead guy, here's the other dead guy."

"The other dead guy?"

"Long dead. Bones."

"You're sure it's . . . human?"

"Oh, sure. Skull tells you that. Doesn't say male or female, not yet, but we'll find out which. How long ago, maybe. Helluva thing."

I agreed, stunned. Whatever I might have expected, it had not been another body. "Any indication how the thing was set off?"

"You see a tin can in there?"

"There was a coffee can, with a plastic top and toilet paper inside."

"Got me a hunch the contact was under the can. Like a mousetrap, with a spring. Take off the weight, *bammo*. Don't know where the bomb was. Back in a crack in the stones, maybe. Not under him, or he'da gone up, not down. Helluva thing."

Down at the bottom of the hill, I told Grace Ron was gone. She held on to me and cried. Another car came along, parked, and emitted an eager-looking young man with a microphone. I got Grace into the car, shut and locked the doors, and told her to stay there for a moment. Then I sought out the deputy and gave him my card.

"His sister's in no shape to be interviewed," I said. "I'm going to take her home. She's a Denver cop, you can reach her there or at home—I've put her name and number on the card."

"No ideas about this, huh?"

"Maybe tomorrow," I told him. "Right now I'm baffled."

Which bafflement continued on the long drive down on the mountain.

I took Grace to my house. The last thing she needed right then was to be left alone.

two

OF COURSE THE whole thing was on the news that night and the following morning as well as up front in the morning paper. DEATHS ON LAND PROPOSED AS THINK TANK, blared the headlines. Amelia Wirtz was quoted as saying she hoped the whole thing would turn out to be an unfortunate accident.

"You can't believe it was intentional?" she asked me on the phone.

"Look, Amelia, all I know is, the thing was done by explosives. Explosives are not accidental. Lightning is accidental."

"Could he have been struck by—"

"I smelled it! There's a smell to dynamite. It's not state-of-the-art, but that doesn't mean it can't kill."

"Maybe there was some left there from years ago, and it was struck by lightning."

She was grasping at straws and I told her so. "Do you really think there could have been a cache of dynamite there that you hadn't found in what? Thirty years? Unlikely. Very unlikely."

"It's depressing," she said. "The only saving grace is that the young man didn't lose a long life."

I heard her to say "saving Grace," and it wasn't saving Grace anything. I started to say so, then realized what she had actually said. Grace would not have agreed. Grace was, as usual, believing this was her fault. Grace believed she should somehow have protected her brother from all the hounds of hell or heaven, despite his spending his entire adult life playing bunny wabbit at the greyhound track. Her grief was real and agonizing, and the only real saving grace was that she would have felt it sooner or later. Ron had been doomed possibly to a long and probably to an agonizing death. Maybe the time would come that she would see the very suddenness of it as a blessing for her and for Ron himself. I'd had some experience with long-drawn-out dying, and it wasn't something I'd wish on my worst enemy. So to speak.

I'd offered to spend the day with her, but she'd gone to work that morning as usual.

"I'd only sit around crying," she said, her jaw clamped uncompromisingly. "Work's the only thing that helps when you're this sad."

Cop-shop immediacy no doubt made this true. It wasn't always true in the antique business, which is often so leisurely as to be almost comatose. People do not generally knock the door down exclaiming that they must immediately spend ten thousand or twenty thousand or more on some aged piece of craftsmanship, and this morning was no exception. I was not distracted. Grace was on my mind, and I couldn't stop worrying about her. Mark's long face didn't help. Nor did Eugenia when she came up to my office with tears in her eyes, discovering, so she said, that she'd felt quite an affection for the young man.

"He did so beautifully with the old pieces, Jason. I really . . . I really grieve over him."

She sounded surprised. I wasn't. Eugenia's outside is

Mt. Rushmore, but her inside is Earth Mother. I went down to the basement with her, and we admired Ron's last work on the Gothic Revival secretary. This was the piece I'd spotted the maker's mark on, a desk below and bookcase above, dating from about 1840 and made by J. W. Meeks of New York. Amelia Wirtz's grandfather had no doubt brought it with him when he moved west to begin ripping and tearing. I knew I'd seen something similar, so I looked through several resource books on Victorian furniture, and lo, there was the twin to the bookcase (structurally, if not apparently) as owned by the Metropolitan Museum of Art.

The secretary was fairly simple for a Victorian piece, about seven and a half feet tall, a two-doored cupboard below a pullout desk shelf and a rolltop disclosing three small drawers and some pigeonholes, then two glass upper doors covering a couple of bookshelves. The lower doors were paneled in a quatrefoil design that was echoed by the brass detailing on the glass lancet doors above. One of the brass-trim assemblies was in place; the other had been removed and stored in one of the lower shelves. One upper door sagged on its hinges, and the whole thing had been slathered with repeated coats of paint. Until now, I'd never seen the piece as the maker intended it.

Ron had left it virtually clean, the rosewood glowing softly through the slight haze the stripper left behind. A few tight corners of the quatrefoil paneling needed a little more work. Once the hinge to the sagging door was repaired, the whole thing could be rubbed down and revarnished. The brass fittings for the upper doors would need to be straightened and polished, and a replacement escutcheon found for the keyhole to the rolltop. The glass was missing from the upper doors, but a corner remained, enough to identify what kind of glass had been used originally. Two replacement brass knobs would be needed for the rolltop as well. Someone had removed those, perhaps to use on something else. I had boxes full of period hardware in the basement, stuff I'd picked up here and there and kept just for such purposes.

"It's beautiful," said Eugenia. "Really beautiful."

"Grace tells me he was always good with his hands."

"He started well with the little davenport desk, too."

He hadn't gotten far with it. He'd stripped the one drawer and had begun on the mahogany lid, a lid much like the one that covers a piano's keys. In fact, the davenport looked much like a thirty-inch-wide spinet. The top, at eye level when seated, bore a little fretted gallery, a place to put a few books or ink and pens. The desk shelf extended on two carved supports, and the casters were hidden by bun feet. It was designed to be rolled wherever one was sitting, beside the fire in the winter or beside an open window in summer. The Victorians were indefatigable correspondents. Travel was slow, and phones hadn't been invented, so they wrote endless letters at all kinds of little desks and escritoires and secretaries. This was definitely a woman's piece of furniture, and the age of it would indicate it might have belonged originally to Janet Wirtz's mother, Amelia's grandmother. I wondered briefly why Amelia hadn't passed it on to her son's wife, then remembered what she thought of her son's wife and shelved the question.

We stroked the desk lid and said kind words about Ron's work, and after a while went back to work, both of us slightly cheered to think that during his last days he had done something he had obviously enjoyed. No one works that carefully unless he likes it.

My desk calendar reminded me that I had said I would look at Valerie French's apartment today. I called her office number. She said yes, she was ready, she'd take off from work and meet me there. She worked at the University Medical Center, just off University Boulevard, and had a ground-floor apartment in an anonymous building just three blocks away.

I got there in about ten minutes and she was waiting for me. The door opened while I was coming up the walk. There was a minuscule hallway, made more minuscule by the table she had in it, and then, to my left, a living room. She had conveyed disaster during our first meeting, and she had not misled me.

"It's awful, isn't it?" she asked, staring at my face.

"It doesn't make a statement," I said placidly. "Or perhaps it makes several contradictory ones. Where did you get those two chairs?" They were against the far wall of the dining area, separated by a small buffet.

"I bought them," she confessed. "It was the only time I ever went to a garage sale. I liked the way they looked, except somebody varnished them or something."

The two chairs were obscured by the "throws" across their backs. Whenever I see a "throw," I want to add the necessary second word, "away." I removed them, folded them, set them aside. The chairs did look coated with a dark varnish. "Where?" I asked again. "What part of the country? West Coast, right?"

"How did you know? I guess they look sort of Oriental, right?"

"Rather, yes, but that's not how I knew." They were matching armchairs, low-backed, the top rail flaring slightly at the ends. The splat was in five vertical parts joined by small rectangular blocks. Barely visible under the heavy coating were the dark, exposed pegs at the joints and an inlaid design on the center splat. The arms had stepped handholds, curved splines, and the seats were upholstered in something nondescript. They had plain, H-pattern stretchers, set rather low, which contributed to the slightly Oriental look. I upended one. Metal feet. Mahogany. Under all that dark coating, the inlay looked like fruitwood and stone. Malachite. Lapis, maybe.

The buffet between was similar. "Did you buy this the same place and time?"

"Oh, no. I found it in a secondhand furniture place. It just seemed to go with the chairs, so I bought it."

"How much did you pay for it?"

"Too much." She flushed. "Almost a thousand dollars."

"Considering it's worth fifteen times that, at least, I'd say you got a bargain. This was made by Greene and Greene, in California; Pasadena, I think. First decade of the nineteen hundreds. It's Arts and Crafts, of course. Not a style I'm crazy about, but these are marvelous examples of the genre."

Her eyes were very wide. "You're teasing me."

I shook my head, grinning at her. "I wouldn't do that, Valerie. Maybe you have more taste than you think."

"Oh, but I don't. Just look at this place!"

It was dreadful, in a homey way. Nothing went with anything. Various pieces had been acquired, not planned. What made it interesting, however, was that almost everything was good. The sofa was just a sofa, probably a sofa bed, to give her a guest bed, but it had clean, classic lines. The easy chair was just a chair, but it, too, was well proportioned. The coffee table was wonderful, half of a marvelously carved door fitted with a simple bronze frame and glass top. There was a good rug in one corner, where it did no good. I wandered through to the bedroom. A very nice four-poster bed, too small for queen, too short for the twentieth century, which meant it was made before sizes were standardized. "The bed?"

"Salvation Army. Nobody wanted it because it won't fit a mattress. I had the mattress factory cut off a regular one for me."

"Why did you buy it?"

"I liked it."

And so it went. She had probably a hundred thousand dollars' worth of stuff in the two rooms, all of it looking faintly shabby and nervous about the company it was keeping.

We sat at her dining-room table—a very nice piece of marquetry, Ron would have loved it—which had a broken leg and was supported at one end by a pile of books. I wrote a list of the pieces of furniture I had seen in the two rooms, gave it to her, and told her to number them, starting with her most favorite piece and working her way down.

When she'd finished, after a lot of erasing and renumbering, I said, "Mark and I could decorate this apartment for you, selling you pieces to go with some of what you have, redoing your curtains and wall coverings. We could make it look great. Then you marry what's-his-name—"

"Espy Gryphon."

"Right. Then you marry Espy and move out, putting all our work to naught. You move in with him somewhere else, right? And you'll have a bunch of stuff you don't need and don't want, money down the drain. So, what we could do is redo the walls and curtains and whatnot, and recover these two chairs you're in love with, and find you some pictures. We will also take the things you're not using over to our place, for either storage or consignment, depending on how things work out, and lend you what you need to make the place look all of a piece."

"Is that . . . playing fair?"

"It is not only fair, it's sensible. You can pay for the whole shebang with the sale of one piece. This table, for instance. Or the four-poster bed. Also, I will personally undertake to give you some basic information so that you can sound authoritative about the pieces you're keeping. What about silver? What about china?"

She had neither. I told her we'd borrow some, from somewhere. We reaffirmed the date by which this would all be done, and I trotted off home, musing over the vagaries of taste. Her taste was flawless. She just didn't use it!

After I got back, I told Mark and Eugenia about the deal I'd made with Valerie French. Eugenia made sensible comments, but Mark was strangely silent.

We had just finished discussing it when Grace phoned. She had been in touch with the Clear Creek Sheriff's Office, who had asked for help from the state crime lab. She said they needed an explosives expert, someone who could tell them where the charge had been set. I kept my mouth shut. I'd seen enough of the effects that I could have told them, but it wasn't something I wanted to get involved in. The charge had been set high in the rock wall in the north side of the chimneylike privy niche. Had it been set anywhere at the back, the stones would have been blown outward. Had it been set low, the force would have crushed Ron against the wall rather than downward. As it had happened, stone fragments had been blown out of the north wall—leaving a definite cavity—some landing at various distances south, toward the terrace, some crashing against the opposite side of the chimney, to fall downward, forcing what was beneath them into the shaft below. Examining the stones for weathering would prove which ones were newly exposed, for forensic purposes, but you could tell by just looking. The newly exposed stone was gray, light-colored, the surface irregularly crystalline. The old stone was dark and water streaked, and the surfaces were smoothed by wind and water.

"They don't know how it was set off," she said. "I guess they'll find out."

I said a few soothing words. She hung up, leaving me to think about setting things off in general. The bomb could have been set off by radio, or by an electrical impulse, through a wire. There were many fissures in the stone that wire could be hidden in. There were also, however, lots of small creatures around, and as every electric company repairman knows, large-scale havoc can be caused by very small-scale beasties. A mouse-sized pair of jaws can easily pinch two wires together and short-circuit very large arrays of equipment.

If I'd been setting the charge, I wouldn't have used an electrical detonator unless I'd intended it to go off almost immediately. It could have been rigged the way the sheriff's deputy had assumed, with the trigger under something heavy enough not to be moved by a mouse or chipmunk, but light enough for a man to move without difficulty. The toilet-paper can with a rock on top would have done nicely. Lift the can, a spring snaps shut, the circuit is completed, the thing goes off.

On the other hand, if I'd expected the explosive to sit

there for days or weeks, I'd have used a battery-powered receiver and set it off by radio.

And if, as Amelia suggested, it had been there for years?

Well, it simply couldn't have been. When I'd first seen the rock chimney, I'd looked at it closely, admiring the verticality of the shaft, the practicality of the use Amelia had put it to. There were small fissures, yes, but all of them were exposed to the weather. If one is storing explosives, one does not put them out where sun and rain can get at them. One puts them away, in some dry, safe place. So, to my mind, it was obvious that the explosives had not been there long.

There was always the possibility this was a completely random, practical-joke kind of thing perpetrated by some idiot who didn't know what he, or she, was doing. That didn't make sense, but then, until we knew how the thing had been set off, nothing made sense. Speculating about who, why, or when was useless. Until or unless they found parts of the thing, we wouldn't know whether it had been set a month ago or while we were mushroom hunting.

About four-thirty I quit pretending to work and went over to Grace's. When she showed up, wan and miserable looking, I insisted she shower and change and go out with me for a quick supper. "No place fancy," I promised. "Just a quick supper, and I'll bring you home."

She mumbled and vacillated, but I got her into and out of the shower and dressed. I'd forgotten it was Monday night, when a lot of the restaurants are closed. We were only five minutes from downtown, so we parked across from the Brown Palace and got a table at the Palace Arms. Grace ate very little and passed up dessert, which I'd seldom if ever seen her do. I kept my promise and took her home, sitting beside her when she collapsed bonelessly on the couch.

"That car," she said. "The one that let Ron off the other morning."

"What about it?"

"Did you see the license plate?"

I had. It was a Colorado plate, and I told her so. Also I'd noticed the letters on it, JZN, because they almost spelled my name. The numbers I hadn't looked at.

"Do you know what kind of car it was?"

I didn't. In recent years carmakers seem to have been contesting for anonymity. No car looks unlike any other car unless it's at least twenty years old or painted with some wild design. This one had been anonymously four-doored, and that's all I remembered.

"It had a bumper sticker, but I couldn't read it," she said. "I did see that same color up on the mountain."

She might well have. "I saw the same blue, yes," I agreed. "While we were mushroom hunting. And, likely, only one current manufacturer is using that particular blue."

"Could it have followed us?"

"I suppose it could have, Grace. It was Sunday. There were a lot of cars on the highway. You think this was someone out to get him?"

"I ... I got to thinking, maybe it was somebody out to get him, or anybody with him. Like the Colombians, you know, the drug dealers. They kill anybody. Wives. Kids. The idea is to scare people witless. Maybe ..."

"You don't think Ron was mixed up in something like that?"

"I don't know what he was mixed up in. But if all that talk about his *friend* was even partly factual, someone might have been trying to send that *friend* a message. If the bomb got you or me, Ron would transmit the message. If the bomb got Ron, Ron would be the message." She wiped her eyes. "It's all I can think of."

It made as much sense as anything I'd come up with. "Does he have any real friends here who would know what he's been up to?"

"Some people he's known for years. From before he moved. I know he got together with them at Christmas a few years ago. And I think they kept in touch."

She got up purposefully and went over to the chest that stood along the wall between the bedroom and kitchen doors. One of the large lower drawers held a canvas rucksack, which she brought over to where I was sitting. It held clothing, a Walkman, some tapes, a dog-eared high-school annual, Class of '81, and, at the bottom, atop a clutter of papers and envelopes, a spiral notebook with a rubber band around it.

"Ron's journal," she explained. "He kept everything important in here."

She opened it carefully, putting some of the things in it aside. Loose snapshots. A receipt for a Photomat place. A few small, dog-eared notes with their original envelopes, a couple of them with Denver return addresses.

"This guy," said Grace, holding up a small envelope. "Brew Tyrell. Brewster, I think. A family name. He and Ron were friends when they were kids. I know Brew saw him that Christmas Ron was here."

She took the note out, read it, flushed deeply, and put it back again.

"What?" I asked.

"Just a friend saying he'll always be a friend," she

whispered. "Look, it's dated a long time ago. It must have meant a lot to him."

Tears threatened to overflow once more. "Come on," I urged her. "What's he written in the book?"

"Poems," she whispered. "He was always writing poems." This was obviously painful for her, so I took the book from her hand, sorted out the envelopes and letters, and handed them back to her.

"You figure out the names that might be useful. I'll follow up on them."

"We will," she said firmly. "We both will."

We ended up with half a dozen names, four men, two women, all of whom had known Ron before he moved away. "I wanted him to stay here in Denver," she said musingly. "But he said my being a cop stifled him. Stifled his new friends, more likely. Not these people." She pointed at the list we'd made. "The people he knew in school were good people, but I can't say that about the new people he'd met. I told him he didn't need to worry about cops just because he was gay, particularly not a female cop like me, but the crowd he'd gotten in with didn't see it that way. They didn't like cops, period. I asked him why he picked people like that. He said they were exciting. I suppose they were. I told him they were dangerous. He said he knew it, he didn't care. They were into that whole . . . cruising thing."

She folded Ron's papers, put them back in the notebook, closed it with its rubber band once more, and restored it to the rucksack she'd found it in. "You take this," she said. "If these names don't pan out, maybe you can find something else useful in it."

We chatted a bit longer. I asked her what she wanted me to do with our mushroom harvest, which was still in the trunk. She told me to bring them in, she'd cut them up and thread them to dry. I put the rucksack in the trunk and carried in the harvest, then stayed to help with the cleaning and slicing while she strung the slices on stout thread and hung them from cupboard handles. When I left, about an hour later, the whole place had that woodsy, fungusy smell. Mushrooms won't dry that way where the humidity is high, but in Denver's dry air, it works very well.

I went home and took Bela for a late-evening run, fed him and Schnitz, then got out a bottle of wine I'd been saving and put on some music, all in aid of thought, so I told myself. A little later the phone rang; Mark, asking how Grace was. I told him.

"By the way, Mark, can you explain something to me? What does Grace mean when she says Ron was into that whole 'cruising' thing?"

An uncomfortable silence. "I'll come over," he said. "Pour me a glass of whatever you're having."

I turned on the gas log in the fireplace—no more wood-burning fireplaces in Denver, not with our pollution problem—and got out another glass. Mark arrived a few moments later, letting himself in the shop door downstairs with his own key and hollering on the stairs to let me know he was coming up.

"You asked about cruising," he said when he'd settled down across from me in one of the deep leather chairs. "It's not something I understand at an emotional level, because it never fit my notion of who I am. It has a lot of sadism and masochism to it, and to my mind that spells self-hatred. I don't relish the idea of promiscuous anonymity, a kind of ships-in-the-night lifestyle, where the ... participants have never seen one another before and may never see each other again."

"You're talking about what? Bathhouses?"

"Anonymous encounters anywhere, on any stamping ground at all."

"Prostitution?"

"Sometimes."

"What? Transvestites?"

He frowned. "That's no doubt a very visible part. Raging queens. Transvestite hookers. Affected passion in public. Pretty boys gushing over one another." He made a face. "The homophobes often talk about homosexuality as a lifestyle. Being gay is not a lifestyle, but cruising is."

"You don't approve?"

"No. Most homosexuals don't focus their whole social or professional lives on their sexuality any more than straight people do. Most heterosexuals aren't compulsive seducers, rapists, or pedophiles, even though some are, and neither are most gays. It upsets me that the whole gay pride thing has become a carnival for the sexually insatiable wacko fringe."

"Wacko fringe?"

He sipped thoughtfully at his wine. "Don't catch me saying this in public, but I've thought about it a lot. Maybe it's happened because gays were in the closet for so long. Their emotions were hidden, repressed. Some dealt with it, but for others, it was like living in a pressure cooker. They became habituated to it, habituated to the danger, to living on the edge of sanity. Rather like being . . . oh, I don't know, a foreign agent or something. Constantly looking over your shoulder. Eventually, when the repression let up, some simply went overboard."

"Understandable," I murmured.

"Oh, I understand the nut fringe all right. What I

don't understand are the apologists who now try to make a philosophy out of it."

"Like de Sade with cruelty," I said. "Like Don Juan with seduction. Like Crowley with demonism."

He grinned. "My, aren't we widely read."

"Not particularly," I said. "I took a course once on the history of sexuality in art. Different ages and cultures allow varying things to be shown in art; nudity, cruelty, blood and gore. We are, by the way, the first human culture to avidly display gore—blood and guts—in art, if you can call that kind of movie art. Which is beside the point. You object to philosophizing."

"The current preachers of promiscuity talk a lot about freeing sex from identity; about the intense creativity that can be liberated with the sexual impulse. About promiscuity having a lot to do with male socialization. Piffle. They picked up the banner of the sexual revolution: anything goes between consenting adults. Some of them forget the adults part and say anything goes. This is a minority, I'm talking about, Jason. A small minority, but it has become so vocal, so visible, that it's getting its own peculiar behavior identified as typically homosexual behavior. The extreme is being seen as the norm, and opposition to that extreme is hurting the rest of us. It's become the current issue, the way free love and drugs were in the sixties."

"Like Falwell howling about women's libbers who want to turn to witchcraft and sacrifice their babies?"

"Very much like that. If you're for women's rights, you must be for abortion, witchcraft, sacrifice of babies, and probably cutting off men's penises as well. If you're gay, you must be promiscuous, a spreader of HIV, a pedophile, and quite possibly a murderer. This conveniently ignores the fact that infanticide is most common in cultures where women have no rights and that virtually all wife beating and child abuse is committed by heterosexual males."

He frowned, annoyed with himself or me or the world in general. "Why did you want to know all this?"

"I want to know if there's anything there, in that lifestyle, which might have motivated someone to kill Ron Willis?"

He shifted uncomfortably, thinking. "Since he had AIDS, the most obvious idea would be that he infected someone, but that doesn't necessarily play. There's a lot of risk taking going on, a lot of what I'd call fatalism, or even nihilism."

"In what way?"

"Well, take the time a few years back when public-health people shut down the bathhouses in order to slow the spread of AIDS. You'd think everyone would approve, particularly those most at risk, but instead, there was an outcry. Even though the bathhouses were prime facilitators of infection, the existence of the bathhouses gave legitimacy to who and what the patrons were. Or thought they were. So they objected to the shutdown."

I frowned into my glass, not understanding.

He scowled in return. "The straight analogy might be other sexually transmitted diseases. Men have known for decades that condoms protect them from disease, but the more macho a guy is, the less likely he is to use condoms. You know?"

"Sex taking precedence over safety?"

"As it always has with some people. If sex expresses love, then you want it to be safe because you love your partner, you love yourself. If sex expresses excitement, power, domination, or violence, however, then safety isn't as important as the risk and the rush. If a hooker infects a guy, he might go back and beat up on her—that expresses his power over her—but he wouldn't protect against it in the first place because that wouldn't be macho. Macho is taking risks. It's like safety helmets for bikers. A person who rides for fun doesn't mind wearing one, but a person who rides to express his go-to-hell persona won't wear a helmet, though that won't stop him from suing the other driver when he ends up paralyzed. The freedom to risk becomes a political statement. Aided and abetted, may I say, by the Civil Libertarians."

I made an unbelieving face, and he laughed.

"Really. Health departments have had regulations dealing with sexually transmitted diseases for years. Syphilis, for example. If you get it, the department can chase down all your contacts and all their contacts. But not if you have AIDS. AIDS testing is anonymous. No one has a legal right to get the names of contacts. No one has a legal right to identify known carriers. That's civil rights, Jason."

"The fear of dying hasn't stopped it?"

"Not among the nihilists who already have it and don't give a damn. Not among those who're attracted by the danger! The danger is part of the thrill. The sexual equivalent of skydiving or free climbing. That may be true, though it wouldn't be for me. I'm too . . . conservative."

I refilled my glass and sat back down again. "So, boiling all this down, if Ron was into that, then he could have spread the disease, but you don't think that would make anyone angry enough to kill him."

"It's just unlikely. Anyone in that life might be exposed two or three times a day, any day in the year. The disease doesn't necessarily show up until months or years later. Anyone in that life would find it impossible to identify who infected him. Only monogamous people can say for sure where they got it."

"Not a likely motive, then."

"You said Ron was into drugs, and drugs are a more likely motive. If Grace is right, he wasn't mean or malicious, but one can do a lot of damage just witlessly stumbling around."

"Grace gave me a list of names, people he knew before he moved to California."

"I doubt you'll find much help there. I'll ask around, see if anyone here knew what he was up to. I don't move in the circles he did, but I have acquaintances who do."

"Grace blames herself."

He snorted. "The time is coming when we won't know who to blame. My father blamed my mother for the way I turned out. Suppose science finds out how to diagnose homosexuality and change it in utero? Will the gay community—forgive the phrase—allow that? Hell, right now you've got deaf people who don't want deaf children undergoing surgery that will give them some hearing. Deaf people say the deaf way, with sign language, is complete in itself, it doesn't need fixing. Right now you've got couples choosing to pass on genetic deformities rather than adopt. They decide a fifty-fifty risk is worth it to condemn a child to lifelong deformity, and if that isn't sociobiology talking, I don't know what is. 'We're deformed but we get along,' they say. 'We're deaf, but we get along. We're homosexuals, but we get along.' "

"You're very intense about it."

"I decided a long time ago, Jason, that an unselfish desire to have children is a poor second to the purely selfish desire to have a carbon copy of oneself, warts and all. At least it is where my father is concerned."

"Confusing," I allowed.

"Some days it inclines one to the monastery."

"All of which isn't the problem confronting me right now," I said in a surly voice. "I'm a simple, straight individual who simply and straightforwardly wants to get married."

He yawned, looked at his watch. "Grace will come around to it eventually. Right now she's got to get her grieving over with."

"It will help her if we find out why." I checked the clock over the mantel. Almost midnight.

"Then find out why, Jason. Amelia wants that, too. I talked to her this evening."

"I'm surprised she still wants me involved, after this."

"Amelia's got a good head. She's reliable." He hoisted himself out of the chair and stretched. "See you tomorrow, but I'll be in late. I've got to pick up some fabric samples for the curtains and slipcovers for your friend Valerie."

We said our good-byes and he departed. I heard the front door bolt go *thunk* behind him. I sat where I was for a long time, trying to think my way into Ron's life, as it had been. I have never courted danger in my life. When I was a kid I'd done things I was told not to, simply because I was told not to, adolescent rebellion asserting my control over my own life, but they weren't dangerous things. I'd done the same in the navy a few times, skirting insubordination by fairly narrow margins. Always, I'd kept the limits in mind. Like Mark, I'd been too conservative to get myself in much trouble.

Though perhaps it wasn't really conservatism. Mark

and I both had excellent imaginations, and it was imagination that saved us. When one can clearly imagine the trap springing, one does not put one's head in the noose. If one cannot imagine the noose, however, if one has never seen a noose, or if one believes nooses are only for others, then one goes on taking tea with the hangman's daughter, playing dice on the gibbet, putting the rope around one's neck, just for kicks, and eventually the trap springs while one is on it.

Ron could have believed that nooses were only for others. Grace had always talked the hangman away from Ron. Grace had always deflected the reckoning.

Which brought me right back to where I'd been some hours before. There was nothing that could be done about it until the crime lab came up with some facts. Ron probably wasn't killed because of his lifestyle, but that was opinion. And a device set days before would obviously have had nothing to do with Ron. Only one set that day, after we got there, could have had one of us as the intended victim.

Certain people who had once wanted to kill me were long gone, and to the best of my knowledge, no one else existed who had any reason to want me dead. Cops made enemies intermittently, so someone might conceivably want Grace dead. Without some facts to go by, cogitating over it was a waste of time. I went to bed, resolving to put it out of mind for the time being.

Tuesday morning, after Mark showed up, I went down to the Denver Main Library and spent the rest of the morning looking through architectural magazines, making a list of names and addresses, avoiding those with a tendency, as Amelia had put it, to build monuments, and paying particular attention to people in the western United States. Then I dropped in on a client

who managed one of Denver's better small hotels and
chatted with him briefly about staffing. He loaned me a
couple of hotel management texts, took me out to lunch,
and told me a dirty joke about the Rockies.

I spent the afternoon browsing through the texts,
making notes. By about four o'clock, it was clear that
before going any further, someone needed to define precisely how the place was to be used. Building a facility
for flexible use was no problem; staffing it definitely
would be. The staff required for twenty participants was
different both in quality and kind from that required for
fifty. The staff required for twenty who spent only a few
days would be different from the staff required for
guests who spent two weeks. If someone else did the
shopping, one cook, one pantry person, one dishwasher,
and one wait/busperson could prepare and serve breakfast and lunch, five days a week, while working only
forty hours. The evening meal would require a cook, an
assistant, two pantry people, two wait/buspersons. Assume the evening cook was also the chef who would
plan the meals and do the shopping. If these people
didn't work overtime, weekends would require a second
set of people who might, however, work long days and
do all three meals. So, we'd have around ten full-time
staff and five part-time staff for the kitchen, all of
whom would need to be housed on the place.

If there were fifty participants, the staff needs went
up, way up, and I wasn't out of the kitchen yet.

Maids or stewards needed an average of thirty to
forty-five minutes to make up a small single room and
bath. Twenty single rooms would require ten-plus hours
daily. It would take an additional three or four hours to
do the laundry. So, that was two full-time jobs, seven
days a week, which meant at least three people on var-

iable shifts. Another maintenance person or person and a half would be needed for windows, public areas, plus there'd be some groundskeeping.

One might consider a different style, one less hotel-like, more like a summer camp. One could have only a busperson/dishwasher and short-order cook on duty at breakfast and add a pantry person to provide a buffet lunch at noon, letting people wait on themselves. This would vastly reduce the staff needs. If linens were changed once a week and people made their own beds, the need for maids would be reduced. What did Amelia envision for entertainment? A game room, a card room, a library? Before I went any further, I wanted to talk to her about her vision of the place.

I phoned her office and left a message, made a quick circuit of Jason Lynx Interiors, to be sure the doors were locked, then fed the animals and took myself over to Grace's.

She was just out of the shower when I got there, damp hair in feathery strands and cheeks brightened by the steam. I told her she looked better.

"I feel some better," she admitted. "I made the funeral arrangements today. Well, not funeral, I guess. I'm having Ron cremated. I called my cousin in Minnesota. He's got the farm now, the one we used to visit in the summer. Uncle Bern still lives there, too. It's where Ron was happiest, when we were kids. I thought it would be nice to put his ashes there." Her eyes filled, and she turned away from me.

I put my arms around her and held her. "Are you going up there?"

"Maybe. For a few days. My cousin invited me."

Her phone rang and she answered, then hung up. "Damn people," she said. "Someone has been calling

me and hanging up ever since it happened. One of
Ron's so-called friends . . ."

She started to cry. I put my arms around her again.
"Grace, when you go, think about us. I want to get married."

"Jason," she said fretfully. "I—"

"Shhh. You don't need to say anything now. Just think
about us. Don't think only about life ending. Think about
it beginning, too."

She turned toward me, her eyes blazing. "Will you
find out who killed him?" she said challengingly, as
though it were a dare. "Will you do that for me?"

"I'll do my best," I said, shocked. For that moment
she looked fierce, lips drawn back, teeth showing, a
mama carnivore that had lost her one cub. "You realize
it might have had nothing to do with him. It could have
been meant for you, or me."

"It didn't kill you, or me. I want to know who killed
him! I'm not going to think about getting married until
I know who killed him!"

She drew a deep breath, then sobbed. "I didn't mean
that the way it sounded. I didn't want it to kill you, Jason. Or me."

There, just for a moment, I'd wondered if she would
have chosen it to happen to me rather than Ron. Their
mother had been gone since Grace was thirteen. She
had protected little brother as though he had been her
child. Biologically, I suppose, young take precedence
when it comes to protection. The male of the species is
supposed to look out for himself.

I took her out for a pizza. The minute we got back to
her place she called the airlines to make a reservation
for Minneapolis. She would rent a car to drive to the
farm, some two hours from the city.

"Can't your cousin fetch you?" I asked.

"Hours out of a farmer's day are hard to make up," she said. "Besides, I really sort of want some time alone."

She got a reservation for Thursday morning. She'd already arranged for a few days' leave. She was obviously not in the mood for company. I told her I'd drive her to the airport. She thanked me absently, almost as though I'd been a mere acquaintance, and I went home feeling dismal and abandoned, wondering if I should have offered to go to Minnesota with her. She'd said she wanted some time alone. Nonetheless, sometime tomorrow I would offer, just in case she changed her mind.

There was a message on my machine from Amelia, telling me she would drop in at the office in the morning. I neatened up the place a bit in honor of her visit, then spent an hour listening to music and thinking. Trying to think, even though there weren't enough facts available to think about.

Amelia, when she showed up on Wednesday morning, was in a ruminative mood.

"Bones," she said. "Have you any idea at all about these bones they found up there?"

I shook my head. "People die. People die in strange places, and have been doing so for at least eight thousand years."

"Oh, come . . ."

"Really. They found human bones up in the White River National Forest that evidently date back eight millennia, deep in a twisty cave, where someone maybe crawled to get away from someone or something and then just died. Perhaps he'd been wounded. Maybe he was sick."

"Eight thousand years," she said in awe. "I must have missed reading about it."

"He didn't make good copy," I admitted. "No artifacts, for one thing. A few smoke smudges on the wall to show he may have carried a torch. Not much to make a story out of, not like the iceman they found in Europe."

"You think the bones they found at my place are prehistoric?"

I shook my head at her. "No. The ones in the national forest were preserved because they were protected deep in a cave. The shaft up there at your place isn't protected at all. It probably has several openings. The rescue men said there were bats."

She shifted uncomfortably, and I read her mind. Perched on that privy, one would not like thinking about bats flying around below. "I never . . . saw bats."

"Nonetheless, there were bats."

"He, your fiancée's brother, he didn't suffer. . . ."

I told her what I'd told Grace. "The rock hit him suddenly, with overwhelming force. The cause of death was listed as massive skull fracture. He was dead before he dropped."

"We don't know about the bones, do we? Whether they . . . he was dead before he dropped."

"We don't even know it was a he, yet. We don't know how the person died or how old the remains are."

"Could someone have fallen in there, and then just starved, unable to get out?"

An uncomfortable thought, but possible. "How long have you had your one-hole plank over the shaft, Amelia?"

She frowned, thinking. "My father owned that land. He died when he was about sixty, and the year after he died, I started camping up there. It was when Kennedy was president . . . what, sixty-one, sixty-two. I was in my early twenties, just starting practice."

"I thought you said you bought the land?"

"I did. From the estate. It and some money and odds and ends of furniture and keepsakes were left to my father's brother, my uncle Maddox. Father probably had no idea what the place meant to me, or he'd have left it to me. The happiest memories I had were of that place. Every summer Father and Mother and I used to go up there for picnics. I remember how excited I was when I found the cave. I'm sure Father knew about it before, but he pretended I'd discovered it. For such a predator, he could be very sweet at times. He showed me the spring, how to follow the paint spots to find it. Back then, you couldn't see it from anywhere except right above it. It didn't spurt out the way it does now, it more or less trickled down the canyon wall. You had to lean way out to even see it. It was our secret, his and mine, a secret spring, all our own."

"We'll have to have it tested and see how much there is."

She nodded. "The water level's a lot higher now than it was when I first saw the place. We kept up the picnics, even when I was in high school, but in my senior year, Mother died. She was only forty-two. A young woman! Maybe the place reminded Father of happier times and made him grieve too much, because he never went there after that. He warned me off the place, too. Rattlesnakes, he said, but I think it was grief. It was his place, and if he didn't want me to go there, I wouldn't." She sighed, looking for a moment wistful.

"But I always remembered the place as a happy one for me, so when Father died a few years later, I went up there and camped out, something I'd always wanted to do. I explored the place thoroughly, fell in love with it all over again, loved the cave, loved the way the water jetted out of the stone. I called Uncle Maddox. He lived in Chicago at that time. I asked what he was going to do with the property. He said he didn't want the place, didn't intend ever coming back to Colorado, didn't know why Father left it or the other stuff to him, said he didn't need any furniture, didn't want any keepsakes, give the money to charity. So I did, and added ten thousand for the land and the furniture. . . ."

Her voice faded. She'd lost track of what I'd asked her.

I repeated the question. "When did you put the plank up there?"

"When I camped up there the first time, I decided I was going to make the place comfortable. Right after I bought the land from Maddox, I had the plank cut for the privy and some others cut and drilled for the hole over the spring, and I put them in place the next time I went."

"Why did you cover the spring shaft?"

"Because I turned my ankle on a loose rock and damned near fell into it on that first camping trip. I didn't want to risk it, and though it was unlikely anyone else would find the place, I didn't want some animal falling into it and fouling the water."

"You used the water?"

"It's where I get my cooking and washing water when I camp, just drop a bucket down and haul it up."

I looked at her formidable arms and shoulders with sudden appreciation. Fifty or so feet of rope and a full bucket would make a considerable load.

She saw my appraisal and laughed. "I use a tackle,

Jason. It's in the tin trunk, with my sleeping bag and cooking stuff and the nylon line. The cover to the spring is drilled to hold it. You clamp it on the side of the cover, then shift the cover over, and the tackle's right above the shaft. My own invention. I was so proud of it!"

"I'm surprised the wood has lasted this long."

"It's teak," she said. "I meant it to last. That place was special to me. I never wanted it to change, not ever. I wanted it just as it was, adding the least possible, taking nothing away. So, the few things I did add were supposed to weather and get gray and last as long as I did. Well. They almost made it."

I objected. "They haven't come near, yet. You've got decades to go. Tell me something, weren't you ever worried about staying up there by yourself?"

Her brow furrowed thoughtfully. "When I started going up there, no. I felt perfectly safe. The kinds of people who went to the mountains weren't the kinds who bothered women, or so I told myself. Later, yes, I worried about it. The last few years I've carried Mace and a gun and strung a few trip wires to prevent anyone sneaking up on me."

With that as preliminary, we started talking about the institute, her forehead lines becoming deeper and deeper as I went over the notes I'd made thus far.

"Lord," she said at last. "Such a complexity."

"Your land isn't Aspen," I said. "It isn't Vail. And it certainly isn't near enough to Denver to allow people to commute. All the people who work there are going to have to live there. The only way that will make economic sense is to have the place in use year-round, or at least most of the year, maybe closing down for one or two months midwinter. What you can't do is close it down after each session and then open it up again for the next one. If you want good staff, you'll have to guarantee steady employment."

She scowled. "It would make more sense to do it somewhere else, wouldn't it?"

"It would be easier. I'm not sure that means more sensible. Isolation has one advantage, and that is that people will probably focus more on the purpose of the institute than on socializing or sight-seeing as they might in some more touristy place."

She sat staring at the wall across my shoulder. "What if we took twenty acres or so along the road and built houses?" she asked at last. "What if we recruited families, all of whom would work for the institute? Daddy's a chef and Ma's a housekeeper and the kids are busboys or dishwashers, and the place is open nine months a year and they have three months off?"

"It could work. If you can find people with the right talents who are willing to live out in the wilderness. You'd need a little redundancy, to allow for illness or accident or the unforeseen problems that always crop up."

"I'll think about that," she said, rising and smoothing her skirt. "I feel a little foolish. You've done more thinking about this in two days than I evidently had in several years."

I shook my head at her. "You had a vision. I don't think visions are subject to analysis. You read about saints or angels appearing to people, saying things like 'Build a cathedral here,' or 'Lead the armies of France.' Somehow they never go into the engineering or logistics."

She laughed. We shook hands. She departed.

Mark stuck his head in. "How you doing?"

"Pretty much status quo. I've given Amelia something to think about. She's given me something to think about. I believe the explosion took some of the gloss off the institute idea for her."

He made a face. "She's decided not to do it?"

"No. She's a bit more aware of the isolation, that's all. A place that's great for camping out is not necessarily great for other purposes. Also, I think she's concerned about the bones."

He lifted the eyebrows. "Bones?"

"She's been camping up there for thirty years. She wonders how long the bones have been there. I'm sure she wonders who, as well."

She wasn't the only one who wondered. Grace called that afternoon to tell me an investigator from the state crime lab planned to go up the mountain and down the shaft to see if there was anything else there.

"Anything that might help identify the bones. A belt buckle, maybe. Contents of a pocket. Cloth fragments. Shoe soles. Something."

"Have they found anything to tell them how the device was set off?" I asked.

"Fragments of metal spring." She knew as well as I did what that meant. Ron had somehow set off the explosion.

I told her I'd be glad to go with her to Minnesota if she'd like company. She repeated her earlier statement, sounding very remote. She wanted some time alone. She was getting a ride to the airport with a friend of hers who was flying to New York. She'd call me when she got to her cousin's place.

Since Grace was my only link with the police investigation, I couldn't expect to learn anything else until she returned. Unless I found something out myself. And why not? I told Mark where I was going and suggested he check late that afternoon to be sure I'd made it back unscathed.

I put on some well-worn jeans and a T-shirt, the new hiking shoes, stuffed a flannel shirt and a jacket into the car, grabbed a few odds and ends from the kitchen, and invited Bela and Schnitz to go for a ride. For a wonder, Schnitz accepted the invitation. Unless it's a necessary trip to the vet, I never take the animals if they don't want to get into the car. A hundred twenty pounds of unwilling dog is a hundred twenty pounds too much, and an unwilling cat of any size is no fun yowling from a carrier and a fatal error in judgment if he's loose.

I kept a Schnitz harness and two leashes in the glove compartment for occasions like this. The only other supplies I thought I'd need were in the garage: a coil of rope, heavy gloves, and a hatchet. We set off, Bela upright on the backseat, looking out the window, Schnitz on the seat next to me, purring loudly. With Schnitz, purring could mean he was happy or it could betray anxiety. In this case, it was anxiety. He was still getting used to riding in the car and needed the sound of his own purr to reassure himself.

After a while Bela lay down, then Schnitz fell asleep, and everything was very quiet. When we turned off the highway on the Fall River Road, the animals wakened, and the rest of the way to the property they were both intent on the scenery. When we arrived at the land, I fished the harness and leashes out and made sure both critters were firmly anchored before I opened the door. Once Bela had sniffed his way around a little and knew where I would be, I could let him loose. Though I sometimes let Schnitz loose, today, with dense woods all around, I thought he should be attached to something while I went down the hole.

The bucket, line, and tackle Amelia had mentioned were in the cave. Nothing there seemed to have been bothered. The tackle was sturdy enough, though the line wasn't heavy enough to bear my weight. I'd figured as much. The coil of rope in my trunk would fit the tackle. Now all that remained was to find something I could put over the privy shaft to attach it to.

An hour and a half later I had the rig set. A stout sapling bridged the shaft from side to side, well wedged in. The tackle was attached to the sapling, and the rope to the tackle, sixty feet of it pulled through and knotted off so it could not pull out and strand me down below.

Flashlight in the pocket. Gloves to prevent rope burn, and a hard hat to prevent being brained by falling debris. I kept one in the trunk of the car for use on those rare occasions when Jason Lynx Interiors was involved in extensive remodeling or new construction. I dangled myself awkwardly over the shaft and lowered away. It felt like more than fifty feet, though it wasn't. I could see the knot in the pull rope, above me, still eight or ten feet below the sapling.

The shaft widened at the bottom. Up top, it was just chimney size, but the floor was the size of a large closet, if one counted the fissures and channels going off on all sides. Something hit my head with a crack, and I looked up. Bela was looking down at me, whining, dislodging a few more pieces of gravel as he moved around. I said his name a few times in a cheerful voice, and he decided I was all right. He lay down with his paws over the edge and his head on his paws, nose pointed down.

I began a laborious search of the hole. Piled guano

proved the rescuers had been right about the bats, though all of it was back in the larger fissures. There was no smell. The air flowing through the crevices was fresh and colder than the outside air, cooled by the stones through which it poured. The rock beneath me was dry, littered with sharp broken fragments and several big rocks, the fragments of the privy plank beneath them. Evidently the narrowness of the shaft had kept any very large boulders from coming down.

Any human use of the privy had been so sporadic that dung and urine had simply dried away or washed away into cracks along the floor. Around the edges were a few packed wads of toilet paper, obviously rain-sodden and dried many times. One of them looked newer than the others. There was nothing else at all, and that didn't make sense. The place should have accumulated some dust, at least rock dust from the explosion!

I tramped around, finally realizing that the center of the floor was higher than the edges. The stone was slightly convex, which meant that rain and melting snow simply washed all detritus away. It had rained recently, enough to flush the place clean.

I focused on the cracks along the floor. Anything too large to be washed down would hang up at that point, as the paper wads had done. My flash caught something shiny. A gleam. Something down and inside the crack. If I pushed at it, I might push it farther. I lay down and put my eye as close to the crack as possible, shining the light in from the side. It was definitely metal, thin and curved. I needed something to hook it out with. Nothing I had with me quite suited that purpose.

Sighing, I put the flash back in my pocket and hauled myself up and out of the shaft. It had been considerably easier going down. Once out, for some reason to do with aching shoulders, I was loath to go back below. Schnitz yowled angrily at me from the shady place I'd anchored his leash. Bela whuffed. It wasn't their usual mealtime, but it was mine. We'd have a bite before the next descent.

I took the animals over to the cave, rolled Amelia's sleeping bag out on the sandy floor, and sat on it to share the potluck I'd brought from home. A little bread and cold chicken. A little cheese. Olives. Schnitz refused olives, though Bela took one politely and spat it out when he thought I wasn't looking. Milk from a thermos cap, the first one for me, one for Bela, a half for Schnitz. A glance at my watch, which said get on with it, it was already two o'clock. I rolled up the sleeping bag and went back to the privy shaft, detouring by the car to pick up a wire coat hanger, part of my emergency kit.

Back down the rope with the coat hanger, which had been bent into a flat hook. After an awkward few moments bending and shifting, I managed to get the wire behind the metal and jiggle it loose. It had some other stuff with it. When I got it out in the light, the metal turned out to be a ring and the other stuff turned out to be fingerbones held together by shreds of whatever. Skin. Muscle.

I'm not particularly squeamish, but I didn't want to touch them. Finally, I took out a handkerchief, wrapped the whole thing up, and put it in my pocket. I was about to start up the shaft when all hell broke loose above me: Bela barking, Schnitz screeching like a banshee, someone yelling, a hideous growl from Bela, the like of which I had never heard from him before, and a clatter of stones. I got out of there in about one third the time it had taken me previously, but when I hauled myself out, Bela was gone, Schnitz was gone—the rock I'd fastened his leash to was overturned—and somewhere down the mountain was a good deal of confused noise ending with the revving of a car engine and a sound I took for a shot.

I didn't even think. I just ran for the road. When I got down the hill, the dust still hung in the air and Bela lay to one side growling to himself. There was blood on his shoulder. He was licking it, and when I came up to him, he looked up at me from opaque eyes that, for the moment, did not know me. Then he whined miserably. He'd failed to maim the miscreant and he felt badly about it.

I knelt down to examine the wound. I couldn't tell whether he'd been grazed by a bullet or cut with a knife. Whichever, the red line ran across his shoulder, not into it. "Stay," I told him, turning to go back up the hill. He stayed, licking at his shoulder while I went hunting.

Schnitz was halfway up a tree, one of those nearest the rock terrace. The leash was tangled around a branch. He couldn't get down. Eventually, I got up. Then, with Schnitz on my shoulder, I went back to the shaft, disassembled the climbing gear, put the tackle back in the cave, and carried the rope and our other odds and ends back down the slope to the car. Bela was right where I'd left him.

He whined when he got to his feet and yelped when he climbed into the car. The shoulder hurt. I sat in the driver's seat and shook with an unpleasant mixture of anger and fear. Bela is among the friendliest of animals. He barks, but that's mere announcement. He growls seldom, and then only at people he believes are up to no good. So, whoever the invader or invaders had been, they had shown some hostile intent that the dog had picked up on. Mere sneakiness could have been enough. I've noticed that dogs will growl at skulkers while ignoring people walking openly about their business.

Whatever, at least one invader had been armed. Maybe this had been a chance passerby who had seen the Mercedes and decided to try a little wilderness mugging. How close had he or they come? Close enough to see the tackle over the shaft? At what point had Bela taken umbrage?

Bela, still busy with his shoulder, wasn't telling.

I reached into my pocket for the keys, encountering the handkerchief-wrapped packet. Almost unwillingly, I took it out and unfolded it. A ring, and the bones of a finger. Not touching the finger, I took up the ring and peered at it closely. A simple gold setting of three oval stones. I didn't recognize the stones, a deep greenish blue, not emeralds. Inscribed, on the inner face. *Forever. A.* And numbers, maybe a date, which I couldn't make out.

We went down the mountain expeditiously, not fast enough to be stupid but as quickly as traffic would permit, going straight to the vet's office, where Bela was given a shot of antibiotic and had the area around the wound shaved and doused with antiseptic. I got a week's worth of antibiotic capsules for him, one every morning, one every evening.

Dr. Carson said it was a gunshot. "We see a few every year," he said. "Dogs shot on someone else's property. Dogs shot on their own property. Evil dogs that need shooting. Nice dogs that no one could be mad at." He went on to tell me about six or seven dogs and their owners, including a good bit of gossip and conjecture.

He was a good vet but a terrible busybody, at least so Grace always said.

He ended with, "This is just a flesh wound, no bones or nerves involved. Let me know if it shows any signs of infection. By the way, how did it happen?"

I told him we were picnicking in the mountains and that I thought someone had shot at Bela without seeing him. There was no good to be achieved by adding a murder and a mysterious skeleton to Dr. Carson's repertoire of interesting tales. Neither did I intend to give the finger and the ring to the police. Grace was too upset to be bothered with it just now, so I'd wait until she returned to say anything about it.

I did show it to Mark the next morning. He immediately put his own hand down next to the bones, comparing the length of his fingers. "A lot smaller than mine," he said. "Do bones shrink when they dry?"

I had no idea. Wood does, of course. I'd had no experience with bone. We got out a magnifying glass and had a look at the numbers engraved inside the ring, 8957.

"Some private meaning," said Mark. "Scriptural reference, maybe? Or page and line of a book of poems, or a favorite novel? What are the stones? Peridots? They have that chartreuse color. Or maybe tourmaline."

I shrugged. "I'm no jewelry expert. Maybe when we find out how long the bones have been in there, it'll give us a clue."

"Odd, having two bodies down the same hole, separated by—what? Decades, at least?"

"It's a perfect oubliette," I said. "And the spring is even better. When I saw the spring, the first thought that went through my mind was what a wonderful place to hide something you didn't want anyone to find, ever."

"You weren't thinking of a body, were you?"

"Not at that moment, no. I was thinking more in terms of evidence that couldn't easily be burned or destroyed. A murder weapon, maybe."

"Here we go again!"

I flushed. There was already an actual murder before us, Ron's. We didn't need the complication of an older, even more mysterious one. I wrapped the bones and ring in their tissue, put them in my bottom desk drawer, and changed the subject.

"I can't do anything useful about that until Grace gets back. What's on the Jason Lynx agenda that needs attention."

"As I mentioned the other day, we have two new clients. You've only seen one of them."

I raised my eyebrows. That's right. He had said two.

"The other one came in a week ago, asking for you. He has a very interesting problem for you, as soon as you have time."

This was said with such complete innocence that I immediately smelled a rat. "What are you up to, Mark?"

"Not a thing." He managed to look hurt and gleeful, both at once. "We have a man with a problem, and you are our preeminent problem solver. I have no idea why you should find anything suspect in that."

"Who is he?"

"His name is Wilson Credable. He has lately inherited a large property from his mother, who had it from his father, who died, one suspects, from an excess of wrath."

"Not the Credable Castle!"

"The same." He giggled.

As well he might. That monstrous structure had been

a blot on the urban scene for at least half a century. When it was built, in the late 1800s, it had commanded an extensive acreage so far east of Denver that it was thought unlikely the city would ever go that far. The city had, alas, gone that far and farther, and the Credable Castle now loomed over near suburbia, an exuberant octopus of tottery towers and eroding battlements.

"What's his problem?" I snarled. "A bulldozer or two, some well-placed explosives, and the job's done."

"He doesn't inherit if he pulls it down."

"He has to keep it?"

"Not only keep it, but live in it."

"Why would anyone . . ."

"Wilson was indiscreet. He told his parents the place was an eyesore furnished mostly with tasteless excrescences. Papa, Crispin Credable Junior, was always proud of the place, so he took a nearly fatal dose of umbrage. Papa left everything to Wilson—Mama having a life interest—but only if Wilson lives in Credable Castle and learns, so sayeth the will, to value his patrimony."

"I have a hunch there's more."

"Not a lot, no. He has to live there. He can't sell it or tear it down. Papa Credable was in his eighties when he died, but Wilson is a child of Daddy's later years, so he's not a lot older than you are, Jason. I told him you'd understand his predicament."

I began to get a glimmer. "He can sell the contents?"

"Nothing in the will refers to the contents. Only to the house."

"He wants me to come see him?"

"As soon as possible."

Mark made the call. I changed into something more conservative, just on general principles, and drove out to the castle. The approach is by a perfectly normal suburban street, with well-trimmed lawns on either side, and then one comes to a seeming cul-de-sac fronted by tall iron gates beyond which rears a great forest of untrimmed trees. Behind and above the trees looms an enormous pile of gray granite, like the wild shores of northern Scotland, fiercely defendable. One expects pennants and a flourish of trumpets. Or maybe a bagpipe, on the battlements.

I'd seen pictures of the place before. About once every ten years some new reporter for one of the two Denver dailies decides it would make a nice feature, usually sometime around Halloween. The quasi-familiar gates were open, the drive was through deep shade, the front door was double and twelve feet high, made to look even taller by being at the top of a flight of granite steps. Though somewhat prepared for the place, I wasn't prepared for Wilson, an apple-cheeked little man with a lisp and a ponytail. Something told me Daddy had more than a few hasty words to hold against his son.

"So you're Jason," he said. "Mark has told me all about you. Come in. Don't trip over the draft excluder. It was windy last night, so I strung it out along the bottom of that door. The weather stripping keeps coming loose."

The draft excluder was about three feet long, three inches in diameter, and completely covered with beads patterned to represent a diamondback rattler, even to the quite real rattles at the end of the tail. It felt like it was full of dried beans. "I've never seen one like that before," I murmured, appalled.

"And never shall again, I don't doubt. Grandmama

had a great deal of time on her hands for fancywork, and so did Mama."

"Snakes aren't quite what one thinks of when designing beadwork," I murmured.

"You miss the point," he said crisply. "Snakes are already designed as beadwork. Grandma Rose copied him, scale for scale, from a real one. One fancies she kept it alive just for that purpose."

He led me farther into the great hall. Stairs wound upward into crepuscular gloom. Light fell through stained glass. At the end of the hall an enormous grandfather clock ticked solemnly, each tock a footfall. There wasn't a cliché missing.

"We're going to the parlor?" I asked. "Or is it . . ."

"The grand salon," he replied, leading me down the hallway, left turn, down three steps, through an arch. Grand salon, indeed. High ceiling supported by marble columns surmounted by complicated capitals. Coved, painted ceiling with ornamental plaster. Huge fireplaces, two of them, manteled and overmanteled in marble of at least six colors. Blue. Green. White. Pink. Gray. Black. I found myself tallying. Ornate chairs and sofas, covered in damask. Complicated draperies of more damask, heavily fringed in gold. Étagères, laden with curiosities, fringed carpets in faded colors, threadbare in spots. That fashionable clutter so dear to the hearts of Victorians. Not a square foot of bare wall, not a square inch of bare table, not an upholstered arm or headrest unantimacassared. A gigantic, gilt-framed oil hung over the fireplace, echoing another across the room: the nearer a portrait, the farther a bellowing stag athwart dark and misty mountains.

"I find it oppressive," he said. "Damned oppressive." He led me through the room into a dining room of like proportions. Oak table and chairs, sixteen of them. Crystal chandelier, somewhat cobwebby, china cupboards built in on both sides, bevel-glass doors above, paneled below, an acre of tortured oak carved in deep relief: fruit and dead rabbits; flowers and dead pheasants. The carpet in here was turkey red, old as the hills, about thirty feet long and fifteen feet wide. We went from there into a series of pantries, from these into the kitchen—cavernously antediluvian, with an open arch leading back to servants' quarters—from that into another, smaller dining room, and thence into what I suppose would be called a morning room. Smaller than the grand salon, at least, with only one fireplace, a piano, bookshelves, window seats, more comfortable furniture. Sprawled about were three young people, each with a pile of books, one with a laptop computer and the other two with notebooks.

"Members of our Excelsior group," he said, introducing us. "Angel Garcia, Ann Louise Washington, Paul Lo."

They rose variously, said how do you do, also variously. Paul was polite, Ann Louise sincere, Angel wary. I murmured something about not disturbing their work, and they went back to what they'd been doing. When we reached the front hall, I asked Wilson about the Excelsior group.

"It's a tutoring group. It started with just me, but I've got a dozen other well-educated ne'er-do-wells involved."

"Ne'er-do-wells?"

"People who had expensive educations, who are living on family money, like me, wasting all that tutelage. I've got two other dilettantes like me and nine so-called housewives. We each take two to four young people and provide study space, resource material, computer use, plus personal supervision. The three in there are studying English drama and verse right now. It's what I'm best at. Meantime, I'm boning up on African history, on Mexican and South American literature, in translation, regrettably. They also need more math. They need more science. I'm auditing college courses in both. When I was in school, I simply wasn't interested."

"Your interest now is the most interesting thing I've seen here," I said, intending to be flattering.

"What you've seen is just the center of the house," he said plaintively, disregarding the compliment. "You haven't seen the library, the billiards room, the study, the conservatory, the gardener's suite, the garages-cum-stables, or the children's dayroom. Upstairs are three floors of bedrooms and baths; en suite, as one might say. Grandpapa did build in a lot of baths."

"What, exactly, does the will provide?" I asked him pointedly.

"There's money," he said, with perfect candor and calm. "An income. I'd like to keep it. I can't have it unless I live here with my 'family.' I am not allowed to tear it down, though once I'm dead, the next heir may tear it down if he or she wishes. The next heir is all too ready to do just that. My cousin, Edward, who every now and then makes threatening noises, who has within the last few days stepped up the annoyance, who now has the unmitigated gall to use my phone as a message service! Edward is son of Papa's next oldest brother, Admar."

"You had no siblings?"

"I was the only chick in this barnyard."

"You don't want to live with it the way it is?"

"The problem is, I can't continue to live in it the way

I am, a bachelor, if Edward can prove the will requires me to have a family. Besides which, one cannot call it living," he said, glaring fiercely in my direction. "One might possibly call it drowning, or suffocating, but one could not call it living."

"You can shut all of it up but three or four rooms and use those," I suggested.

"Unfortunately, Edward is poised to challenge my inheritance on any possible grounds. The will is clear. I and my family must 'dwell in and maintain' the entire house."

"And your family."

"A not-so-subtle hint. Thus far the attorneys have held Edward at bay. When I turned forty-five this year, however, Edward claimed I was past the age of marriage, that my time had run out."

I considered this while looking back through the arch at the morning room. That room at least was not impossible. If some of the trees outside were thinned, it would get the morning sun, and the paneling was simple enough to be elegant. Take down eighty percent of the pictures, put some plain carpet into it, something not so busy as the Axminster currently in use, remove half the furniture and reupholster the other half, the morning room would at least be livable.

We wandered back to the grand salon. I sat down on a worn silk covered *confidante*. Wilson offered tea. I accepted. He trotted off, returning in a few moments with a tray.

"You don't live here alone, do you? You've got to have help with this place?"

"There's a cleaning crew that comes in every week, a contract gardener who mows the lawns and does the watering. Then I have a local woman who launders and does a little cooking for me. Mostly I eat out."

"You have enough capital to remodel some, if that's what you decide to do?"

"You mean, make a livable apartment or something?"

"Something."

"I have very little usable capital. The investments produce a steady, reasonable income on which I can live out my days in comfort. In addition to meeting the expenses of maintaining this monstrosity, there is enough for wine, for decent dining, for one's small charities, for the necessities of life, but there is no big money to tap. I thought maybe some of the excess furnishings might bring something to be prudently invested. Or at least to fix the roof!"

They would, certainly. "Let's be sure we understand each other," I said. "You can sell some or most of the furnishings, but you and 'your family' still have to occupy the house. You can't tear it down, but you could remodel if you had the money."

"So my attorney tells me. Anything more than that, Cousin Edward will come roaring down from Wyoming. Cousin Edward is a man's man. Though older than I by at least a generation—Uncle Admar, unlike Papa, moved expeditiously to his reproductive duties—Edward rides and ropes and shoots varmints and brands cattle. I am sure he dreams of setting a branding iron to my shrinking flesh and claiming Castle Credable for his own. Perhaps I should put a moat around it. Water is the only challenge that Edward cannot meet! Of course, he blames even that on me."

I didn't follow up on this conversational tidbit. "When we finish our tea, let's see the rest of the house," I suggested, and for the next two hours that's what we did.

He gave me a bit of the family history while we were walking through room after room after room. Grandpa Credable, Crispin Credable the First, had a wife, five unmarried sisters, eight children, and a railway fortune when he moved to Denver in 1890. Credable Castle was built to house all those sisters, all those children plus those yet to come, plus all the servants the moneyed classes at that time considered necessary to serve such a ménage. The first wife, Grandma Minerva, died in 1899.

"One supposes she had been ill for some time," said Wilson. "Though she was comparatively young, there were no children born during the last ten years of her life."

In 1900, Crispin the First was married again, to Grandma Rose, begetting in rapid succession: Crispin Credable, Jr., 1901; Ethelia Credable, 1903; Carolyn Credable, 1905; and Admar Credable, 1907. By that time the elder Credable's sisters had been married off—they were dowered extremely well, said Wilson—and the first lot of children, separated by at least a decade from the second lot, had either died or scattered. Of the twelve Credable children, only Crispin Credable Jr., Carolyn, and Admar survived their father. Crispin Jr., fell heir to the monstrous pile in 1925, when he was quite a young man, certainly unwed, and quite probably—so said Wilson—without issue.

"I don't think Papa was at all interested in sex. He didn't marry until he was almost fifty, and a lack of interest in matters amatory would explain certain tensions between Mummy and him that were evident to me as a child. Even though he never managed more than me—if, indeed, it was he who managed me—it didn't mitigate his or Mummy's expectation of their only heir. I, mind you, was supposed to emulate Grandpapa and beget an enormous horde. It was my bedtime story for more years than I care to remember. I have only to close my eyes and I hear Mummy's voice in my ear. 'When you grow up, Wilson, and have lots and lots of babies.' If they were so set on lots and lots of babies, why didn't they adopt! Or why didn't they give the place to Uncle Admar! By all accounts, he'd have reproduced for 'em.''

He sounded quite petulant about it.

"What do you do?" I asked. "How do you spend your time? In addition to the tutoring, of course."

"For shame! You can't tell? My dear boy, I'm an actor. It's only amateur theatrics, but we do have fun."

"And what made you think of Jason Lynx as a way out of your difficulty?"

"Didn't Mark tell you? It was Amelia Wirtz who told me all about you. She told me you had all sorts of clever you'd never even used yet. Dear Amelia. She's a patron of our theater group. Though it sounds unlikely, the lord high executioner—her papa—and the castellan—my papa—were the greatest of friends."

three

T HE CASE OF Wilson Credable—whose name was also Crispin, it turned out, though he refused to be called the Third—presented an intriguing problem that bobbed about in my head like a cork on a fishing line, not quite signaling a catch. Selling off some of the family impedimenta would not be difficult. Taken individually, many of the pieces were interesting and valuable, even beautiful. Taken en masse, as poor Wilson was obliged to take them, they were no doubt as suffocating as he said.

There are still a good many large houses around Denver that were built and furnished during Victorian times. I encounter one every now and then, usually when elderly parents have died and children or grandchildren are trying to deal with all that clutter. The Victorians themselves must have dealt with it by spending a good deal of time out-of-doors, on porches, in summerhouses, traveling or vacationing. One sees photographs of the ladies reclining upon the sward in their white shirts and boaters, their full gabardine skirts and laced boots, surrounded by wicker baskets and painting gear. Perhaps this outdoor life was an escape, whether they realized it or not, from all those things they heaped up about them back at home. They took fresh air as an antidote to dim and dusty rooms that could never be anything but dim and dusty, despite the constant efforts of one or more parlor maids.

The Victorian way of life—at least for the middle and upper classes—almost required the acquisition of stuff. There was the ritual of the grand tour, the obligatory long trip to Europe from which travelers returned laden with memorabilia, each bit of which had to find some pride of place: lamps, tables, chairs, hangings, paintings, carpets, sculpture—the list was endless. There were the summer holidays that produced similar, though smaller, assortments of souvenirs; the visiting back and forth that produced still more. Then there was all that "fancywork" with which women—those with servants—occupied much of their time: beadwork, wax flowers, poker work, shell boxes, silhouettes, découpage, china painting, watercolors, pressed flowers, and of course needlework in all its varieties; embroidery and petit point and tatting and crocheting, as though it was the particular destiny of women to fill the universe with lace collars and antimacassars.

The early Victorians collected things; later travelers collected both things and photographs of things; both to the same purpose—to make recollectable certain occasions they might otherwise forget. Despite the memorabilia, in time the occasions were forgotten, leaving behind only the things or the pictures of the things to confuse and bedevil later generations. Wilson Credable was so bedeviled, lost in a jungle of other people's lives.

Still, furnishings weren't his real problem. Cousin Edward wouldn't make an issue of furniture, but he would make an issue of Wilson's having no issue, so to speak. I discoursed on all this to Mark over a simple supper in my kitchen, two heads supposedly being better than one.

I concluded, "Wilson says his father and Amelia's father were buddies. You've described Amelia's father as a—"

"A very hostile, power-hungry man. According to my father, whose older associates had run-ins with him."

"All right. But Wilson believes the elder Credable to have been gay—or perhaps asexual. Wouldn't old Wirtz have rejected such a friendship?"

"I doubt Wirtz would have known," Mark offered. "Back then, sexuality was kept very quiet, whether hetero, homo, or bi, and by all accounts, Wirtz wasn't very perceptive about people. You know he was called the lord high executioner, like in the *Mikado*? Supposedly, he had a little list, and it was wise not to get on it. One of the local journalists did a biography after his death—unauthorized, need I say? It was called *One Very Angry Man*, and several of Wirtz's acquaintances and business colleagues were quoted as saying Wirtz was much given to threats and bluster and general hatefulness. I asked Amelia about it. She said yes, he really was a terror to live with, she didn't know how her mother had managed it."

"She would have seen a side of him that others didn't, perhaps?"

Mark made a face. "Wirtz was born around the turn of the century. So was Credable Junior. Wilson's father and Wirtz were contemporaries, both born and brought up in east Denver at a time when it was a fairly small town. They may even have attended the same schools."

"Public schools?"

He leaned back and considered this. "Neighborhood schools were pretty well segregated by race and social class. Could have been public school. Could have been private school—one of the country day schools—or military school. There's a military academy down in Roswell, New Mexico, where some of the middling gentry used to send sons they didn't quite know what to do with."

He said it almost bitterly.

"You, Mark?"

"I was sixteen at the time it was threatened. It remained only a threat. Mother reminded Father that it hadn't worked in other cases."

"Hadn't worked?"

"Had not 'made a man of' other sons and heirs. There was at least one suicide she trotted out as exemplary. The military was always the venue of last resort, wasn't it? If your son didn't go into the family business, didn't go into holy orders or a learned profession, he could always go into the army."

"Very British," I opined.

"Well, American upper classes tended to be Anglophile up until the last few decades. None of which has anything to do with poor Wilson's problem."

"You speak as though you know him. What kind of person is he, really?"

"I've met him. I know him mostly by reputation. He's said to be enormously kind. He volunteers for all sorts of good causes. He almost single-handedly supports a tutoring program for bright minority kids who should be but aren't doing well in school."

"I saw some of them at his place. He said something about amateur theatrics?"

"With the kids, yes. He picks minority kids who speak abominably—à la Professor Higgins—and makes them memorize great hunks of highfalutin' English.

They put on shows and all Wilson's friends are commanded to buy tickets and attend. I've been, a few times."

"Are they any good?"

"On occasion, yes. And they're never painful, never embarrassing. Wilson wouldn't let his kids be embarrassed."

I nodded, understanding. "He seemed lonely to me."

"Even before Wilson's mother died—she was an invalid for a number of years—Wilson had a very good friend living with him. The friend died last year. Not AIDS. Something quite unrelated. I've been told Wilson was devastated, and since then he's redoubled his good works."

"Who's his lawyer?" I asked, thinking of the will. "I would much like to check on the provisions of the will."

"Amelia, of course. They're very close."

I was surprised. "There's at least ten years' difference in their ages. How did they get friendly with one another?"

"I really don't know how it came about. You'd have to ask Amelia."

Which I did later that evening, by phone, after thanking her for thinking of me anent Wilson Credable.

"You are trying to keep me busy, aren't you, Amelia."

"Someone needs to take you in hand," she said severely. "Why don't you marry that nice girl and settle down?"

"Nothing would please me more. If I can get her to agree. Which she is not in the mood to do at the moment."

"She has other things on her mind. She loved that bothersome brother of hers, didn't she?"

I said she had indeed, and still did. "Speaking of bothersome, would you mind telling me what your involvement is with Wilson Credable?"

"Our parents were friends. That is, Hector Wirtz and Crispin Junior were friends, as were Emmeline Credable and my mother, Janet."

"But not all four?"

"I wouldn't go so far as to say the men were friends of the women. Back then, intersex friendship wasn't considered appropriate, much less necessary. The sexes intersected, so to speak, publicly at the table, privately in the bedroom. Elsewhere, they were largely segregated. We two families used to take ritualized vacations together back in the fifties, sans servants, at which time I was usually told to mind the baby—Wilson, that is, though his mommy always called him Crispin the Third. Actually, she called him Threesy, which he quite hated. On occasion the chatelaine and her son would be invited to our house for lunch, then Mother and I would be invited to the castle, quid pro quo. When he got to be a little older, six or seven, he'd take me around the castle while my mother and his played cards with his uncle Admar and aunt Carolyn. Wilson had all sorts of fun cubbies and hiding places. He was also a lonely little bastard. I suppose I was, too."

"Lonely little bastard?"

"In his case, I use the word in a suppositional sense. When he got to be older, he went through that thing many unhappy kids do, doubting that his parents were really his parents—more particularly doubting that his father was really his father. He doted on Emmeline, his mother. She was a sweet woman. She went on inviting me for lunch, even after Mother went off to Mexico and died."

"In Mexico?"

"She fell ill and died there. As I was saying, it was I who told Wilson he was gay, as a matter of fact, when he was about fifteen. It had been obvious to me for a couple of years. He then wondered, in this voice of incredulous discovery, if he might not have inherited the tendency. I told him he was either his father's son or not, but he couldn't have inherited anything from his father unless he was his father's son."

"Since Crispin the Second, Crispin Junior, was friendly with your father, did you ever think your father . . ."

She snorted. "Lord, no, Jason. I don't think my father was gay. I believe he was simply disgusted by any human contact whatsoever. It wasn't that he loved men, it was that he didn't love anyone. I never saw him hug or kiss Mother or even give her—or anyone—a warm handshake. Certainly he never did me! I firmly believe he consummated his marriage to my mother only because consummation is required for a legal union, and I'll wager he did it in three minutes flat and never touched her again except with a gloved hand. That consummation resulted in me, and I've blessed the law for my existence ever since." She laughed at my sudden silence. "I've shocked you! Lord, what a priss you are."

Silently, I agreed. Intimate revelations did tend to make me uncomfortable. Once you know something very personal about another person, the person is changed. It is almost as though one must begin again with this more complicated person, making the acquaintance anew on a more convoluted and tentative basis. Which was all well and good with someone

much-liked, or loved, like Mark or Grace. Such friend-
ships tend to be convoluted anyhow, the deeper the
twistier. With certain others, however, those who were
mere casual acquaintances, when I learned more than I
wanted to know, it was difficult afterward to be with
them at all. I had to adopt a role first, put on my glazing, take up a manner of smooth and inconsequent com-
placency, a social face. Grace—who first made me
aware that I do this—dislikes it extremely. She says it
makes her think she is consorting with a mannequin.

I said nothing of this to Amelia, but merely agreed
that I was a bit stuffy about other people's sex lives,
and if I'd thought about it first, I'd never have asked the
question.

"What are you going to do for dear Wilson?" she
asked, still amused at me.

"I don't know, Amelia. I can sell his furniture, that's
no problem. There's quite a good market for Victorian
bric-a-brac, and that house can only benefit from a
decor-ectomy."

"Well, Jason, as for the rest of his problem, you
might think of Wilson as a possible murder victim.
Mark has told me you're very good with murders. If
you pretend Wilson is dead, maybe you can think up
something that would have prevented his demise. He really will die if he is thrust into the world on his own.
Living as a third-generation Credable quite unfits one
for serious work of any kind."

"You don't mean die, Amelia. I mean, surely that's
overstating the case."

"I mean die. He hates that old place with a passion,
but it's his shell. He's a little old hermit crab rattling
around in some vast chambered nautilus, but he'd be

dead in a minute without it. The world would eat him up! Think of something for him, Jason. Be useful."

I tried being useful, cudgeling my brain about Wilson Credable, and I was still at it when Grace called from Minnesota about ten. She sounded weary and no more relaxed than when I'd seen her last.

"I'm staying a few days," she said. "I haven't seen Uncle Bern and the cousins for years. I'm making it a family visit."

"You sound tired, love."

"Well, we went out by the pond, where the willow trees are. Ron and I used to play there, with the branches down all around us. We pretended we were Indians, or pirates, or castaways. We put his ashes there, under trees."

Her voice touched a chord inside me, a melancholy sound, the faint reverberation of old loss. "It sounds very peaceful."

"It is." Long silence. "Jason . . ."

"Yes, love."

"I've been thinking about what you said."

"So have I."

Long silence, which I broke by asking, "You want me to go over and feed Critter?"

"I took him to Margo's." Margo runs a small boarding kennel out of her home in Aurora. "We'll talk when I get back."

And that was it. No promise. No rejection. Just, we'd talk when she got back.

In my bedroom, Bela was already curled up in his dog bed, nose under one paw. Schnitz was on his side of my bed, his back pushed up against the pillows. He opened one yellow eye and glared at me, revving up his purr. I gave him a skull massage, working my fingers down his backbone to his tail, which twitched apprehensively. Schnitz did not like people fooling with his tail.

I read for a while, not with any great concentration. Something was teasing at me, something about Wilson Credable. About eleven, I gave up and turned out the light. In the middle of the night I awoke, said "Aha," very loudly into the silent room, then turned over and went back to sleep. In the morning, I distinctly remembered saying "Aha," but I had no idea why.

Credable Castle had to be inventoried if we were going to sell any part of the furnishings. Friday morning I called Wilson, explained the matter, and asked if there were any inventories done when he had inherited from his father. For purposes of estate valuation, there should have been, but he claimed no knowledge of such. I talked to Eugenia about it, and we decided the two of us would spend the next couple of days doing a few of the first-floor rooms while Mark saw to Valerie French's problem, which he consented to do with a slight sneer. It was perfectly obvious that something about the Valerie French situation annoyed him, but I hadn't time to follow up on it just then. I called Wilson back; he said "Excelsior," by which I took it he meant onward and upward. Certainly he wasn't referring to packing material at this stage.

"I've never seen the inside of the castle," Eugenia said, sounding almost eager. "Is it dreadful?"

"It's not what I'd call livable. It's Victorian in spades."

"Bric-a-brac," she said in a tone of anticipation. "I love bric-a-brac."

To each his own, I thought, parking outside the half

flight of granite steps that led up to the balustraded terrace outside the front door.

"Oh, goody," breathed Eugenia.

She flushed when I gave her a look of surprise. "Goody?" I asked.

She shrugged. "We might discover something wonderful."

Quite true. We might. I was not counting on it, however.

Wilson let us in and waved toward the grand salon. "I'm working with the kids in the morning room. I'll join you in a bit." He turned back through the right-hand door while I marched down the threadbare Orientals to the stairs, Eugenia trailing behind.

"Oh, my," she whispered, when we reached the steps. "Good heavens."

In all the time we have worked together, I have never seen her in such a mood of unbuttoned eagerness. She is usually tough as a sergeant major and stiff as a cob. I cleared a dozen objets d'art from the nearest table to make room for my briefcase. We each took a clipboard and a set of forms and started around the room, I clockwise, Eugenia counterclockwise.

"Do we do cupboards?" she asked in a small voice utterly unlike her usual manner.

I turned, looking where she was looking. The cupboards were built into the paneling, all along one wall. I hadn't even noticed them until that moment, and the thought of what might be inside was daunting.

"Not today," I said firmly. "Today we'll just do what's on display."

A quarter of an hour later Wilson came to help us. That's what he called it. What he actually did was emit a stream-of-consciousness monologue, mostly to do with memories evoked by whatever item he was looking at at the moment. Since this was usually not an item either Eugenia or I was attempting to identify and list, it proved a bit distracting.

"That's Grandfather," he said, peering at a huge dark oil painting above the nearer fireplace. "Crispin Credable Senior, with Grandma Rose and three of the youngest: Papa, Admar, and Carolyn. In the dining room there's a picture of him and Grandma Minerva and the first brood of Credables, eight of them. He never did a picture of my aunt Ethelia. She was retarded. She didn't live very long. If this place were haunted, Grandpa would be the haunt. Think how he would feel if he knew! All those sisters, provided for and married off, and not a surviving child from any of them. All those children of his own, and only my papa, Aunt Carolyn, and Uncle Admar left to attend the funeral."

"It does seem tragic," said Eugenia. "What killed them all?"

"Every one of Grandpa's sisters died of diabetes. It ran in the family, ran rampant, one might say, for three of his children died of it as well when they were quite young. Of the five who lived to grow up, the two youngest sons died in World War One, one son was killed in a train wreck, Aunt Livvy died in childbirth, along with the baby, and the eldest, Aunt Gertrude, went mad when she was about twenty and passed on years later believing she was the Grand Duchess Anastasia. Those were all Grandma Minerva's children. Except for Ethelia, Grandma Rose's children did a little better. Uncle Admar went prospecting for gold in the mid-fifties and was never seen again, but my father lived until 1982, and his sister, my aunt Caroline, is still alive, in a nursing home. She's ninety-something, and still bright as a button."

"I thought you told me you had a cousin Edward?" I asked, fascinated despite myself at all this genealogy.

"Uncle Admar's only son. Born during a brief marriage when Uncle Admar was a young man, just out of college. Edward and I are the stingy last twigs on what was once a burgeoning bush, the family Credable."

"Is Edward married? Does he have children?" Eugenia asked, pen poised.

"He is not, he does not. He, too, is neglecting his Credable duty to reproduce." Wilson flung himself down on a Renaissance Revival sofa, making it creak audibly.

I flinched. The deep-buttoned jacquard-upholstered piece had an interesting split back, as though two armchairs and a love seat had snuggled up to one another and melded into one piece of furniture by losing all the arms but the outside two, all the legs but the outside four, fragile walnut stems far too delicately turned and castored to take abuse of the sort Wilson was handing out. Eugenia evidently thought so, too.

"Sit up straight," she admonished him. "If you're going to loll, do it in that!" She pointed toward a heavy armchair with matching footstool, both so carved and ornamented as to make their purpose difficult to ascertain.

Wilson shuddered. "The loathsome thing might eat me! What is that chair? I've often wondered if it hadn't been designed as an instrument of torture."

"It's high Victorian," she said in her usual haughty voice. "The highest. Sort of exalted Jacobean crossed with Rococo Revival. They were still showing furniture like that at the exposition in Chicago in the early 1890s, even though simpler designs were gaining ground. Your grandfather probably brought it with him from the east. It may have belonged to his father."

"Don't you know exactly how old it is?" he asked, suddenly suspicious. "How can you appraise it if you don't know—"

"It's worth what someone will pay for it," I told him. "What someone will pay for it depends on the market, on the quality of the piece, and on the provenance. Knowing to the day how old it is won't help sell it if no one wants it. Knowing precisely how old it is might help sell it if someone wants it and also wants to be sure it's 'authentic.' What 'authentic' means can vary. Authentically old. Authentically by a known maker. Authentically in period. Authentic as to materials. Not all antiques have intrinsic value."

"He means things like Revere silver or Frank Lloyd Wright furniture," Eugenia explained. "Or something fashionable or collectible at the time it's sold. Something a bank would lend money on."

"At least these things are Credable," he said with a smirk.

"There is that," I agreed. Everything in the room was at least Credable. I turned the chair over, found a maker's mark, and showed it to Wilson, telling him I could look up the maker and in that way establish the approximate age of the piece.

This satisfied him for the moment. He told us it was time for him to check his students' work and wandered away. At noon, he came trotting back to tell us he'd prepared lunch for the six of us. Surprised but grateful, we took a break. Wilson's three students were bustling around in what once had been the servants' dining area off the kitchen. We were introduced around again, and each one of them came up with an apposite remark; how very pleased, have heard so much about, how nice to have you with us. We lunched on excellent sole and salad, rolls and butter, accompanied by general conversation. Wilson was giving the signals, and each of them had obviously been primed to take part.

"How long have you lived in Denver, Mrs. Lowe?" This was Angel, making small talk, rather stiffly.

"Are you finding the contents of the house interesting, Mr. Lynx?" This was Ann Louise.

"Mr Credable tells me you once worked for the Smithsonian?" This was Paul Lo, and he actually sounded sincere. We managed to get smoothly through the encounter, and when we'd shared a ripe melon, I thought I saw Wilson give a little wriggle of satisfaction, like a music teacher after a successful recital.

Eugenia and I returned to our task while Wilson and his students went on with theirs. By late afternoon we were almost finished with the dining room, except for the contents of the china cupboards. We'd peeked in. We'd both gasped. Most of the value in the two rooms we'd inventoried would be in those cabinets. I'd spotted a tea set that looked very much like a Mueller design from the Union Porcelain Works, an American factory that produced some of the finest decorated porcelain in the world during the last quarter of the nineteenth century. Eugenia was struck speechless by a whole shelf of dusty Belleek, which is a particular favorite of hers. Jason Lynx Interiors doesn't do a great deal with porcelain, but one must either know about it or know someone who does. I resolved to bring a specialist with us when we returned.

Since Wilson had gone to take his students home, we let ourselves out, not without a certain trepidation. I had

no idea if there was anyone else in the house or if all
the hundred doors and windows were locked. The very
thought of what vandals could do to the place made me
shudder, and evidently Eugenia had similar thoughts,
for she tried the latch determinedly at least three times
before she would leave it.

Saturday, Mark and I conferred about Valerie, or
rather Valerie's apartment. I watched for the slight annoyance I'd noted before, not finding any. Perhaps I'd
been mistaken. I spent the rest of the weekend in sloth,
except for balancing my checkbook, paying my bills,
and trotting about in the park with Bela. I did call
Toddy Fairchild, who knows porcelain as few people in
the country know porcelain. He also knows pottery, and
glass, or anything else made out of clay or sand and
fired in a kiln or melted in a furnace, and he was delighted to be asked to view the Credable collection. I
talked to Grace a couple of times on the phone. She
sounded distant and melancholy, so I didn't press.

When we resumed our inventories on Monday, Toddy
kept saying "oh, my," and "gracious," and "well, really," little verbal firecrackers going off in strings.
"Cameo glass!" he exulted. Cameo glass is made in layers, then carved away to show a light design against a
darker background, or vice versa "Oh, do look! Silvered
and engraved. This looks like an exposition piece!"

I'd explained to him what the deal was, and he promised to do the valuation for nothing if he could have
first crack at the contents.

"Won't he undervalue the things?" Wilson had asked,
somewhat apprehensively. "I mean, if he's going to be
first to buy them. . . ."

"He merely wants to submit a sealed bid for a particular selection. We'll publicize the list and others will

bid as well. I'm working on the same basis. You sell me what you want to sell me, if I'm high bidder."

He still looked doubtful.

"By the way, Wilson, since you can't find the earlier inventory, you know there may be taxes to pay on all this."

That set him trotting off to the family accountant and left Eugenia and me to finish up with the contents of the morning room, the study, and the billiards room. Pantries and conservatory we left for later.

Toddy wanted to know all about the Credables, and I filled him in. "I knew they either entertained a lot, or there was a huge family at one time. There's a frightful lot of china in this place."

There was a frightful lot of china. Service after service, all of them large enough to set sixteen to twenty places. Most of them decorated with gold, which meant they had to be washed by hand. We hadn't even looked at the cut crystal yet, of which there were shelves full.

"How much?" I asked Toddy. "Rough estimate?"

"A zillion," he replied, his eyebrows drawn together. "Rough guess. Of course, to get that, one would need to take time. You won't get near that if you sell it in lots."

I passed this information on to Wilson when he returned, bearing the inventory sheets, which had indeed existed, somewhere in the accountant's dusty files. He chortled, a little gargle of pleasure. "Really! How wonderful! How soon can you get it out of here—just in case Edward comes roaring down like the north wind. Anything for sale needs to be gone before he gets a court order. Amelia thinks he may try for a court order."

I conferred with Toddy, and he said he could have experienced, bonded men by the end of the week to pack the stuff under his personal supervision. After a look at the accountant's inventory lists, we discarded them as useless. Whoever had made them up had simply lumped things into categories like "Miscellaneous Household China," or "Assorted Glassware." We made up our own lists, small groupings of similar things to be offered for sale. Toddy would circulate them and take a small commission on the things he himself didn't buy. After a moment's thought Wilson agreed to this.

"Which of it do you want to keep?" I asked him. "There are some very nice things—"

"None of it," he said firmly. "Not a bit."

"I think you should pick some out and keep it," I told him significantly. "For your family."

"I have no—" He stopped, mouth open. "Oh."

"Your grandfather was born in 1850. He begat your father when he was fifty-one. Your father was forty-nine when he begat you. You're only what? Forty-four or -five? You still have time to have a family." There was something rather stretched about this line of reasoning, but I plowed on. "At least, so far as Edward is concerned. Keeping some of the dinnerware will help establish intent, at least. Don't you think?"

He did think, and we spent a pleasant hour deciding which of the many sets he was going to keep. He settled on two of the best, in my opinion, though Toddy thought otherwise.

"Uncle Admar always liked these," Wilson said, stroking a dinner plate in bone china, the rim chastely decorated in dark blue and gold. "They're simpler than some of the others. Besides, blue was his favorite color."

"How do you know so much about Uncle Admar?" I asked him. "You'd have been only about seven when he went off prospecting."

"I know. But he lived here, he and Aunt Carolyn. Papa was never around, but Uncle Admar was. He read to me and told me stories. He taught me to play ball. He was like a real brother to Mama."

"And he really went off hunting gold?"

"Well, all that business about hunting for gold, that's just a thing to say, a story people made up. Uncle Admar used to talk about seeking his fortune; then, when he disappeared, Amelia's father said he must have gone delving for gold. It was kind of a joke, because he'd gone off on little jaunts before without telling anyone, and everyone expected he'd come back, but he never did. I always thought it was a little late for Uncle Admar to go off like that. He was fifty. Most people go seeking their fortune when they're much younger, don't they? I would have, if my fortune hadn't been dumped on me."

I told him we'd do our best to excavate him.

"Exhume," he said gloomily. "I've been buried in all this. Room after room of it!"

His words, for some totally indiscernible reason, reminded me of waking in the night and saying "Aha." Now, what was floating around in my head that I couldn't get hold of!

I was not given time to worry over it. Wilson was off on another tangent.

"What shall I do about Mother's jewelry?" he asked. "She had whole boxes full of it up in her bedroom."

"Do let's look!" cried Eugenia, so nothing would do but that the four of us go up to look at Emmeline's jewelry. There was a lot of it, some of it very good, all of it valuable.

"Why aren't these in a safe-deposit box?" I demanded, holding out a sapphire-and-diamond parure:

necklace, bracelet, earrings. "Honestly, Wilson, this isn't the best place for all this."

"I like looking at them," he said, a bit wistfully. "Mama used to let me play with them when I was little. When she got ready to go out in the evening, she'd let me spread them all out on her bed and try them on. When Mother and I went over to the Wirtzes', Amelia and I would play with her mother's jewelry, too. We used to dress up and admire ourselves in the mirror. Janet Wirtz had a lot more than Mama did, things her mother left her, great huge sapphires and rubies and diamonds. She had an emerald necklace twice the size of this one."

"How long has your mother been gone?" Toddy asked.

"She died in 1990. She was only sixty. She married my father when she was only seventeen."

"Well, then," Toddy told him sternly, "you've had several years to play with Mama's things, and now you'd better pack them off to the bank."

"Really," said Eugenia in her nannyish voice. "Really you must, Mr. Credable."

He was sulky about this for the rest of the afternoon, as a man might be who had too few amusements to spare any, though he cheered up by the time we were ready to depart. The four of us were standing outside on the drive, at the foot of the broad granite steps, when a large, expensive car turned in through the wrought-iron gates and came sedately toward us. The impression of bankerly soberness was somewhat belied by the pair of polished horns that graced the hood. Longhorns. At least four feet across.

"Oh Lord," murmured Wilson. "Oh gracious Lord."

"Who is it?" Eugenia asked.

"Cousin Edward," he said. "I knew he was somewhere in the wings, just aching to make an entrance."

"No disclosure," I muttered. "Don't say why we're here, Toddy, Eugenia. Follow my lead. Wilson?"

"Oh, very well," he muttered. "What are you going to say?"

I hadn't any idea. Probably something vague and misleading.

The car slowed and stopped. The driver's door opened, and a tall, extremely handsome man emerged, tugging his sleeves down, running one hand across a smooth abundance of white hair. He was that movie-hero type that ages well, perhaps with considerable help from makeup artists and surgeons, his skin lightly tanned, only very slightly lined, and his face fixed in an expression of lofty detachment that was belied by a pair of extremely watchful eyes. Except for the eyes, he could have been thirty.

"Cousin Threesy!" he said in a charming voice that oozed affability.

Beside me, I felt Wilson stiffen and begin to simmer.

"You must be Edward Credable," I said, stepping forward to offer my hand. "Wilson has mentioned you often."

"Cousin Eddy," said Wilson, with an attempt at savoir faire. "How nice of you to drop by. This is Jason Lynx, Eugenia Lowe, Todman Fairchild."

"You're the decorator fella," said Edward. "'Melia mentioned you."

"You know Amelia," I said with as pleasant an expression as I could muster.

"Since she was a kid. Used to come to lunch with her mom, played bridge with Dad and Aunty Carolyn and Aunty Emmy. I met her when I was home from school, and we chat every now and then. Well, Willy, how's the homestead?"

Wilson murmured. "As always, Eddy. Credable Castle doesn't change."

"Must be anticipating changes. Why else have a decorator, hah?" He smiled on me, his eyes piercing.

"Some of the draperies are simply gone with moth," said Eugenia haughtily. "Not to mention the unspeakable condition of the carpets."

"Ah." His eyes softened slightly. "Just furbishing up, cousin?"

"It seems appropriate," said Wilson. "One wouldn't want the place to fall to pieces. By the way, Edward, did the person who called here for you last week reach you all right?"

"Can't recall anyone mentioning they called here," Edward drawled. "Though anyone might have, considering the last name and all. And how 'bout you, Willy? Found yourself a helpmeet yet?"

Wilson blinked rapidly. I saw the glimmer of tears and said hastily, "Wilson, if we're going to make that date with the fabric people, we really have to leave now."

He gulped. "Of course. Quite right. I am sorry, Eddy, but I can't be hospitable right now. Are you in town for long?"

"Going back tonight," Edward answered, his brows drawing in across the top of his nose, making him look intent and raptorial. "However, I'll be back soon. Whyn't you and me make a date for lunch, talk some things over."

"I'll call you," Wilson said. "I'll call you this weekend."

And with that, Toddy got into his car and drove off;

the rest of us got into my car and drove out the gates; and Edward came right behind us, those horns right on our tail. He stayed behind us. I sighed.

"Looks like we're going to the fabric house," said Eugenia.

"Looks like we are," I said. "Hope to God they're still open when we get there."

As it turned out, it wasn't necessary actually to go in. He stayed behind us all the way down Monaco to Seventeenth Avenue, down Seventeenth to the downtown area, where we switched over to Eighteenth Street and headed for lower downtown, where the wholesale houses are. When we turned off on Wazee, however, Edward's car continued smoothly on, toward the overpass to the highway. We had made our point, but he had also made his. He didn't believe us and wasn't going to take a thing on faith.

"He's going to harass me," said Wilson. "He's determined to do it even though he doesn't need the money. He's been very successful."

"Family money?" I asked, turning the car around to go back to the castle.

"The Credable family? You mean did he inherit from Admar? No. Admar had no inherited money at all. Edward is into coal. He started as some kind of mining supervisor, in the bowels of Wyoming, so I understand, which is one vast coalfield with a few antelope running about on it."

"A self-made man."

"He had to be. Admar had nothing to leave him. All Admar got from Grandpa was a small allowance and the right to live at the castle during his lifetime."

"That seems hardly fair."

"Admar was six years younger than Papa, and

Grandpa was a firm believer in primogeniture. He wasn't about to divide things up. Grandpa assumed Carolyn would get married, though she never did. He assumed Admar would take up a profession, but Admar wasn't interested in law or medicine and certainly not the church. He was fascinated by printing, and he wanted to go into business. He asked my father for a little capital, to set himself up, but Father wouldn't give him anything at all, which I thought at the time was most unkind. I think Edward hates me because of my father. I don't blame him really."

"I thought perhaps Edward's mother's family had money."

"Oh, no. They were blue-collar people, and she was only a child, seventeen—the first, one supposes, of Admar's many conquests. She was pregnant, you see. He did the honorable thing, though he was only twenty. The marriage didn't last. I'm told she hated Credable Castle. In any case, she ran off, leaving Eddy behind to be reared by Grandma Rose. Probably Edward hates me for that, too. At least I had a mother while I was growing up. On the other hand, Edward inherited Uncle Admar's good looks. Quite irresistible, Admar."

"You really think Edward threatens this suit because of the way your father treated his father?"

Wilson sighed. "Why not? Or the way my father treated Edward himself. It's as good a reason as any other."

We returned Wilson to his rockpile and we to our more modest one.

"I don't know which of them to feel sorry for," said Eugenia thoughtfully. "Edward certainly wasn't treated justly, but then, Wilson wasn't either. Family expectations are the very devil." She went off into the showroom, saying over her shoulder, "It is a pity Wilson doesn't have a family. He would be a very pleasant, easy man to live with."

This struck a chord. Something I'd been thinking? That kind of helpless seeking feeling for a thought one knows is there, somewhere. I stood at the foot of the stairs, reaching for it. Nothing. I couldn't get hold of it.

I went upstairs and gave Mark the inventory sheets we'd worked up, suggesting that he decide which of the items Jason Lynx Interiors should bid for and how much he would suggest we bid. That would keep him busy for some little time and leave me to burrow into my subconscious. That plan went immediately astray.

"Jason." Mark came to the door. "What's this skeleton clock like?"

I took the form from him. "Marked J. Lowe, Over-Darwen, therefore British. I'd say eighteen forty to eighteen sixty, give or take."

"What does it look like?"

"Like a clockwork with its skin removed, under glass, all its little gears going tock-tock and a very complicated chiming mechanism. Rather Gothic in style. I didn't listen to it do the hours, but I did notice it was working. Why?"

"I was thinking of Timothy Ballock. You know how he is about clocks."

Oh, indeed. Whatever we might pay Wilson for the clock, Mr. Ballock would pay us twice. Ballock the Clock, we called him. A wealthy man and an indefatigable collector.

I nodded affirmatively but dismissively, and Mark went away, only to return in five minutes. "Jason, this étagère with the fiddle-back veneer . . . ?"

And so it went for what little remained of the after-

noon. I resolved to take Mark with me the next time I
went out to Credable's.

Amelia called about five-thirty, just as I was about to
go out for dinner. She asked if I'd heard from Grace. I
said not since the day before. She asked if I'd thought
any more about the bones. I said no, I'd been too busy
with Wilson.

"I've always thought Wilson quite interesting," she
said. "This work with young people . . ."

"He had three teenagers there this week, studying
like mad. He's obviously fond of them and they of him.
By the way, I met Cousin Edward today."

"You did," she said flatly. "How is he?"

"You don't sound as though you care," I said.

Long silence. Then a sigh. "I was a naive girl in
many ways, Jason. I've told you how Mother and I used
to visit the Credables. Emmeline was very sweet, she
kept on asking me to lunch even after Mother was gone,
and she'd sit me down for little motherly talks. On one
such occasion I met Edward. I was a pretty girl, though
that may be difficult to believe now. Not as pretty as my
mother—she was extraordinarily beautiful, and she
didn't live long enough to lose it. Still, I was nice looking, and I was eighteen. He was thirtyish, quite enough
older than I to have known better. He was an accomplished seducer, a talent he no doubt learned from his
father. I did not escape unscathed."

"He spoke as though you were friends," I managed to
say.

"He probably thinks we are," she said. "Nowadays it
would be called date rape, but Edward's character for-
mation antedates any consciousness of sexual guilt. He
no doubt considers seduction by means of misrepresen-
tation, lies, or threats, to be part of the repertoire of a

gentleman. I'm sure if he thought about it at all, he thought he was doing me a favor. He does call me every now and then, mostly to keep tabs on Wilson. At such times he likes to pretend I am the family attorney, responsible to all the Credables."

"Uncomfortable for you," I said, acutely conscious of my own discomfort.

"At one time it was," she said firmly. "Now I manage total savoir faire. His calls are a good way for me to check up on him. His ego demands that he let little things drop. Names. Places. It tells me what he's been up to. Up until now he's only made vaguely threatening noises. I can't understand this sudden sally. What's he after?"

"Well, he says he's after dropping in on Wilson and making a date for lunch next week. I think Wilson may be in for a hard time."

She promised she'd keep an eye on the situation.

I phoned Minnesota. Minnesota didn't answer.

I fed the animals and went out to dinner at Tante Louise, mostly because it was nearby. I was lackadaisical about ordering, more so about eating. The food was good, but I wasn't. I was the only diner in the place who was eating alone. I skipped dessert, had coffee, went home, and called Minnesota.

Minnesota still didn't answer.

I didn't feel sleepy, didn't want to read. So I took out the inventory and began to look up references, similar items sold at auctions, similar items sold at estate sales. I have a dealer in New York and friends in half a dozen other major cities. We share sales catalogs, faxing annotated sheets back and forth. Then there are the magazines on antiques, not always reliable as to description but copiously illustrated with photographs. It is possible, with a little diligent work, to come up with a pretty fair valuation of many items.

Never all, however. I couldn't find anything similar to the skeleton clock. There was nothing similar to a prie-dieu chair upholstered in needlework (lilies) and blue velvet, the apron inlaid with olive oystering (an inlay cut of small branches, showing the growth rings, and so called because of the resemblance to the concentric growth of oyster shells). Prie-dieu chairs came into favor among the pious during the mid-Victorian period because of women's voluminous, often hooped, skirts. If a lady knelt at an ordinary prie-dieu, with the kneeling bench perhaps six to eight inches from the floor, her skirts billowed up behind her to expose more of the lady than modesty allowed. The prie-dieu chair has a heavily cushioned seat sixteen or more inches from the floor, for sitting or kneeling, and a narrow back with an upholstered top on which hands can be primly folded. The prayer angle permits skirt dangle, so to speak, and modesty is thereby preserved. Later in the century, straighter skirts were the fashion, so this particular chair was probably something the family had had a long time before moving to Denver. At any rate, I found a few prie-dieu chairs cataloged, but none like the Credable one.

At eleven, I gave up and called Minnesota. Yet again, Minnesota didn't answer. I snarled a bit, then went to bed, only to lie staring at the ceiling wondering where Grace was, where her uncle was, or his family. Farmers aren't supposed to be away from home, or so she'd always said. So what had happened?

Maybe she'd returned home. I phoned her house. It gave me the busy signal. All right. She was either home, talking on the phone, or it was busy because someone was leaving a message. I waited a few minutes and tried again. Still busy. Not damned likely.

Bela whined, picking up on my disturbance. Here I was, out of touch with Grace for a little over a day and having a full-fledged anxiety attack over a busy signal.

I got up, threw on some clothes, took Bela with me, went out to the garage, and got the car out. I was just pulling out, the car window open, when I heard a small voice from across the alley.

"Where are you going this time of night?"

It was my elderly neighbor, Nellie Arpels, craning forward from her wheelchair to peek through a crack in the gate. I stopped the car and got out.

"What are you doing up?" I demanded.

"I couldn't sleep," she confessed, putting up a hand to tidy her white hair in its bedtime net. "I kept seeing your bedroom light go on and off, on and off. I thought maybe you were sick."

"Worried," I confessed. "Grace's brother died. She took his ashes to Minnesota where her uncle lives. She told me she was staying a few days. Now I can't reach her, and there's a busy signal at her house."

"She's a very sensible girl," Nellie said. "She won't let anything happen to her."

"Nonetheless, I'm just going over to her house to check. Be sure she didn't come back without telling me."

"You call me," she demanded. "When you get home."

I promised I would. I wheeled her back into her house, the former garage, which her daughter and son-in-law had converted into a self-contained ground-level apartment for Nellie, where we were greeted by Perky, Nellie's white cat, then I waited until Nellie locked the

door after me before I went back to the car and took off
in some haste.

It was only a five-minute drive over to Grace's place.
Less than fifteen minutes had elapsed since I got the
second busy signal. I knew when I drove up in front
that something was wrong. The side door was standing
ajar. The hallway of the original house, a three-story
turn-of-the-century Queen Anne, is now the hallway
leading to the four apartments Grace has built into the
place, two ground-floor, two upstairs. The front door of
the original house is the door used by the tenants. Grace
mostly uses the back door, out of her kitchen, and
there's also a side door out of her bedroom, which was
originally a dining room. She never uses the side door.
I'd never seen it open. In fact, she had a dresser across
it.

It opened on the side porch and was the door most
hidden from the street, being behind an abundant
growth of lilac. If I hadn't been looking at doors, knowing where they were, I'd never have spotted it. Bela and
I got out of the car. He'd been here before. He knew the
place. He looked at the house, his head up, ears slightly
forward. When I moved, he moved at my side, forsak-
ing his usual herd-dog shamble for an erect, watchful
gait. No growl, just alertness. It occurred to me it might
be the first time he had seen the place at night, un-
lighted. It was probably the first time I'd seen it that
way, come to think of it. There wasn't so much as a
glimmer in all three floors.

We got onto the wraparound porch without a sound.
No creaking boards. Grace and I had fixed them all. I
had a flash in my pocket, but for some reason, I hesi-
tated to use it. We went very quietly around the corner,
facing the open door. From inside came sounds, pull-

ings and scrapings, the glow of a flashlight. Bela erupted from my side in a flurry of claws on wood and a tocsin of barks mixed with growls. Whoever was in there, Bela did not like them one bit.

There were a confused several minutes during which I tackled one dark form as it erupted from the door, was struck by another from behind, lost hold on the first, and found myself on hands and knees, trying to clear my head while Bela licked my face. Upstairs a window opened.

"What the hell is going on down there?" someone asked plaintively. "Gracie?"

I recognized the voice. Ann Barrant, Grace's long-time second-floor tenant. Wobbling, I went out onto the lawn where she could see me.

"It's Jason Lynx, Ann! Somebody broke into Grace's apartment."

"Good heavens! You want me to call the police?"

"Please. I'll be inside. Tell them I'm here, please, so I don't get shot!"

Tell them or not, I ended up with my hands against the wall while I was being patted down, and only very narrowly escaped being handcuffed. Fortunately, one of the cops knew Grace and had met me.

"How many?" he asked, when I'd had a chance to sit down.

"Maybe two," I replied. "I had hold of one, but I got hit from the back. That could have been another man, or it could have been Bela."

"There's blood on your face."

I put up my hand, found a trace. "Bela?" I said.

He came over, whining, red smears obvious around his mouth.

"He bit somebody," I said.

"When he or they attacked you."

"He was just defending me. He's not an attack dog."

Someone came over and wiped some blood off Bela's muzzle and put it in an evidence bag.

"What do you think they were looking for?" the quasi-friendly cop wanted to know.

I looked around at the mess they had made of Grace's house. Kitchen cupboards were open, drawers were open, contents dumped on the floor, cushions were thrown off the couch, desk drawers were dumped. The place had been well and thoroughly searched. Not vandalized. Even so, it would take some doing to repair the incidental damage.

"Any ideas?" The cop nudged at me.

"From my personal knowledge, she didn't have anything here except what you see. They didn't take her stereo, or her typewriter, or her TV. She had no jewelry worth mentioning. Maybe it's connected to her brother's death. . . ."

And then we were off to the races, culminating in an interview with a detective from the local precinct who was, he said, in liaison with the Clear Creek County Sheriff's Office.

"What brought you over here this time of night?" he asked me, after he'd asked me everything the other cop had asked me twice over and had had a lengthy whispered conference in the doorway during which I'd fallen into a half doze.

I looked up, startled, taking a moment to realize the question had been addressed to me. I told him about the busy signal, explained by the fact that the phone was off the cradle on the floor, ending up with, "I was worried about her. She's been really upset about Ron's death."

"She responsible for it, you mean?"

"No, I do not mean! He's her baby brother. She's always taken care of him."

"Oh. Like that."

"Like that. Yes." I was suddenly inexpressibly weary, and even more worried about Grace than earlier in the evening.

Grace's phone rang. I stumbled erect, trying for it, but a cop picked it up first. He mumbled into it then handed it to me. Nellie, worried because I hadn't called.

"Who's that?" the detective wanted to know. I told him and he made notes about Nellie and my midnight conversation with her. Evidently I was no longer suspected of complicity or duplicity or whatever.

"Look," I said. "I've been trying to reach Grace for some time. Her uncle's place doesn't answer. Could you get the Minnesota police to find out what's going on?"

"Yeah, well," he said, brushing me off. "You go on home. You look like you could use some sleep."

I insisted on staying until they were through so I could lock up. The lock on the side door was broken and the doorstop and frame were splintered, but I knew where Grace kept her tools, so I ran some long screws through the door and into the frame. It would have to be repainted anyhow, where the thieves had jimmied it open. It was almost four when I got Bela into the car and started for home. By four-thirty we were in bed, both soundly asleep.

At five o'clock the phone rang. Grace.

I was tired enough to be annoyed. "Where have you been!" I demanded.

"Right here," she snapped. "Where have you been? I've been calling you for the last several hours."

"At your house," I told her, going on to rant and rave about burglars and thieves and what might be missing.

I told her I'd screwed the door shut from inside, that the windows were okay, that neither of her tenants would be inconvenienced.

"I called you to tell you I'm coming home tomorrow," she said in a small voice. "Can you meet the plane?"

I told her I would, though meeting planes is no longer an easy or convenient thing to do. Denver has moved its airport twenty miles out into the country without having provided a light-rail system as a sensible alternative to thousands of private cars burning millions of gallons of gas, making smelly clouds of pollution.

I slept in. Mark looked in on me about nine, then went away when I told him I'd been up all night. I got up about noon. Grace's plane was at three, and it would take that long to wake up, have lunch, and get to the airport.

"Amelia called," said Mark. "There was something on the news about your being attacked. She wants to know if it had anything to do with what happened last week."

I'd mentioned it to the police, but it was a way-out theory at best. I suppose I looked annoyed. Mark shook his head sympathetically. "She's a lawyer, Jason. Always thinking ahead."

"If Ron was the target last week, I suppose last night could have been connected," I said. "If Grace was the intended target, I suppose it could have been connected. If neither of them were the intended targets, then how could it?" All of which didn't come out sounding as logical as I had thought it was.

"Go have some lunch," Mark said.

I did as ordered. I scrambled some eggs and made toast, chewing and swallowing while grimly concentrat-

ing on what possible connection there might have been.
Ron had said . . . what had he said? That a friend of his
(probably Ron himself) owed someone some money.
Call someone the villain. Ron owed the villain a considerable amount. The villain or his henchmen had picked
Ron up and threatened him, so Ron had made attempts
to come up with the money. And, presumably, since
he'd been dropped off unharmed, Ron had come up
with something. A name, a number, a promise, a plan.
Something. Some way to get himself off the hook.
Someone to borrow it from. Maybe one of those old
friends who had sworn to be friends for life.

So, the villain or his henchmen accepts this promise
or plan of payment, puts Ron into the shiny blue car,
and drops him off just outside Grace's place with a few
final words about "Monday." The next day. A day's
grace, perhaps.

Then Ron goes to the mountains and ends up dead.
Then somebody fires a gun at Bela. Then a thug or two
breaks into Grace's place. Looking for what? The plan?
The promise? Did Ron tell them he'd get the money
from his sister?

It was half-assed even as theory. There was no proof
to make it anything but fiction, and as fiction, it stank.
It did not explain why, if Ron was coming up with the
money, they went ahead and killed him. Unless the killing was done by someone else. Apropos of what?

It made me even grumpier than I'd been before. I got
out to the airport in plenty of time, bought a magazine
to while away the twenty-minute wait, and then waited
at the head of the concourse for Grace to show up,
which she did eventually, looking very pale and sleepy.

Once we were in the car, I asked why I hadn't been
able to rouse anyone at her uncle's house, and she said

there'd been a storm that brought some trees down over phone lines, effectively wiping out communication for a couple of days.

"Nellie said you could take care of yourself."

"How did Nellie get into this?"

I told her. She blinked like an owl, obviously having trouble staying awake. Well, if she'd been up all night trying to call me, she probably hadn't had more than two or three hours' sleep. I reached over and gave her a one-armed hug, and she snuggled into my side with a sigh. We drove to Margo's place and picked up Critter. He half climbed over Grace's shoulder, looking out the car window as we went on.

"Have you talked to any of Ron's friends yet?" she asked.

I gave her a brief reprise of what I'd been doing, starting with finding the ring and Bela's being shot. I told her about Wilson Credable. "That's pretty well taken up my time since you've been gone. I thought I'd wait until you got back to start digging at Ron's friends. They're more likely to talk to you than they are to me, anyhow."

"Not today." She sighed. "I can't even move today." She tightened her arms around the huge cat, who purred deeply.

I took her home. She took one look at the place and the tears started down her face, so I stayed to straighten up. It wasn't as bad as it looked. She couldn't find anything missing or really destroyed, except the mushroom strings. They'd been thrown onto the floor and walked on. I swept them up and put them in the garbage. She wandered around, putting away the things that had been pulled out, and in an hour or so we had the place looking relatively neat.

"What were they looking for?" she asked me.

I sat down beside her and explained my theory, the only one I'd been able to come up with. ". . . somehow Ron convinced them he could come up with what he owed them. That he had it, maybe. Or that he could get it. Or that you had it. Or that he had something he could liquidate."

"That's barely possible." She sighed again.

"So, when he died, they came looking for whatever he had told them he had."

"Why did they kill him?"

"Well, if this hypothesis is true, they wouldn't have. Not until he had done whatever he'd promised to do."

"Somebody else killed him."

"Somebody else set off an explosion. Which killed him."

Tears ran down her face. "I'm tired, Jason. Nothing makes sense and I can't cope and Minnesota wasn't a rest, and I'm tired."

I hugged her, chivied her into her bedroom, into one of the long T-shirts she sleeps in, then unpacked her suitcase for her, talking quietly about nothing while she fell asleep, Critter draped across her stomach. I checked all the locks carefully and let myself out. It was almost six. Suppertime. Surprisingly, I was hungry. I decided to drive out to Cherry Creek Mall, see what attracted me when I got there. The traffic was light, rush hour long since over.

I'd gotten as far as University when I noticed the blue car behind me. The same metallic shade as the car Ron had been in. I slowed. It slowed. I speeded up, so did it. I turned right on Sixth. It stayed behind me. I turned off on Monroe and pulled over to the curb. Parked. Got out. Started walking back to the car that had parked halfway down the block behind me. It reversed, the wheels screamed, and it backed onto Sixth and sped away toward the west. So much for that. They'd been behind me. They would have my license-plate number by now. If they hadn't had it all along.

It was definitely time to talk to Ron's old friends.

Wednesday was better all around. I got up at the usual time after a night's undisturbed sleep. I had coffee, a shower, more coffee, breakfast, and was at my desk by the time Mark arrived. He reported progress on Valerie's problem: new curtains ordered, decorator coming this week to rush wallpaper and paint; the Arts and Crafts chairs at the upholsterer's, who was also making drop-everything-do-it-right-now slipcovers for the sofa bed and the easy chair. The furniture Valerie would send to us was being picked up today, and Mark gave me the list of what would go back to her place out of our stock. He would rent some pictures from one of the art dealers we had an arrangement with.

He wanted to see some of the items on the Credable inventory, and I told him to call Wilson, make a date, and go look at them. Toddy called to say his men would be ready to work on the morrow. Two days, he thought. Maybe three. They would work on Saturday, if necessary. I told him to take a service for eight out of the rather simple design that was banded in green and gold and also from the cut crystal and silver. I needed it to lend to Valerie.

About noon, Mark returned from the castle with copious notes. I told him to keep in mind that the place had to retain enough furniture to be livable, since that was where Wilson would continue to live.

"He's thinking about building a theater in the grand salon," said Mark, shaking his head.

"Dining room would make a better theater."

"Isn't it too small?"

"At least there aren't marble pillars in the way."

Grace called about noon, sounding only a little more like herself. She'd slept in. She'd talked to the cop shop, asking to use some vacation days and take the rest of the week off, and they'd okayed it. "Let's talk to Brew Tyrell," she said. "I called him. He'll be home tonight."

On the way there, she wanted to hear about my going down the shaft up at Amelia's place. I repeated the story. "A ring?" she said wonderingly. "A finger?"

"Back at the shop. I'll give them to you, and you can turn them over to the investigators."

"A man's ring, or a woman's ring?" she wanted to know.

I hadn't tried it on. Mark hadn't tried it on. Some slight squeamishness about that. I admitted I didn't know. I described the engraving once again.

"Eight-nine-five-seven," she murmured. "August ninth, nineteen fifty-seven? Or, European style, September eighth."

"There's nothing to indicate it's a date. I thought it might be scripture, or a page number, or something."

"I suppose," she said in a dissatisfied voice. "Eight thousand pages is a pretty big book."

"Sets of encyclopedias have that many pages. So do multivolume dictionaries." It probably had nothing to do with Bibles or encyclopedias. It was probably someone's birthday, or anniversary.

Brewster Tyrell lived in Cherry Hills Farms, where money begins showing itself off in immense houses cheek by jowl with dozens of other immense houses. The Tyrell domicile was a pseudo-Tudor with a complicated roof, surrounded by recent shrubberies that made the approach a winding one, left, then right, then a swerving brick walk to the front door. Grace rang, and he answered. About Ron's age, thirty maybe. Medium height, sincere brown eyes, smooth face, strongly curved mouth, delicate jaw. What I'd think of as a classic face, handsome in a sculptural way. Grace introduced me, and we were ushered into the study just off the entry hall. From the back of the house came the sounds of women talking, children yelling cheerfully.

"My sister's visiting," he offered. "With her three and my three, it's a houseful."

We were seated, he offered drinks, Grace shook her head, but I accepted a glass of wine. Brewster sat across from Grace and leaned to take her hands. "I was so sorry to hear about Ron. I've worried about him a lot. He just seemed to lose his way, didn't he?"

Grace's eyes brimmed over. She fumbled for a tissue. I gave her my handkerchief.

Brewster sat back. "Too many of the kids I went to school with at East, God, there must be six or seven out of our class alone, dead; drugs or alcohol or AIDS. It's sad."

"Had you heard from Ron recently?" I asked, giving Grace time to get herself together.

"He called me at the office last week. No, week before. Early in the week he died. He wanted to borrow some money." His mouth twisted. "God, I wish I'd loaned it to him!"

That brought Grace out of her cocoon. "No, Brew. You know better."

"It might have prevented—"

"He was dying anyhow. He had AIDS. It wouldn't have prevented anything."

Shocked silence. "I didn't know. He didn't tell me."

"How much did he want to borrow?" I asked.

"Fifty thou, but he'd settle for half that. He said twenty-five would keep the vultures off his neck."

"Did he say why?"

Brewster sighed. "I'm ashamed to say I didn't ask. I just assumed it was drugs. It has been with Ron, for some years. Even before he left Denver. Even in high school. There in our senior year, he always seemed to need a little something to get through the days. I could never figure it out. He was smarter than I was. Smarter than nine tenths of the kids in our class. But he just couldn't take ... burdens. Demands. Frustrations. I don't know. He buckled."

"You told him no," said Grace.

"I told him, honestly, that I didn't have it. I could have raised it, but I wasn't tempted to. I didn't think he was good for it, and he didn't give me the impression it was life or death. If I'd known ..."

"It wasn't your fault," said Grace. "Any more than it was mine. I kept bailing him out, and he kept jumping back in."

"Did he say anything else?" I asked. "Anything that would tell us who was after him, or why?"

Brewster shook his head, slowly, thinking. "We didn't talk very long. He caught me at a busy time. After I turned him down for the loan, he didn't have much to say."

"If you think of anything, will you call us?" Grace asked.

"Who else would he have talked to?" I wanted to know. "Who else might he have gone to?"

He stared thoughtfully at the floor. "He was fairly tight with Will Chappy at one time, and Will called me a few days ago, asking about Ron." His face changed, oddly. "Also Margaret Pace. They stayed in touch. She went out to California, and I know she saw him there. She told me so."

Will Chappy and Margaret Pace were on our list. Brew took an address book from his desk and gave us the addresses and phone numbers.

"Are you and she friends?" I asked.

He flushed, shrugged. "Well, we were. I had to locate everyone because I was in charge of the Class of eighty-one tenth reunion. I traced down everyone, got everybody's address I could find."

"Did Ron come to the reunion?"

"No, but Margaret did. That's when she told me she'd been out to California to see him."

I finished my wine. He uttered a few more platitudes, sincerely meant. Grace thanked him for his time. We went back out to the car.

"Dinner," I said. "The wine made me hungry."

She answered absently, not even suggesting a restaurant. Though Margaret Pace's name had been on our list, something about Brew's use of it had surprised her.

four

SINCE WE WERE already southeast of town, we went to dinner at the Wellshire on South Colorado Boulevard. Being Wednesday and early, it wasn't crowded. We had a drink and ordered dinner. Grace visibly softened and bloomed, the soft sounds of crockery and voices working on her like a piece of music. Grace likes restaurants. They're her natural milieu.

"So," I said, when she was contentedly finishing off the last of my dessert. "Who is Margaret Pace?"

She sat back, frowning very slightly, a spoonful of chocolate mousse halfway to her lips. "She's a person Ron adored in high school. The only girl or woman he ever showed any interest in. She comes from a very wealthy family. It always surprised me that she went to a public school; I'd have thought she'd have gone to St. Mary's or one of the private day schools."

"The kind of girl whose family would just naturally arrange for her to have a French-speaking nanny?"

"Right. Then she'd get lessons in riding, music, and ballroom dancing, and probably a year or two in Europe, polishing her French, before she started college."

"Ron adored her?" I found this odd.

"He was hopeless about her. Even though he wasn't

139

in her social class. He wasn't invited to her parties. Her parents wouldn't have allowed him in the house."

"Why? Because he was poor, relatively speaking?"

"Because he wasn't anybody. Not a banker's son, a doctor's son, an eminent lawyer's son. His family hadn't gone to Harvard or Yale. He didn't ride. I remember one time he spent a week desperately trying to figure out how to take riding lessons, just so he could meet her, casually, on horseback."

"He adored from afar, I presume."

"He wrote her poetry. He bought her books. He tried . . . oh, Jason, it was heartbreaking. Can you remember?"

I could. Those first, shattering ill-fated romances. I'd had a couple. Strangely, now, I could hardly remember their names, much less their faces, but then! Oh, yes, I could remember.

"So? What happened?"

"Nothing happened. She was his fairy princess, and he was the swineherd. He got me to teach him to dance, hours and hours, then he went to the senior prom, hoping for one dance with her. I don't think he got his dance. He wouldn't talk about it. She went away to school. He stayed here. He quit pretending. I think she was his last hope of being . . . straight. Or maybe it was something much loftier than that, something symbolic, mystical. Romeo and Juliet, doomed lovers, I just don't know. Anyhow, when she left, his life began to unravel. He moved away. I didn't know he'd ever seen her again."

"We need to talk with her," I said, fishing in my pocket for the card Brewster Tyrell had given us. "We've got an address. An apartment building, right in our neighborhood."

"In our neighborhood?"

"Well, Polo Club."

"That's more like it. She's still Margaret Pace? Not a married name?"

"Which doesn't mean she isn't married."

"No, of course not. Right. I'll call her." She finished off the chocolate mousse, wiped her lips neatly, and went off to find a telephone. I had another cup of coffee and watched bemusedly while the buspersons cleared the table and the bill materialized at my elbow.

In time, Grace returned, shaking her head. "She said to come over. She sounded . . . Jason, she sounded drunk."

"Why the surprise?" I murmured.

"People like that . . . they shouldn't get drunk. They don't have any reason to get drunk."

"You are a dreamer, Grace. Rich people get drunk, and use drugs, and commit suicide. They simply do it more expensively than other people. Maybe it's a good thing if she is drunk. It may make her more talkative than otherwise."

We paid the bill, retrieved the car, and drove to the Polo Club, not the gated community, but the apartment house. There was no parking space space near the building, so we parked at the far edge of the lot. Inside, across from the office the concierge sat at his curved desk, and he called upstairs before letting us through the doors into the elevator lobby. The elevator ran up the side of the atrium, all very imposing, and on the top floor the door opened onto a private elevator lobby: marble floored, skylighted, with a whole oasis of potted palms. The apartment door stood open in the opposite wall, framing a red-haired beauty whose natural habitat could have been the cover of *Vogue*. Or *Playboy*. She simmered against the doorframe, leaning into it, as though it were someone else's body she lusted after.

She was drunk. Not awfully, just slightly. A little waver in the walk, a little too much concentration in the manner. The soft garments she wore—trousers and a flowing shirt—rustled as she came toward us, a silken pouring of fabric across perfumed skin, erotic as sound and scent could be. She was lean but not thin, with a boyish, athletic muscularity. I saw why Ron would have been attracted to her. She had an androgynous eroticism, an almost asexual sensuality.

"I'm Margaret Pace," she said, a throaty murmur, her eyes sliding over both of us like a caress, peering beneath her lashes.

Grace introduced me. Margaret took my hand and gave me a smile, frankly invitational. Grace's brows went up. I kept an impassive face, made necessary—made possible!—by Grace's proximity. We moved from lobby to entry, from entry to living room: leather and deep Orientals and a few well-chosen bibelots against full-length windows giving on a roof-garden allée of potted trees with a bronze nude at the far end. Not Venus. Diana, with a bow. Not lover, but huntress. Over the goddess's shoulder the sky was full of city lights against a far horizon of broken mountains. Very nice.

"So Brew sicced you on me," she said to Grace, all graciousness, with only the slightest slurring. "You're who again? Ron's sister?"

Grace nodded her head slightly, her eyes wary, as though puzzled by something.

"Grace is Ron's sister, yes," I said. "She's also a policewoman."

"Oh, I know," she said with a gurgling laugh. "Don't

I know. Ron talked a lot about Grace. Let's go outside. We can talk better outside."

We went through sliding glass doors onto the southeast corner of the roof, along the allée, then turned left to a marquee like a Persian tent, flowing draperies around an arrangement of teak furniture, softly cushioned in what looked to be watered silk, the whole decorated with potted orchids and candles in glass chimneys. A fair-weather paradise. Someone here was responsible for putting out the furniture and taking in the furniture and trimming the trees and providing a continual rotation of potted plants. There wasn't a twig out of place, not a yellow leaf or a faded bloom. All very well tended. And the lady of the house, also well tended.

"You want a drink? Something?" she asked, indicating a carved teak chest, Balinese I guessed, that had been outfitted as a bar.

I accepted a brandy. Grace shook her head, no. Margaret poured herself a generous dollop of Irish, dropped in one ice cube, and sank into the nearest chair.

"Lynx," she said, giving me that same invitational smile. "That's a big old cat, isn't it?"

"Not one that would do well as a pet," I agreed.

"Oh, well. Pets are boring. Give me the wild ones anytime."

"Did you know my brother well?" Grace asked, moving in on this seductive sequence like a little terrier.

"Better than you did," she challenged.

Grace's face paled, as though she'd been struck. I took her hand in mine. "Let's not get off on the wrong foot here. Grace didn't know him well. I didn't know him well. Ron didn't want us to know him well. That's why we're here. He's dead, and we need to know why."

"Inconveniently dead," she said. "Very damned inconveniently dead."

Grace moved angrily, and I squeezed her hand to keep her quiet. "Why would that be?"

"He owed me money," she said. "Or stuff. One or the other."

"Drugs?" asked Grace, suddenly all cop, no judgment in her tone, just looking for information.

"Well, since he turned me on in the first place, it was his duty to keep me supplied, don't you think?"

"When did he 'turn you on'?" I asked. "While you were in school together?"

"I wasn't in school together." She sneered. "Not together with anyone. Muzzie favored the egalitarian virtues of public school. Daddy favored the aristocratic power of private friends. So I went, but I didn't mingle. Daddy saw to that."

"When did Ron give you drugs?" I repeated. "Before he left for California?"

"Then, and since."

"Why did he?" I pressed. "At first. Was it him, or you?"

"I was pissed," she said, leaning toward a jade box on the teak table. She took out a cigarette, lighted it with a gold lighter, blew smoke in my face. "At Muzzie and Daddy dearest. And here was this brainy nerd following me around as though I was the Holy Grail. So I thought I'd have some fun. I told him to get me some stuff and I'd give him a date. So he did."

"Did you give him the date?" asked Grace, without inflection, ominously indifferent.

Margaret shrugged. "I think I did, but who knows? I was away somewhere at the time. On a trip."

"When was this?" I demanded.

"Right after we graduated," she said. "At the prom, actually. That's when we made the deal. I had a couple of weeks before the family shipped me off to be polished. I did not want to be polished. I was in looove." She mooed the word, cowlike, mocking herself.

"With Ron?" Grace asked.

The woman laughed infectiously. "Ron? Funny-funny."

"Who then?"

"Old Brew. True Brew. True-blue Brew. But he wasn't good enough for Daddy. Or even for Muzzie dear. His father was only an accountant. He was middle-class! Muzzie said I could do better."

"He seems to have done well for himself," I said.

"Oh, True Brew did well for himself. I think he succeeded just to rub Daddy's nose in it. And I did badly for myself. Just to rub Daddy's nose in it. Brewster has babies. I don't. Brewster has a good marriage. I don't. Between us, we made our point, didn't we?" She turned aside, light gathering at the corners of her eyes. "I went to that damned tenth reunion just to see him, dance with him. All I could think was, Oh, God. I was so in love with him. . . ."

A long silence. Margaret shook her head angrily, went to the bar, and returned, her glass refilled with darkness, no ice.

Grace said, "Brewster said you went to California to see Ron."

She frowned with concentration, each word considered. "I went to California several times, and when I was there, I saw Ron. I didn't go there to see him, but once I was there, I called him. He was my connection, right?"

"How did you know where to get in touch with him?"

"We kept in touch. Then the last time you told me." She jutted her chin toward Grace. "I called you from San Franciso and said I was an old friend of his. You told me where he was."

Grace nodded slowly. "I remember. Last month. I didn't know it was you."

"Oh, hell, lady, join the club. Anymore, I don't know who's me."

I brought the conversation back on track. "You asked Ron to get drugs for you recently? When exactly was this?"

"Like she says, a month or so ago," she said, leaning her head back to stare out at the sky.

"What was your relationship?" I asked wonderingly. "Was he just your pusher? The guy you went to to get drugs?"

"What else?" She looked at me, sipped her drink, shrugged. "You think he still cared about me? Hell no. I told you. When we were kids, he thought I was the Holy Grail. Once he knew I was just like anybody else, he didn't care anymore. We taught each other what we really were, didn't we? I was a hetero slut. He was a gay pusher. We're losers, both of us."

Grace's hand tensed under mine, her face darkened. I murmured soothingly at her, and she subsided.

"Did you talk to him?" I asked Margaret. "While you were in California, did you spend any time together at all?"

"Sure. We always went down to watch the ocean. I like watching the ocean. It doesn't give a damn."

"What did you talk about?"

"Mostly . . . people we used to know. This last time

he had some ice. I'd used crack, but I'd never tried ice before. I liked it. He said he'd get me some more. He said he was coming home, he'd bring me some more, or get me some when he got here. I gave him my money, all I had. I told him to get me lots. A year's supply."

"Did he?"

"When he got here, he called and said he had it, but he had to have payment for it. I'd already given him all the money I had. I couldn't pay him any more."

I looked at the luxury around us and frowned. She smiled at the expression.

"Daddy won't let me have any cash. He pays the bills, but I can't have any cash. And everything in this place that's salable, he's got engraved with his name and address. And he's got somebody watching me whenever I go out, just in case I try to sell something, or invite anybody up; you know, somebody who might pay for the privilege." She laughed like a gleefully hateful child. "He pays that idiot downstairs to spy on me. He has an account with the cab company. And restaurants. And the grocery store, even. And the cleaners."

"It's like jail," said Grace.

"It's just like jail. Right." She started to say something else, but her phone rang. There was an extension on a nearby table. She went to take the call, turning her back to us.

I heard her murmuring, "Yes ... Yes ... I knew about it. He called me.... Well, I don't want to talk about it now.... No. It's none of your business."

She put down the phone, returned to us.

I picked up where we'd left off. "So if your father controls your expenditures, how did you get to California?"

"This year Daddy cut off my credit with the airlines

and hotels, so this time I had to save up. I bough
clothes, then I took them back and got cash refunds
And I've got a deal with a cabdriver. We split what h
overcharges Daddy on his bills, just like I do with th
delivery boy at the grocer's. That's how I buy my li
quor. You can't put a lot away that way. It takes time
It took me months to get enough for California becaus
I wasn't going to come back. I was going to keep o
going."

"But you didn't."

She shrugged. "I gave Ron what I had to buy ic
with, so there wasn't enough to keep going. I shoul
have run away when I was eighteen." Her eyes went t
the phone, rested there. "I should have run away wit
Brew. He asked me to, but I was too much Daddy's gir
It's too late now. I'm too used to this. . . ." She gesture
inclusively, the world, the view, the allée of shorn trees
Herself.

"You're killing yourself," said Grace. "Just like Ro
was."

"Not fast enough," she murmured around the rim o
the glass, which was already half-empty. "Not nearl
fast enough."

"Let me get this sequence straight," I said. "Ro
brought you drugs from California?"

"He called me when he got here, like I told you, an
he said he had what I'd ordered. I don't know where h
got it. Then he called me again a few days later. Satur
day, I guess. I was watching Saturday Night Live. H
said he knew where there was more ice in one plac
than anybody had ever seen and old friends were th
best friends. I said it didn't matter, I couldn't pay hin
any money. He said right, it didn't matter. He sounde
funny, high, crazy."

"He still needed money to pay for this 'ice'?"

"Who knows? Whatever."

"How much money did he need? When he first asked you?"

"Fifty thousand."

"Did he sound desperate?"

"Didn't he always." She laughed. "Always desperate. That was Ron. Love, hate, fear, anger, joy, whatever, it was always desperate."

It didn't make sense to me. Why would he say it didn't matter? "What did he say when you told him you didn't have the money?"

"The first time? Or the second time?"

"The second time. Saturday night."

"That's when he said it didn't matter, ice got him in the hole, ice got him out of the hole, then he laughed like crazy."

Grace had been following all this, her eyes intent. Now she asked, "Did you know he was dying of AIDS?"

Silence. A sudden stillness of body and face, motion arrested, the word barely audible. "AIDS?"

"Did you tell him you wanted to die?" Grace asked. "When you were in California, did you do something besides ice? Did you share a needle with him? Did you have sex with him?"

Eyes widening in sudden intelligence. "Not Ron!"

"Why not?"

"Because ... because he wouldn't do that to me."

"Not even if you told him you wanted to die?" Grace persisted. "I think he would. If you said you wanted to die, I think Ron would say, hell, why not? She wants it, why not? Kind of a last gift to a girl he once adored."

Margaret lurched to her feet and ran back into the

apartment. We heard her feet clattering on marble floors, the slam of a door.

"I guess we'll let ourselves out," said Grace in a stiff angry voice.

"You really had it in for her," I said wonderingly. In all the time I had known Grace, I had not seen this quietly raging person.

"Ron wasn't a nothing," she said furiously. "He wasn't a nerd, a device, a connection. He was my brother. I loved him. People like this . . . they killed him."

"She didn't set the bomb."

"She set him up for the bomb. She asked him to get drugs for her. He did. That's what got him into the mess, whatever it was. Just the way he always did things, monkey see, monkey do, monkey no think about consequences. He owed somebody for the stuff he got for her! She wasn't worth it!"

"Maybe not just for the stuff he got for her. Maybe some for him as well," I suggested.

"I don't know, Jason. All I know is, she wasn't worth it."

"She has the same problem Ron had," I said gently.

"She has everything!"

"Ron did, too. Life, health, a good mind. But he couldn't accept who he was. It's the same for her. Her father won't accept who she is, so she can't."

"It's not the same," she said stubbornly, pressing the ground-floor button in the elevator.

We rode down in silence. I saw no point in arguing about the relative merits and demerits of Ron and Margaret. Margaret had been quite right when she said they were both losers. Ron had said as much to Grace when he told her he didn't have to be anyone anymore. Margaret, in her own way, was also saying it. She didn't have to be anyone either. Cushioned in luxury, she could live out a short or long life, thinking and regretting as little as possible.

As we let ourselves out of the lobby downstairs, a man brushed through the door between us, not excusing himself, going on to enter the elevator we'd just left. I gave him a dirty look, but he was staring at the ceiling, head back, preoccupied, only his bushy mustache visible. I thought for a moment he might be Margaret's father—he had that bankerly look—but he wasn't old enough. As we went through the lobby the concierge came from the hallway behind his desk, hands busy adjusting his trousers while head nodded a gracious goodbye. When we got outside, we stood there indecisively, not sure where we wanted to go next. Grace was screwing up her face, kicking at the sidewalk. I hugged her.

"You're right," she murmured. "I was rotten to her."

"Rather, yes. But understandably. You were right when you said she may have gotten Ron killed."

I kept my arm around her as we walked across the lot to the car. Except for the traffic shushing by on Cherry Creek South and on Colorado Boulevard, the evening was very still. All the houses and apartments around us were closed against the night, light showing through draperies, if at all. There were no dog walkers, no evening joggers. Stars were beginning to break through the haze, those few bright enough to do so. Faint stars find no place in city skies. A comment, perhaps, on success. If you're a faint star, forget it. The broken line of the mountains wasn't visible from where we were, but the last of the sunlight had faded to dark violet above the city glow.

When we got to the car, I looked back, at the top of the building where the line of pollarded trees made a darkly scalloped border against the sky. There was pale movement among them, Margaret no doubt, come back to her penthouse garden to drink the night away. I was tempted to go back, try to help. . . . What help could I be?

Instead, I asked Grace if she wouldn't stay with me that night. She said a few unconvincing words about being alone, and even though I thought she'd been alone enough, I couldn't talk her out of it. Considering the mood she was in, I was careful not to mention marriage or any other important topic. I talked instead about Valerie French and her putative in-laws. About Wilson Credable and his family history, about all the great-aunts and siblings who had died, about Admar and Edward and his tussle over Credable Castle.

"So there's only Wilson and Edward left," she murmured sleepily.

"And Aunt Carolyn," I said, as drowsily as she. "She's in a nursing home somewhere. She's about ninety, I think Wilson said."

"If she still makes sense, it would be fun to talk with her. I'll bet she has some stories to tell about growing up in that place, with all those relatives."

"I think most of the relatives were gone by the time Carolyn was born. By that time the sisters would have been married off and most of the older children would have gone out on their own."

"Still," she whispered. "It would be fun to talk with her." A moment or two later I heard her kitten snore, a very lulling sound. Like infant surf. I drove to my house. She wakened slightly, saw where she was, and stiffened.

"I said I wanted to go home."

"I'm taking you home. I just want to get that ring I told you about." I went upstairs to my office and got the rolled tissue out of the desk drawer. "The ring," I said to her as I slid back behind the wheel. "The finger."

I walked her to her door. She was being remote, chilly, so I gave her a chaste kiss on the cheek and departed. Then I went home and spent a frustrated hour wishing she were there with me. I told myself to be sensitive, to be forbearing, to let the lady get it together, but it didn't make me feel any better.

When the Bela alarm put its nose in my ear at about seven-thirty, I got up yawningly, showered, shaved, brushed my teeth, wandered into the kitchen to put on coffee, turned on the radio to catch the weather forecast and early news.

". . . Margaret Pace, daughter of industrialist Benjamin Pace, found dead by early-morning joggers, evidently having fallen or jumped from her rooftop apartment . . ."

I called Grace's house. No answer. I called the cop shop. She wasn't available. Five minutes later she called me, full of recriminations at herself, at us. "Jason. That man who pushed between us when we left Margaret last night, in the lobby. Did you look at him?"

I fumbled with memory, which proved recalcitrant. "I thought he was stocky, but that could have been his topcoat. He was wearing a dark hat. He had a bushy dark mustache. When I glared at him, he was looking up at the ceiling of the elevator. I didn't really see his face. I thought he looked young, thirty-fivish, maybe."

"They've asked every resident in the building. Not one of them came into the lobby last night at that time.

They were all either in for the evening or out until later."

"I didn't notice the time," I said. "Except ... the stars were just coming out."

"That's what I noticed, too. That placed it close enough. It was about five after nine."

"She didn't jump?" I asked, my sleepy brain finally putting two and two together. "You're saying she didn't jump?"

"There were bruises on her throat, and a piece of broken glass in her hand. Suicides don't jump with glasses in their hands. There was blood on the glass. Preliminary lab findings, it wasn't hers. She'd used the glass as a weapon."

"How could anyone get in?" I asked. "Did she let the person in?"

"It was our fault," she cried. "We went down when she was in the bathroom. The man came through the door when we opened it. When the elevator got up there, she must have thought it was us, coming back. It wasn't a break-in. Whoever went up just walked right in on her."

Midmorning, Amelia Wirtz wandered in without her usual self-possession.

"I heard from the Clear Creek Sheriff's Office this morning," she said in a distressed tone. "They have a partial report from the state crime lab. The skeleton was a woman."

I was less surprised than she. The ring I'd found had seemed a feminine thing. That hadn't ruled out it's being worn by a man, as a keepsake on a pinkie finger maybe, but subconsciously, I'd been prepared for hearing it was a woman. I considered telling Amelia about the ring, but decided nothing would be achieved by doing so. The sheriff's office would undoubtedly query her in good time; better I stay out of it.

"So?" I asked her.

"So, until we get this all straightened out, let's put the institute thing on ice."

The word made me react, recoil, just a little.

"What?" she demanded.

"Ice," I said. "The word has acquired a new meaning." I told her about "ice" as it related to Margaret Pace. And what had happened to Margaret Pace.

Her face clouded. "I know the Pace family. That is, I know Ben. Lord. Margaret was an only child. Was a time, the sun rose and set with that girl, so far as Ben was concerned. He'll be out for blood."

"Whose blood? Ron's already dead."

"You said she was killed. Someone killed her."

"She may simply have fallen," I admitted. "Why would anyone kill Margaret?"

Amelia shook her head. She didn't know.

We sat there, staring at each other, unenlightened. Finally I asked, "What's the next step concerning the skeleton?"

"They're having a forensic anthropologist do a head, you know, in clay. And they're running some genetic studies to see if they can identify race, and some kind of test to determine age. They think now she was Caucasian, around forty, forty-five."

"Teeth," I murmured.

"What about teeth?"

"They could maybe identify her by her teeth?"

"If they had some idea who she is, yes. They know she was around five-foot-six. Her teeth were good. Some of the bones were broken, but there's no sign of

healing, so they were broken after she was dead. O
right before she died. Or—"

"Do they know how long she's been there?"

She shrugged. "A long time. All the time I've been
camping up there. It makes me . . . shivery. What do the
Scots call it? The *cauld grue*? The thought that maybe
she was dropped down there alive. That she died there,
of cold and starvation." She shivered. "Not nice, Jason."

"Let's think about something else. How are we doing
with Wilson Credable?"

"Oh, Wilson is feeling very chipper. He's quite
buoyed up by the idea of selling some of Marley's
Chains."

"Marley's . . . ?"

"Wilson's words. He says he's been weighted down
with worldly possessions all his life, like Marley's
Ghost. Getting rid of some of the stuff makes him feel
young again."

"I don't think Edward will feel that pleased about it."

"Oh, well, Edward. I don't know why Edward is re-
opening this issue just now. He's always felt that since
the fortune started with Crispin Credable Senior, and
since both he and Wilson are grandsons, Edward being
the elder grandson, the castle should have come to him,
but he knows it didn't. Both the will and the law are
quite clear. Why is he doing this?"

"What would he do with the castle if he had it?"

"Stand on the battlements and crow each morning, I
think. Until he got bored. Then he'd sell it. It has nothing to do with logic or the demands of the law. It's an
emotional thing. He considers himself the better man,
that's all. It probably had something to do with his

mother's abandoning him. He's been compensating ever since. I know the feeling."

"Your mother didn't abandon you."

"At the time it felt like abandonment. Even though I was seventeen, not a baby any longer, it felt ... like she'd willfully left me. In my mind, the sequence began with her leaving, then she was gone. There was nothing in between. No farewell."

"Speaking of your father—since he owned that land and left it to your uncle, do you suppose the bones might have been some ... well, something your uncle might have known about?"

"I called Uncle Maddox as soon as they told me it was a woman. He has a full-time nurse-housekeeper because he needs someone to look after him, and she was reluctant even to let him talk to me for fear it would upset him. She was right. He got very upset, told me he hadn't a notion about it, and he wishes people would stop bothering him about that place, he doesn't want anything to do with it. He said it about three times. 'I don't want anything of Hector's. Hector gets mean when anybody fools with his things. Hector can get really nasty.' "

"He doesn't remember Hector—your father—is dead?"

"A lot of the time he seems to be back in the early nineteen hundreds. He talks as though he's ten or twelve years old most of the time. Very much afraid of Hector." She sighed. "It hurts me to say so, but I know what he means. Father could be formidable, and he didn't take kindly to trespass, not by anyone, including Mother or me. We learned not to offer any opinions on his life, business, or belongings. If I told Father his new suit made him look handsome, he might be pleased, but he might just as well go into a rage. 'Damned well better look good,' he'd shout. 'I paid that thieving tailor enough for it!' "

"A hard man to get along with."

"Well, Mother and I learned to stick to generalities at the dinner table. Talk about other people was safer than talk about people we knew. Talk about animals was safer than talk about people. Best of all was talk about sewing or gardening or bridge, since Father had no very strong opinions about them."

"Couldn't have been easy, being an only child."

She shrugged as she rose. "If there'd been more of us, I imagine Father would have generated enough animosity to go around." She smoothed her skirt, picked up her purse, preparatory to departure. "So, we're tabling anything further on the institute? Figure out your time and bill me."

"Ah, Amelia, I've hardly done enough. . . ."

Her voice turned to ice. "Figure out your time and bill me, Jason. This was a business arrangement, and despite all these interpolations, I intend it to continue so."

"Yes, ma'am," I said, shocked.

She bit her lip. "Sorry. I didn't mean to sound unfriendly. This whole thing has upset me more than I like to admit. I feel powerless. I haven't been sleeping well. I have nightmares and come awake with my heart pounding. I'm snapping at everyone. Maybe I should take a vacation."

I nodded understandingly, patted her on the shoulder, and escorted her to the front door. Then I went in search of Mark and Eugenia. I could hear their voices, and finally tracked them to the basement. They were in a spotlighted space in the dimly lighted workroom, where

Mark, in his painting coveralls, was stripping the daven-port desk Ron had started.

"I can't figure out why this was ever painted," he said as I came through the door. "The secretary, yes, it was a little dilapidated, but this piece could have been new. It's a lovely piece of cherry, Jason."

Outside the circle of light stood two catty-cornered stacks of drawers from the davenport. I took the top one, stood it on end, and started to sit down on it.

"Don't," Eugenia said urgently. "You'll ruin your trousers. It's allover blue."

"Oh, right," I said, peering at it. It was heavily coated with blue dust. "What the hell?"

She wiped at the drawer with a wad of newspaper, then dusted her hands together. "Mark says it's chalk."

Mark said, "From a chalk line, Eugenia. Someone spilled the loose chalk. It's in the top drawer, the one on the bottom of the stack."

I removed the next drawer down, disclosing the inte-rior of the third, shallowest one. It held a messy tangle of line, caked with blue chalk. The two halves of the plastic chalk container were there as well, the little windup handle lying centered on a pink square, all that was visible of a larger sheet of pink paper. I lifted the paper out with thumb and forefinger, turned it over: the second or third copy of a sales ticket. Beneath it were other sizes and colors of paper, an untidy stack, each exposed edge blued with chalk.

"These papers are probably trash, but they ought to go back to Amelia," I said. "I thought the drawers were empty."

Eugenia nodded. "They all were, except the top one on the right side. It was painted shut. Ron came to me and asked how to get it open without scarring the wood.

I told him to apply the stripper heavily, all the way
around the drawer, and let it soak in. I guess it finally
softened the paint enough that he could get the drawer
out."

Ron had scraped the face of that one drawer to bare
wood, enough to show that Mark was right. It was a
very nice piece of cherry. I lifted the papers, shaking
them gently, then took them up the stairs to the back
door, where I dusted them off more thoroughly. A cloud
of blue wafted away on the light breeze, and I stood out
there for a few moments, smelling the sunshine. Nellie's
gate was open across the way, and I could see her sitting in the sun in her wheelchair. I strolled over, finding
her eager for company. Nothing would do but she roll
herself into her apartment to get me a piece of tissue paper to fold up the chalky papers in. She asked me what
I'd been doing, so I told her while she arranged the
odds and ends.

"They're all old sales slips from hardware stores,"
she said. "Here's one from a lumberyard. Bannock
Lumber. I remember that place. Went out of business in
the sixties. Somebody bought cement and metal lath
and what's this? A carbon . . . ?"

"Carbide drill bits," I said, reading over her shoulder.

"And trowels. What do you suppose they were
doing?"

"House repairs, maybe. Probably a chimney."

She shook her head at me. "No, not a chimney. A
chimney gets fixed when the chimney sweep says it's
falling apart."

"So?"

"So, the way that happens is the first cold night
comes, and people say, oh, let's have a fire. So they
light the fire, and it smokes. So then the chimney sweep

omes, and he says, you've got bricks fallen down the himney, but it's too cold to fix it now. You'll have to ix it next spring. So the chimney gets put off until pring, or even the following fall. But these tickets are or July. Nobody thinks about fireplaces in midsummer. et's see. What would you fix in July?"

"That's when lawns are being watered or summer hunderstorms drop a lot of rain," I suggested. "How bout sidewalks; patio steps; leaking foundations?"

She was shaking her head over the prices. "Things ure were cheaper in the fifties," she said. "I'll bet the epairman got around three dollars an hour!"

I laughed, remembering what Amelia had said about er father. "If Hector Wirtz set the price, I'm sure ou're right, Nellie. He was quite a skinflint. What was is was his, and he didn't like giving it away."

"Hector Wirtz, Hector Wirtz?" she said musingly. "I now that name from somewhere. Wasn't he an oil-nan?"

"Oil, timber, ranching. Sort of an all-around spoiler, o hear Amelia tell it."

"That's it! He was in the newspaper. He shot a man. Oh, it was a big hoopla."

"He must have got off."

"Oh, sure he did. Money does. This man came to Wirtz's house, and Hector Wirtz shot him for a burglar. Turned out he wasn't a burglar. He was some man who had worked for Wirtz. Didn't matter. Wirtz got off, then he sued the paper for libel."

"When was that, Nellie?" I wondered why Amelia had never mentioned it.

"Oh, it was a long time ago. Forty or fifty years. I re-member, they called him the lord high executioner. Like in Gilbert and Sullivan, you know. Seems like this wasn't the first man he'd killed."

Maybe such details had been kept from Amelia. More likely she simply did not like remembering it. Nellie and I talked a few minutes longer, and then I took the tissue-wrapped packet of papers back to my office and put them into a large manila envelope intending to give them to Amelia, next time I saw her.

I called Grace and offered to fix dinner for us that night. She said maybe, depending. She'd call me.

I don't like Thursday nights. Thursday nights are evidence of the intransigence of time and the irrefutability of Friday. No matter what I have planned to do during a workweek, Thursday night always arrives with more left to do than can be done in one more day. Half of Wilson's Marley Chains were still unvalued. I hadn't looked over Mark's list of things he thought we ought to buy. I hadn't solved Ron's murder. Grace was counting on me to do that. Our future might depend upon it.

So, I told myself sternly, concentrate on that!

There was another name on my mental list: Will Chappy. How many Chappys could there be? I looked him up in the phone book, and there he was, William R., with a home in Englewood and an office in the Tech Center. I called his office. He was in. I told his secretary to tell him I was on my way over, to talk about Ron Willis's death. I yelled down the stairs to Mark and Eugenia, telling them I was leaving.

According to the gold-leaf name on the door, CHAPPY, HANDLY, AND WOODMAN, my quarry was a consulting geologist. The office had a few earnest-looking young people crouched over computers. In a glass-walled room to one side, more earnest faces hovered over a lighted table spread with diagrams of something esoteric, talking seriously and loudly about using high-resolution seismography to describe some geological anomaly with a very long name. Tectonic plates entered into the problem. Big stuff, geology. When Chappy himself came out to escort me back to his office, he turned out to be a rumpled sort in horn-rim glasses, shirttail not quite tucked, tie loosened at the neck, a couple of razor nicks, that comfortable disarray that speaks of unselfconsciouness. He had a corner office; he was not merely one of the flunkies.

"What is high-resolution seismography?" I asked, surprising myself.

"Setting off little explosions and measuring the sound transmission through the earth. Different strata transmit sound differently. You chart it on a computer and it can tell you what's underground. Sometimes we don't even use explosions, we have a big machine that goes *thump*. I thought you wanted to know about Ron?"

I said I did.

"Poor old Ron. I was sorry as hell to hear about him."

"When did you see him last?" I asked.

He faced away from me to stare out the window. "Oh, it's been a while. Christmas, a couple years back, I think. He was home visiting his sister." There was tension in his neck, his jaw. He wasn't telling me something.

"I thought you'd seen him recently," I said blandly. "This last time."

He shifted uncomfortably, gave me a glance from under his lashes. "Well, yes. I didn't want to say anything about it, but yes, I did. He wanted to borrow some money, as a matter of fact. I hated to turn him down."

"But you did turn him down?"

"Well, yes. We've got every dime sunk into our expansion efforts—office in Dallas, office in Anchorage. I told him I couldn't possibly come up with anything right now. Besides, knowing Ron . . ."

"You did know him well."

He shook his head, as though unsure, speaking slowly, thinking his way through the story. "I thought I did. He called me at home, said he needed a favor, I said come on over, but then he showed up with this car full of . . . well, not the type of people I want at my house on a Saturday night—or ever! Here they all were, on my doorstep, and I said sorry, I didn't realize he was with friends, and since we were expecting guests, I couldn't invite them all in. There was some mutter around, then they went back to the car and he came in. Only they didn't all go back to the car, because here came my wife in a few minutes to say two of them were in the backyard."

"Disconcerting," I murmured.

"Ron thought so. He turned white. I asked him what the hell, and he said he owed these guys money, they were probably watching the back door to be sure he didn't run off. I said something to the effect he wasn't much of a friend if he'd bring a bunch of drug dealers to my home, where my children were. He huffed a little about their not being drug dealers, and I said who else? That's when he asked me for money. He said he could pay it back in a couple of weeks, that he'd come into some big money, if I could just trust him for a couple of weeks . . ." His voice faded, and he shook his head angrily.

"And . . . ?"

"And I didn't like what he'd done, bringing those people to my house. So I said no, I couldn't trust him for two weeks, or for one week, or any time at all, and did he take me for a fool, expecting me to believe he'd come into money?"

This time I just waited.

"He insisted it was true, that he'd come into so much money he'd never have to worry again. He said he just didn't want to tell these guys about it, because if they knew about it, they might figure a way to take the whole thing and leave him out in the cold."

"Anything else?"

"I asked him how he got into this mess. He said he bought drugs from these people for a friend of his; of ours, actually. I asked what friend, and he told me Margaret Pace. She was supposed to pay him for it. She couldn't. I said give the stuff back, and he said he'd tried that, but the dealers wouldn't take it, they wanted the money. He'd tried borrowing from Brew Tyrell. I was his last hope."

"And you told him sorry."

"I told him I wasn't in the money-lending business. I wasn't that sorry, to tell you the truth. And ever since I heard about him, I've been feeling guilty as hell. . . ."

"So he left."

"He went out the front door, got in the car, the car tooted, the guys came around from the backyard, and they all drove off."

"What color was the car?"

"Blue. One of those metallic finishes."

I nodded absently. "You didn't believe him for a moment, about his coming into money?"

He laughed. "Where would Ron Willis get money? Hell, his sister runs a boardinghouse, his folks are dead—"

"His sister is a policewoman. She owns apartments."

He raised his eyebrows, made an oddly uncomfortable half shrug. "Well, whatever." He gave me a straight, man-to-man look. "I didn't believe him. Would you?"

I had to confess, I would not have believed him either. I could think of nothing more to be gained from William Chappy, so I left him to his anomalous strata and departed.

I still had the list of names Grace and I had put together from Ron's correspondence. Both Chappy and Tyrell had been on it, so there were two men left, and one woman. It was, however, close to five o'clock, and if I was going to fix supper for Grace, I needed to get at it. Grace is not one for delayed dining. Late suppers are fine, but only as an adjunct to, not a substitute for, three or four sizable daytime meals.

I called the office. She had left a message. She would be over around six-thirty. I stopped at the market and picked up six lamb chops, a bunch of asparagus, half a dozen blue potatoes, stuff for a salad, and a pint of Ben & Jerry's Double Fudge Chocolate Chunk ice cream. When I got home, I put the potatoes on to boil in their jackets, snapped the white ends off the asparagus, garlicked and peppered the chops, and whipped up a dressing of one part raspberry vinegar to three parts olive oil and a great deal of Roquefort cheese. When the potatoes were just barely cooked—this takes a firm potato; if they go floury on you, forget it—I peeled them, sliced them rather thick, put the oil and cheese dressing over them along with salt and pepper, then put them in the oven to keep warm.

Grace was prompt, and so was the food. While we made small talk she ate two chops and two helpings of purple potato before she was able to free up her mouth to make any comments.

"Ron didn't really like Will Chappy."

"How come?"

"Oh, when they were in school together, the story was Will Chappy would do anything for money."

"Such as?"

"Well, it was different things. Selling copies of tests, for instance. Will worked in the office part-time, and he figured out a way to get into the file cabinets. He stole tests and sold copies. At least, that's what Ron said."

"Did you report it?"

She flushed. "I wasn't a cop then, Jason. You know how kids are. They don't tell on their friends, and they expect their family to respect the confidence."

"So it wasn't reported."

"No. Ron and I both understood why he might do it. The family was damned near destitute. The father had been killed in Vietnam and the mother was trying to support five or six kids. William was the oldest surviving son." She chewed, swallowed thoughtfully. "Ron understood, but at that time, Ron had a strong sense of ethics. He believed in the way we'd been raised and he disapproved of Chappy."

Which disapproval he could set aside when he desperately needed money. I didn't say it, however. "Amelia says the skeleton up there on her land was a woman."

"I know. I talked to the state lab people today, when I took the finger over. They were a bit snarky."

"Snarky?" I asked innocently.

"You had no business going down that hole, Jason. Supposedly it was a crime scene."

"I suppose."

"They wanted to know if there was anything else down the hole. They say you probably interfered with evidence."

"There was nothing down there but bat droppings and a few wads of toilet paper, and I interfered with neither. There wasn't a sign of any fabric, any leather, any metal except the ring. There wasn't even any dust."

"They're going to look anyhow. The stones in the ring are tourmalines. Birthstone for October, according to one of the women down at the crime lab."

October was Grace's birth month. "I thought that was opals?" I'd been shopping for a really good opal thinking one would be nice as an engagement ring.

"Opals or tourmalines. They're a marvelous color, aren't they? Prettier than emeralds. She told me there are pink ones, too."

"But you like the green ones."

"Oh, yes." She gnawed the last bit of meat from a lamb bone and sighed contentedly at her empty plate.

I got up and got the ice cream out of the freezer. When she saw the pint container, she glowed. I felt the heat of the room go up several degrees. "I don't know where you're going to put this," I said, waving the container at her.

"There's room."

There always was. I had one spoonful of ice cream and two cups of coffee while she did away with the rest of the pint.

"Okay," she said at last, giving me a melting look. "Now I'm ready."

"For?" My heart leaped.

"For figuring out what happened to Ron."

Well, she'd given me fair warning. It was obvious I

could expect nothing but the status quo until we solved this thing.

She hadn't yet heard about Chappy, which gave me some progress to report.

"The week before Ron died, when he first got back here, he learned that Margaret couldn't pay him for the drugs he'd bought. Then he called Brewster Tyrell, wanting to borrow money. Brewster turned him down. The night before he died he went to see William Chappy—"

"You went to see Chappy without me?"

"You were busy. Just listen. Chappy says he also turned Ron down. On that same night Ron called Margaret Pace, who repeated what she'd told him before, that she had no money. Now here's the interesting part. Despite all this, the people he was with let him go."

Grace cocked her head, waiting.

"When he asked Chappy for the loan, he said it would be short-term because he, Ron, had 'come into' money. I believe Ron was let go because he convinced them he could get the money somewhere," I said. "It's the only thing that makes sense."

"Surely he was making that up."

"So Chappy believed. On the other hand, remember what Margaret said. She quoted Ron as saying it didn't matter if she couldn't pay him: ice got him in, ice got him out. That could mean he'd found another buyer. Maybe he convinced his creditors that he had a buyer."

She fiddled with her napkin, folding and refolding it. "Ron could be persuasive."

"So he persuades them he'll get the money. Then, the next day, they find out he lied, so they kill him."

"Couldn't be," she said. "You're not thinking."

"Why?"

"Because they had to have followed us when we went to the mountains, how else could they have known where we were? And if they followed us, then they couldn't have been checking out his story."

"Cellular phones," I offered. "Some of them followed us, some of them checked out his story."

"So where did they get dynamite on such short notice?"

That was a problem. People don't usually carry explosives around, unless we're talking about terrorists, that is, people who think of explosives as part of their daily stock-in-trade. Which was not impossible. More and more, such things are happening, terrorist attacks that kill innocent passersby, with someone calling to "take responsibility," which is both an oxymoron and a contemptible lie.

"That scenario has too many holes in it. What about Bela getting shot? What were the villains doing up on the mountain?"

I sighed. "And what was the blue car doing following me Tuesday night?"

She exploded. "You didn't tell me that!"

"I forgot," I said lamely. "I guess we have to figure someone is looking for something. That's the only thing that explains everything. Somebody was looking up on the mountain. They didn't find what they wanted. Presumably they went back, after I left, and they still didn't find it. So they looked at your place. They didn't find it. So they started following me around. What they're looking for has to be whatever Ron had, or whatever they thought he had."

"The name of another buyer?"

"It's thin, isn't it? If he had a buyer, no reason to keep the name secret. He could have told them."

"They could be looking for the drugs."

I said, "He told Chappy he tried to give them back. They wanted the money."

"With Ron alive, they wanted the money. With Ron dead, maybe they'd settle for the drugs."

"We could come up with a dozen theories, Grace. The fact is, we just don't know."

"You're giving up," she said, in a hard, angry stranger's voice.

"I am not giving up," I said between my teeth. "I do not give up so long as there's another thing to try or another person to talk to. And while we're on the subject, you might consider that the explosion was not intended for Ron at all. It might have been intended to bury those old bones so they'd never see the light of day."

"That's pretty coincidental, isn't it?" she snarled.

"Not inasmuch as Amelia Wirtz's picture was in the papers that Sunday morning along with the announcement she was going to build on that property. If someone had guilty knowledge dating back thirty or forty years, that person might decide to bury old bones right then, before a construction crew camped out on the side of that mountain. There's no statute of limitations on murder."

She sat there, forehead creased, wanting to yell at me. I could see her boiling. She desperately wanted to blame someone, something for Ron's death. What I'd just said had not been impossible. I wished she could believe that Ron had just died, not been murdered, but just died, as he would have died anyhow. If she could believe that, it would be easier on both of us.

She got up, readying herself to depart, giving me a challenging look. "That may be so, Jason. But if it is, you'll have to prove it."

* * *

Friday morning I went with Mark to Valerie French's apartment. Mark had a key. The painter had finished, the wallpaper was to go up today in the bathroom and kitchen, and we were checking progress. The living-room and bedroom walls were a medium tint of mahogany, a warm soft red brown in a matte finish. All the trim was the same color, one shade darker. The Arts and Crafts buffet stood beneath the living-room window, seeming to glow with reflected color.

"You got that refinished in a hurry."

"Actually, it was only very dirty," he said. "Layers and layers of dirty wax. It responded well to cleaning."

It certainly had. The ends of the ebony pegs showed clearly, and the inlay work was gorgeous, done with marvelous craftsmanship—which is what Arts and Crafts was all about: the best materials and the best workmanship. The problem with the style, from a decorator's point of view, was that most of the furniture had been crafty enough, but short on the arts end. No matter how well the wonderful woods had been put together, most of it had looked clunky and ugly. Valerie's pieces were different. They truly had some art to them.

Mark handed me the sample of the drapery material, the same color as the trim.

"What's on the chairs?"

He dug out that sample, too. A rich green, echoing the malachite inlay.

"So far, so good. Remind me what we're bringing over."

He handed me the list. Dining table and chairs. China cupboard with glass doors. Lamp tables. Dresser and bed. Pictures, odds and ends.

The carpet in the apartment was a neutral cream, fake Berber, slightly soiled. "Carpet cleaners?" I asked.

"They'll be here as soon as the wallpaper's up. We'll put that good rug of hers in front of the sofa. The greens are just right, plus several blues and this coppery mahogany. The slipcovers are plain cream, of course. Anything else would be too much."

"I had Toddy box some of Wilson's china."

"The carton's in the bedroom," he said smugly. "We'll unpack it as soon as our furniture is here."

"You sound pleased with yourself."

"I have a buyer for her bed."

"That was fast work."

He nodded, grinning. "That one item will pay for everything we're doing and leave her a nice bit over. I think it would be lovely if she didn't have to cash Espy's check."

"You know Espy?"

"I know the son of a bitch."

I stared at him. He returned my gaze blandly. I cleared my throat. "Would it be fair to say you don't like him much?"

"Eminently fair."

"You think our Valerie could do better?"

"On any given day of the week, yes. Espy wouldn't know art if it bit him on the ass. All he or his family use to judge anything by is how much it costs Their home is a monument to tasteless magnificence. And look at what she has here, Jason. No training in art or decor, no education in the field, no large amount of money, nothing but her eye, and look what she managed to assemble here!"

He was right. It was remarkable. On the other hand, it had been a hodgepodge. The eye was good, the taste

unerring, but something was missing. I didn't pursue
the subject of Mark's acquaintance with the Gryphons,
though I found it puzzling. It was not, I told myself, my
current puzzle.

Friday morning I wrote the remaining three names of
Ron's old buddies on a legal pad and set about finding
phone numbers and addresses. Jeremy Wilkins. Vaddy
Halved. Jennifer Koonitz. Only one of them was in the
current phone book. Jeremy Wilkins.

I called. A voice answered, neither male or female.
He/she said Jeremy was at work. I asked for the
number. He/she gave it to me. I called it, and someone
answered, "Pete's!"

Pete's what, for God's sake. "I'm trying to locate
Jeremy Wilkins," I said. "Is this the right number?"

"Hold on."

There were going-away, retreating sounds. In the
background a machine whirred a monotone. A floor
polisher? A vacuum cleaner? A door banged. Someone
dropped what sounded like a crate of glassware. Great
banging and shouting.

"Wilkins," said the phone.

I said the bit again.

"Yeah. This is Jeremy Wilkins. What you need?"

"I'm trying to get some information on Ron Willis."

"Shit." Hand over phone, someone yelling. "Will you
guys cut it down!" Then he was back to me. "You can
come on over?"

"Over where?"

"To Pete's."

"Pete's what?"

"Pete's Tavern. In Wheatridge. We're in the book."

And a disconnect. I looked in the book. Pete's Tavern
was indeed there, on Eighty-fourth. I checked out with

Mark and Eugenia, neither of whom seemed to care greatly whether I stayed or went, so I went.

Pete's Tavern was a glossy adjunct to a local bowling alley, different establishment but with a connecting door. The place was shiny as a new dime, gleaming with good economic health, polished floors and tables, clean windows, and the muffled sound of balls rolling, pins falling. Jeremy Wilkins was fat and completely unconcerned about it. His shirt gapped and he didn't care. He drew two beers without being asked, led us over to a corner table, dropped into one chair, and kicked out another for me. I sat.

"A little early for me," I said, anent the beer.

"Never too early," he growled. "Beer is man's greatest blessing; facilitator of youth, appeaser of maturity, succor of age. I made that up."

I raised my glass. "Well, we can drink to it."

We did.

"You being appeased or succored?" he asked.

"Facilitated, I hope."

"Right. What's about Ron Willis?"

I told him about Ron Willis.

"Shit," he said. "That's the damnedest thing. You know, any of the kids in our class, I'd have guessed Ron would have made it big. He was so damned . . . open. Eager, kind of. Didn't have sense enough to cover up like most of us. Hell, we weren't going to put our hearts out there for the world to see, but not Ron. What Ron loved, the whole world saw."

"Margaret Pace?"

"Sure. She was something. She was so damned beautiful it made you itch. Sit next to her in class, most of us'd have to put a notebook in our laps just to keep our modesty intact."

I laughed, then frowned. "She's dead."

He hadn't heard, so I told him.

"Part of the same thing? You think?"

"I think. Maybe."

"Well damn."

We sat in companionable silence.

"Did you and Ron stay in touch?" I asked. "After he went to California."

"Sort of. He called me a couple times. Drunk, or maybe high. Wanting to talk old times."

"Was he in touch with you during the last few weeks?"

"No. We weren't close anymore. We had been, in school, buddies, you know. We were both gay, but he didn't know it and I didn't do anything about it." He gave me a challenging look, which I met without flinching. "That doesn't bother you?"

"Not as much as it evidently bothered him."

"Yeah. There's that. It bothered other people, too. Chappy. He was the big homophobe. And Brew Tyrell. Not that he was nasty; he wasn't. Just couldn't understand it. Thought it was something one could 'overcome.' Brew was into overcoming about then. Very rigorous."

"He stayed friends with Ron."

"I wouldn't say it that way. I'd say he was loyal. That's the thing about Brew. He may not approve, he may not understand, but he's loyal. God, it makes you want to puke."

"Loyalty?"

"The way he did it, yeah. Like the people were irrelevant. Like the promise was the thing. You know?"

I did know. "You think his promise was kept to honor himself rather than to honor Ron," I offered. "You think

Brew stayed loyal because he'd given his word and he doesn't go back on his word?"

"Very much like that, yeah."

"An interesting observation."

"Yeah," he said, grinning into his glass. "I was a brain once. Very perceptive."

"You're not a brain now?"

"Oh, I still belong to Mensa. Doesn't mean much. So I can work puzzles. You still have to buy bread, you know? The gasman cometh."

I took my notebook out of my pocket. "What else can you tell me about Will Chappy?"

"Ol' William. Well. You know that old saw about wolves in sheep's clothing? Will was like that."

I raised my eyebrows, waited.

"He looked like the best-natured guy in the world. Casual. Rumpled. Got that old broad face and that lazy smile. Women were always wanting to take ol' Will in hand, straighten his tie, scratch him behind the ears. He never got better than a C that I know of. Never played team sports. But if there was money in it—ol' Will was right there, and he had all the angles figured out while the rest of us were still moving our lips trying to read the instructions."

"Not always ethical, I hear."

"I suppose not. At that age, though, it didn't mean much. Kids cut corners generally. You grow up, you get married, you settle. I hear he's done well for himself, very respectable."

I admitted he looked very respectable. "I've got two other names here. What about Jennifer Koonitz and Vaddy, what is it, Hal-ved?"

He frowned, fingered his chin. "Something like that. I know Jen Koonitz is dead. She died . . . oh, three four

years ago. I heard about it at the tenth reunion. I think
it was AIDS. She was an addict. She was Vaddy's girl,
and Vaddy was the closest thing we had to a gangster
when we were in school. Maybe he really was one.
Most kids like him, they drop out, you know? But
Vaddy stayed with us. Wasn't until a few years later I
figured out why. The kids in school were his customers."

"Including you?"

"No. Just whoever. I haven't any idea who he sold to,
except maybe Ron, and that's just supposition. Why do
you ask about Vaddy and Jen?"

"Ron knew them. He kept in touch with them."

"I suppose Vaddy's still around. I haven't seen him
for thirteen, fourteen years. I can't imagine why Ron
Willis would have stayed in touch with either one of
them."

"Drugs, maybe?"

"Ron moved away. He wouldn't have been getting
drugs from Colorado. Hell, he'd have been right at the
source where he was."

"Source?"

"Any port city. Isn't that where all kinds of contra-
band come in?"

"Maybe it went the other way."

"Ron was sending drugs to Vaddy?"

"Ron managed to live out there for a good many
years. His sister says he couldn't hold a job, but maybe
he did. Maybe he was Vaddy's supplier."

Jeremy shook his head. "Not the Ron I knew, no. He
wasn't sensible enough. He was smart, but not sensible.
He was a dreamer, a drifter. Once in a while buy a little
for a friend, sure. But be part of a steady pipeline, no.
Ron didn't have that . . . mercenary interest that Vaddy

or Chappy had. Either of them could figure the net profit in a split second; Ron wouldn't add it up if you wrote it on a blackboard for him."

This accorded with what I thought, too. I frowned at the last half inch of my beer, and Jeremy got up and refilled our glasses, then yelled something through to the kitchen, where I heard crockery rattling.

"Had 'em make us a sandwich," he said. "This time of the morning I get hungry."

My watch said after eleven. I hadn't bothered with breakfast, so a sandwich wouldn't be unwelcome. I thanked him and we settled to our table once more. He asked about Margaret Pace, and I told him what I knew, guessed, postulated.

"That was one of those soap-opera triangles," he said. "Ron wanting Margaret, Margaret and Brew madly in love, Brew being the faithful friend to Ron—slightly superior, you understand, very aware and forbearing about Ron's hopeless adoration—then that ridiculous prom night."

"Ridiculous?"

"A regular second-act curtain! Evidently Margaret's ma and pa decided enough was enough with Brewster Tyrell. Margaret wasn't allowed to go to the prom with him. Her pa fixed her up with the son of one of his friends. So, since Margaret had another date, Brew asked Betty Allenby; she was crazy about him, married him eventually. Then there was Ron, the original bleeding heart, a wallflower if there ever was one. And Chappy, who always went stag. He moved in on Margaret just to set Brewster's teeth on edge, and there was poor old Brew, stuck with the gal he came with, and the rich boy, not knowing what was going on. All this was in the Anglo corner, of course. Minority students had their own sets of complications. We had a black prom queen that year, and there were some fights about that, too."

"A disgusting evening was had by some," I suggested.

"Pretty near. Margaret's date got into it with Chappy, then he, the date, went storming out. Then Margaret told off Chappy. Then Ron moved in, knight in shining armor, and took her home, if you can believe that. All this time poor old Brew just watched and kept a stiff upper lip and his date pretended not to see anything. Betty Allenby was one of those cheery girls, always looking on the bright side, perennially busy being all three monkeys simultaneously."

"You saw all this from the sidelines?"

"I was a wallflower, too. My chosen position. An observer of the human parade, you know? That year I was editor of the school newspaper, so I trotted around with my little notebook, doing interviews, taking mental notes like crazy. After I got home, I decided not to print most of it. Too much pain going on. I saved it for my novel."

"Your novel?"

"Sure. When I retire."

I sat there, trying to remember my own high-school days. I hadn't had a sweetheart, though I, like Ron, had adored from afar a couple of times. I was still trying to overcome my own handicaps back then, too insecure to reach out to anyone else. Which was perhaps why I didn't remember the kind of complications that Jeremy did.

"You remember a lot," I commented.

"One day I'll write it all down." He rose to go fetch

our sandwiches. When he returned, putting the plates before us, he asked, "What was Ron into?"

"Ice," I said, lifting a square foot of pumpernickel to disclose a cubic yard of pastrami, awash in mustard.

"Diamonds or graft?" he asked.

"What?" I was busy with the mustard jar.

"Stolen jewelry, or protection money?" He laughed. "Is my jargon out-of-date? I'm stuck back in Bogart days. All those late movies."

"I'm talking drugs," I said. "Ice."

"Like crack?"

"Damned if I know. Margaret Pace told us Ron gave her ice."

"Oh, right. Like crack, only it stays with you. So I hear."

"Well, we have a missing cache of ice. We have a dead dealer—Ron. We have the dead dealer's dead girlfriend—Margaret. We have somebody following me, probably the guy Ron owed money to."

"That could be Vaddy. Was it a local car?"

It had been.

"You say Ron's sister is a cop? She can find out."

Which, presumably, she could. We had our sandwiches. That is, I had half mine and Jeremy took the other half. I thanked him for his time, we shook hands, and I departed. The names on the list were complete.

Back at the house, I couldn't remember in what connection Vaddy Halved had appeared in Ron's correspondence file. I started to call Grace to ask her if I could come over and look at Ron's papers, then I remembered they were in the trunk of the car. She'd given me his rucksack the night we'd made the list.

I went to the garage and fetched it, taking it up to my bedroom, which was more private than the rest of my quarters. Mark and Eugenia did tend to lap over into my kitchen and living room sometimes, just for convenience. I dumped the rucksack on my bed and started through it, piece by piece.

The item on top was a folded square of heavy ivory paper, which, when opened, showed a slanting, powerful hand, black ink, dashing words with plenty of space between. *Dear old boy, apropos the last words of St. Francis, may the equid enjoy the legacy. All the lovely ice shall cool his brow, and of his bones are coral made. Look deep, brother. What can no longer be mine may as well be—Yours.* It was dated three weeks before: July 10.

five

THE REST OF the papers in Ron's rucksack included half a dozen raggedly torn envelopes, ripped open with impatient fingers, the return addresses various: Margaret, Brew, Jeremy. There were a few postcards, a few wrinkled, much-read letters, signed by the same people. I took the note into my office and put it on the blotter, intending to look up the last words of St. Francis in the *Bartlett's*, or go to the library if necessary. Before I could get started on either, the phone rang: Wilson Credable, sounding hysterical and much desirous of my company, my expertise, my advice, or so he said. I tucked the folded note under the blotter, then took it out and put it in my pocket, put on my coat, and went, yelling another farewell to Mark and Eugenia. All I seemed to be doing lately was telling people hello or good-bye.

Wilson dithered, one moment bubbling apprehensively, the next pointing proudly to the mostly empty cupboards in the castle dining room, all the contents packed up and taken away to Toddy's place. The services he had retained were neatly arrayed on the shelves, which for the first time in a decade had been dusted, so he said, by the cleaning crew. Now he was in a quandary over which furniture to keep in the grand salon. He wanted to talk about the room, whether to keep it furnished at all or whether to make some kind of recital hall out of it, or perhaps a rehearsal space for his theatrics. I suggested, as I had to Mark, that the dining room would be more appropriate, inasmuch as it was not broken up by supporting pillars, and that a house this size deserved at least one public room of some pretension. We went around the room together as I told him which pieces I would keep, and why, and which ones I'd get rid of. In most cases, the decision was dictated by comfort.

This stuff really wasn't important just now, not even to him. It was obvious that what he had wanted was company. When he had exhausted his store of comments and "well buts," we went into the morning room and had coffee. I took out the note I'd found that morning and asked him to read it and tell me what he thought.

"Oh, what fun." He smiled. "It's like one of those puzzle crosswords, isn't it? Last words of St. Francis. Well, if the writer means St. Francis of Assisi, the words were, 'I have sinned against my brother, the ass.' "

"How on earth did you know that?"

"In my youth I was much given to reading about saints. I considered sainthood as an alternative." He blinked, then hastened on. "The ass must be the equid in the next phrase, though it's anyone's guess what the legacy is. Ice shall cool his brow, the ass's brow, we assume, and of his bones, the ass's bones, is coral made. That's a Shakespearean reference, of course. *The Tempest.* 'Full fathom five thy father lies; of his bones are coral made; Those are pearls that were his eyes: nothing of him that doth fade but doth suffer a sea change into something rich and strange.' "

"You read it to say the ass is in cold water?"

He giggled. "The ass is up to his ass in something or other. Or, since we've got a Shakespearean reference, we might think of some other ass, Bottom, for instance. Why are you paying any attention to this? What is it?"

I told him it was a note found in the possessions of a murdered man, hoping he'd spot something I'd missed, looking for an insight I hadn't had. He shook his head in amazement and uttered exclamations in all the right places, but he didn't come up with a thing we hadn't already considered.

"It may mean nothing," I admitted. "But it was in Ron's rucksack."

"Well," he said, cocking his head, "then it's all well and good to sit here figuring out what it means to us, but the really salient point is, what did it mean to the young man who was killed?"

A point I had not yet considered. What would Ron have made of the last words of St. Francis, of the word "equid," of the quotation from *The Tempest*. I didn't know. I'd have to ask Grace.

I asked Wilson if there was anything else he needed, and he said yes, he wanted to clear out some of the upstairs rooms while the clearing was good. "I just know Edward is going to come roaring down like the north wind. I want everything gone that's going to go, before he catches on."

"You haven't met with him yet?"

"I'm avoiding his phone calls. He says he has a legitimate interest. He says his father left personal property in this house. I know it's cowardly of me, but I just can't cope with the man. He's such a sneerer!"

I had had that impression also, so we went bumbling off to spend another hour and a half looking at upstairs bedrooms and talking about what could be done with them. Actually, though some of the rooms were damp, with discolored ceilings betraying roof leaks, it wouldn't take much to make others quite livable. Just get rid of the heavy drapes, ninety percent of the stuff on the walls, ninety percent of the stuff sitting on the furniture, reduce the furniture itself by half, and the rooms would open out into pleasant spaces in which people could be comfortable. Some of the wallpapers were oppressive, by current tastes, but they could be replaced. One of them was a striped ocherous ground covered with deep wine-red roses and trailing bows of purple ribbon. In the dim light, which was all the drapes allowed into the room, the twining flowers and ribbons made an allover pattern like giant squid, readying themselves to attack.

"This was Uncle Admar's room," said Wilson thoughtfully. "Maybe he left to get away from the wallpaper." He opened a bureau drawer and shook his head. "It's still got his underwear in it!"

Like a child with a treasure, he started going through the drawers, the little side one that held hairbrushes and handkerchiefs; the top one that held cuff links and watches and odds and ends of keepsakes. Among the keepsakes was a lace-trimmed hanky with a monogram: an *L* or a *J* or even a curly *S*, which he took out and fluttered and speculated about.

Interested despite myself, I opened the closet door to disclose a full array of clothing. "He didn't take much with him when he went off to hunt gold," I commented.

"Oh, he didn't really go hunting gold. I told you. He used to go off sometimes, that's all. When anyone asked, he always said he was going off to seek his fortune. He said it in that voice, you know, the tone, meaning more than mere words. When I was a little boy, he read me bedtime stories. Mother never did, she had trouble seeing in lamplight, but reading to me is where Admar got the phrase. In the storybooks, the heroes were always poor, like Admar, and were going off to seek their fortunes."

"You never learned what happened to him?"

"We never did. Privately, quite privately, because Aunt Carolyn would stand for no criticism of Admar—he was her baby brother, after all—I always thought he went off on a little trip and then just kept on going. He and Father never got along that well, and there was nothing for Admar to do here, especially after Edward had grown up and left home. Reading bedtime stories to a lonely little nephew surely wasn't a career that would satisfy a man like Admar. I really wish Father had given him the money he wanted. A business would have been good for Admar."

"How old were you when he left?"

"Seven. Almost eight. Edward was thirty, and though he seldom visited, he frightened me even then. Once when Admar had been gone for quite some time, Edward had a flaming row with Father. I was in the library window seat, behind the curtain, when they went at it. Edward wanted to know where Admar had gone, and Father told him he wasn't his brother's keeper, Scripture to the contrary, and Admar was a fifty-year-old man, surely adult enough to go and do what he pleased."

"Did you ever ask your aunt—Carolyn?'

"Ask her where Admar had gone? No. I never did."

"Did anyone ever ask her?"

"I don't know. Carolyn had a reputation for being vaporish, that's how my father put it. Dim. Personally, I think she was—is—bright enough. She just chose a preoccupied air to avoid a lot of the infighting that went on in the family. All I can remember about Aunt Carolyn at the time is that she seemed very worried, but Mother kept telling her Admar was a grown man who'd chosen to go off on his own, and about time, too."

We left the room. He paused at the door. "Do you suppose this is the personal property Edward is talking about? Uncle Admar's underwear?"

Then he got a fit of giggles that occupied him all the way downstairs. We had just reached the bottom when the doorbell rang, a tinny clangor quite out of keeping with the shadowy ambience of that hallway. Wilson trotted across the floors, his feet making a little hooved clatter, like a plump little satyr, and I was not far behind him when he opened the door. The anonymous man who stood there said merely, "Wilson Credable?" and, when Wilson nodded, thrust a paper at him.

Wilson took it. The man turned on his heel and left.

"What?" I asked.

He had unfolded the paper and was looking at it in horror. "It's some kind of court order," he wailed. "Cousin Edward has a court order preventing me from selling anything at all in Credable Castle, particularly 'those items of personal property belonging to the late Admar Credable.' "

I took it from him. "Do you mind if I look?"

He shook his head numbly. I read the thing. As he had said, Wilson was ordered by the court not to dis-

ɔose of anything currently in the house or on the
grounds of Credable Castle.

"The china's already gone," I pointed out. "This
thing is dated today. You'll want to ask Amelia, but I
think you can go ahead and sell the china."

"He's going to take everything away from me," said
Wilson hopelessly. "He really is. He's always wanted
to, and now he's going to."

I wanted to shake him. "Don't panic! Get on the
phone to Amelia and see what she says."

"Read the last part," he cried. "You didn't read the
last part!" He went off, presumably to make the phone
call. I heard a slight sound behind me and turned to
meet the dark eyes of the Washington girl, who had
emerged from the morning room into the hall behind
me.

"What's wrong?" she asked me, sotto voce.

I explained.

"Could he really put Mr. Credable out of his house?"

"I don't know the terms of the will, but my understanding is that Wilson gets the house and grounds for
his family. If he doesn't have a family, I don't know
what the legal ramifications are."

"He *has* a family," she said stoutly. "He has us."

"Not in a legal sense," I told her. "Related people.
You know that Wilson's gay?"

"Oh, sure, we all know that. It makes no difference.
He's a kind man. He hasn't nev—he has never come on
to the boys, not once, not even a little. There's some
boys in the program that're gay, and Mr. Credable
won't have them here, just so nobody could ever say
anything bad about the program. And he's always careful that all three of us are together so there's no going

off with this one or that one. You know how people are Mr. Lynx. You know the kind of things they say."

I did indeed know the kind of things that people say

"Just yesterday he say—was saying he wanted you to come talk to us about art so we'd know something about it."

"He's really worked with you on speech, hasn't he?"

She nodded. "The way Mr. Credable says it, every place we go, there's gates. White people, too, there's always gates. And every gate has a gatekeeper. And if you don't speak the language of the gatekeeper, you don't get through, doesn't matter what color you are."

"Some people say we shouldn't discriminate against black street talk," I said, just to see what she'd say.

Abruptly, she lapsed, her vowels broadening, her consonants mushing together. "I had me one a those in grade school, one a those black sistuhs. She didn' figah on black people gon' through any gates at all, so it didn' mattuh how they talk." She resumed her crisp intonation. "I can't imagine working for a major firm in any country if I talked like that, and I told her so. She accused me of being an Oreo."

"How does your mother feel about it?"

"My mother's dead. Before she died, she was for upward mobility. My brother says I'm a race traitor, but then he's in a gang that doesn't speak at all. All they do is rap. I don't care! If Mr. Credable says standard English opens doors, I'll learn standard English."

"He's a good man," I assented.

She went back the way she had come, and I heard voices raised in the morning room, where she was evidently sharing information with the other students. I turned my attention back to the document I was holding, the last part, as Wilson had said. The court order specified that Mr. Credable was to cease and desist allowing underprivileged individuals to meet in or use his home for any reason, as this contributed to the likelihood that assets would be dissipated. It didn't say, "Poor kids might steal the silver," but that's what it meant.

In a short time Wilson came back, his forehead creased, his mouth fretful.

"I'm going over to Amelia's office for a conference, at two. I told her all the china was gone, but she said to have Toddy hold on to it for the time being."

"Which is what he is doing."

"Of course." He rubbed at his forehead. "Amelia says he can't enforce the thing about the kids, and the judge who signed this order has been reversed so often his gears are stripped. She's not so sure about the house. It's silly to feel like this. This huge old pile, why should I care? It isn't a great house, a house of nobility, it doesn't have a long history, it's just a huge old place that a rich man built who had more money than taste. But . . . but . . ."

"But it's your home," I said, wondering that the cliché needed to be spoken.

"Yes. I suppose it is. It's the place I grew up in. It's where my memories are."

"This business about the kids is rotten. I don't suppose you can appeal to Edward's better nature."

"I don't know if he has one. He's never shown me one, not up until now. I might ask Aunt Carolyn. She was always very fond of Edward."

"When you go to see her, give me a call. I'd really like to meet her."

He agreed absently, showed me out, and shut the door behind me with a reverberating, oaken thunk, a very

medieval sound. Such sounds are so much more satisfy-
ing than present-day ones. Pre–high tech, objects
thunked and crashed and clopped, amid a thunder of
drums, a tumult of trumpets. Today things beep and
cheep and whistle. We have come from the roar of the
lion to the chirp of the tree frog, ceaselessly bleating
our identities while the frog-eating bats hover above us.
Cousin Edward was definitely a frog-eating bat.

Poor Wilson. He could only feel secure inside those
walls. Perhaps that is what Edward wanted it for, just to
discomfit his cousin. I very much wanted to ask Wilson's aunt Carolyn if she knew precisely what Edward
wanted with Credable Castle.

Speaking of the devil, Edward Credable was waiting
for me when I returned to Jason Lynx Interiors. Eugenia
met me at the front door, whispering rapidly.

"He's in a dreadful temper, accusing us of conspiring.
I didn't know what to say."

"As little as possible, Eugenia. As far as Edward is
concerned, we were hired to do an evaluation and rec-
ommend conservation measures."

Edward was seated in my office and gave every evidence of being willing to stay there until the following
week, if necessary. The moment I walked in he began
ranting about a conspiracy.

I didn't answer him. I took off my jacket, hung it up
neatly, sat down behind my desk, looked at the mail that
Mark had left there.

"Goddammit, did you hear me?" He pounded on my
desk with a clenched fist.

I looked up mildly. Jacob, my foster father, had been
fond of an expression he called butter-wouldn't-melt. A
kind of guileless stupidity. I've always done it quite

ell. "Everyone in the building has heard you, Mr.
redable."

"Well then, dammit, answer me!"

"Answer what, particularly? Is there a conspiracy?
o. Is something illegal afoot? No. Have we been out
Credable Castle? Of course. Have we done an eval-
ation? Only partly. It will take weeks and weeks to
omplete."

"Wilson has no business—"

"But he must," I said, inspired. "The roofs are leak-
g. The ceiling plaster in several of the upstairs bed-
ooms is already discolored and crumbling. As Eugenia
ld you, the drapes are full of moths, as are the carpets.
the place is going to be conserved, one has to know
hat things are worth conserving and what may be let
o."

He sat down, his eyes narrowed, watching my face as
mongoose watches a snake. "He'll let nothing go! I'm
uing Wilson. I'll subpoena you as a witness. You'll
ave to testify under oath, none of this stuff . . ."

It was mere bluster. He didn't mean a word of it.
Vhat the hell was he up to?

"I'll be happy to say under oath what I've just said to
ou, because it happens to be true."

"I'll get my own expert!"

"Be my guest. Leaking roofs are fairly easy to iden-
fy, no matter how venal the expert."

"He's trying to sell stuff that belonged to my father!"

"What stuff would that be?" I asked, digging into my
ile drawer and flipping through it to pull out the
Credable inventory. "There's a bedroom, on the second
loor, of which the contents are said to be the property
f Admar Credable. There's a bed, a washstand, a high-
oy, a breakfront, two armoires. . . ." I went on, pre-

tending to read, letting memory tote out the contents of that room. "Picture, hung with velvet ribbon, a reproduction of *Bubbles*," I said. "A porcelain vase shaped like a lady's slipper. A hair wreath, probably made in the time of Rose Credable, that is, the last quarter of the nineteenth century. A pair of silver-backed brushes—"

"Crap!" he shouted. "My father had some very valuable items. My father had personal property worth hundreds of thousands of dollars!"

I found this very interesting and completely at odds with what Amelia and Wilson had told me. "I have no idea who owns what," I said, replacing the folder in the desk drawer. "Why come to me? That's a legal question; and it should be put to the family lawyers. If Admar Credable purchased or inherited items in Credable Castle, then no doubt there are bills of sale or documents testifying to his ownership. The matter has nothing at all to do with me."

"You're trying to buy the stuff! That's a conspiracy."

"Not at all, Edward," said a voice from the door. Amelia, and beyond her Mark, hovering, ready to fling himself into action if Edward went berserk. "An offer to buy is simply that. An offer to sell what one does not own would be felonious, yes. It would be up to Wilson to prove he owns the things, or to you to prove you do. One or the other."

"I'm warning you, Amelia! You and your flunky here. What's this stupid business I read about your building some kind of think tank up in the mountains?"

"That matter is on indefinite hold," she said crisply. "I have changed my mind."

"You better get Wilson to change his!"

"The Credable estate was settled when the will was probated. Do not interfere with Wilson's domestic arrangements. Now, if you will excuse us, I have an appointment with Jason."

He left, fuming, uttering threats. "There'll be bloodshed," he cried, halfway down the stairs. "I tell you, there'll be bloodshed."

"What's he really after, Amelia? There was something very phony about all that bluster."

"I don't know what Edward's current agenda is, unless it's to have his own way. Seemingly, that's always been his agenda."

"What brings you here?"

"I thought you might need some help when I saw Edward's car. Who else would have a Wyoming license plate and longhorns as a hood ornament? He's been driving that big car a lot lately, advertising himself. One would think his Wyoming enterprises would need more supervision than he's been giving them."

"And you haven't any idea what he's really up to?"

"I don't. I have not seen Edward in this kind of mood before. I wonder if he is losing his grip. All these histrionics ... At any rate, I'm on my way back to the office now to meet with Wilson. How's he bearing up?"

"Not well," I admitted. "He's fairly fragile. If it weren't for those kids ..."

At which point the coin dropped with an audible clang.

"Aha," I said.

"Aha, what?"

"Aha, I know the answer. Why doesn't Wilson adopt a family?"

"Adopt ... I think he might have some trouble adopting children, Jason. Courts are notoriously conservative about giving gays custody, even of their own children."

"Not children. Adults. I was talking to the Washington girl this morning. Ann Louise. She's an orphan. Why doesn't Wilson adopt some adult children? He's over forty. He could adopt people, say, eighteen to twenty. People who need help with schooling, help with making their way in the world. He's already up to his ears in that tutoring program. From what Mark says, he'd have all kinds of character witnesses."

"I don't know," she murmured, her forehead creased.

Why was it every time I came up with something brilliant, these doubters had to make long faces at me?

"Look, if Edward's only handle on this situation is to claim that Wilson has no family, get him a family!"

"I'd have to avoid Judge Crocket," she said. "He's a homophobe, and quite nutty about biological parenthood. If I could get the case heard by Liz Champion, she'd be great. Are his hands clean, Jason?"

"What do you mean?"

"I mean, no hanky-panky with these kids, right?"

"I should think you'd know him better than that, Amelia."

"I do. But I don't. You know. It's not an area in which I have any expertise."

"Not only has there been no hanky-panky, but according to Ann Louise, he's avoided the least appearance of impropriety."

"I wish I could find out exactly what Edward is up to," she muttered.

"I have the definite feeling he's throwing up a smoke screen."

"I agree. I can't believe he's started all this harassment just because Wilson turned forty-five. I mean, that's no benchmark. Nothing is conferred or accrues to a person just because he's forty-five."

"Maybe his aunt Carolyn can tell us," I suggested. "Do you remember her?"

"Oh, yes. Very well. She was one of the bridge four-some. Find out, if you can. Put it on my bill." She said it offhandedly, thinking about something else.

"I can't bill you for that, Amelia. I'm not a licensed investigator. If I do it, I'll do it because it's interesting. You're seeing Wilson this afternoon. Find out where his aunt is, and call me."

We left it at that. She went off to meet with Wilson; I went back to the puzzle of Ron and why someone had sent him a note containing a reference to St. Francis of Assisi.

That question got nowhere, so I rearranged it. Had someone sent Ron a note containing a reference to St. Francis of Assisi? If no one had, how had Ron come by it and to whom had it been sent?

I put down the inventory list, went back into my bedroom, and got out Ron's rucksack, again dumping the papers on the bed. They were the other side up this time, and the back of one of the envelopes immediately caught my eye, stained as it was with blue chalk. A plain, creamy paper, no address, no return, no nothing. For a moment nothing occurred, but then I recognized the quality of the paper. I fished the note about the ass out of my pocket and tried it in the envelope. Square. Perfect fit. Back into the office to get the tissue-wrapped contents of the davenport drawer. Those also on the bed, sorted and piled like a three-dimensional jigsaw puzzle.

When they were properly lined up, the blue-stained lumberyard receipt lay on top, showing a square of un-stained pink that precisely fit the creamy envelope. When the creamy envelope was put on the pink square

faceup, the entire pile was evenly blue except for one
large square corner. Either I hadn't stacked them quite
right or something was missing. The papers had been in
the drawer before the chalk line was dropped into it.

I called Amelia's office. I dragged her out of her
meeting with Wilson.

"Amelia, this is important. That little davenport I
bought from you. The one that was painted white?"

"Davenport? You mean a couch?"

"A little desk, Amelia. On castors. It looked like a
tiny spinet piano. Painted white."

"That used to be Mother's. I don't know when it got
taken upstairs. That was part of the stuff I bought from
Maddox."

"Part of the stuff your father left to his brother?"

"That's right."

"That piece, specifically."

"That piece specifically. The will said, 'Several items
of white-painted furniture located in the front third-floor
bedroom.' "

"That was the only furniture left to Maddox?"

"The only furniture, yes. Plus some cash and the
land. What is all this?"

"I'm not sure. Where is your uncle Maddox now?"

"In Chicago! At his home there. With his nurse-
housekeeper."

"I need to go see him."

"Jason! He's not even sensible half the time."

"Just give me the address, Amelia."

"Does this have anything to do with anything?"

"Something, Amelia. I'm just not sure what."

Grace was out when I called the cop shop. I left a
message for her on her machine at home. I had to go to

Chicago, it had something to do with Ron's death, maybe, I'd be back probably Sunday. I asked Mark if he could feed the animals for me while I was gone. I made a reservation for that night; Mark drove me to the airport, offering to make me a hotel reservation by phone if I'd call him when I arrived. I was on my way by seven o'clock.

At the airport in Chicago, I called Mark and he told me he'd made reservations for me at the Holiday Inn. It wasn't plush, but it was clean. I'd eaten on the plane, so there was no reason to wander about. I called Grace and got her machine. I watched a late movie and went to sleep with the TV on.

The next morning I had breakfast early. I've always enjoyed hotel breakfasts. If one avoids the steam-table eggs, there's something genial about a hotel at breakfast time. People are likely to be rested, hungry, serious about the day's activities. There's none of that whoop-de-do that runs rampant after the last convention session of the day; none of that voracious desire to cram some little item of away-from-home fun into an otherwise dull schedule. The day's irritations are yet in the future, the night's hopes as yet unconceived. People seem calm and purposeful.

As was I. I called Maddox's housekeeper about nine and was on his front step by ten, an expensive cab ride later. She looked me up and down, tallying me for missing buttons or scuffed shoes. Finding me presentable, she said only, "He may not talk to you. Sometimes he doesn't." Her back, clad in a cotton housedress and rigid as a broom handle, reminded me of Eugenia.

The house was clean and still and a little cluttered with an amazing assortment of objects: ethnic weavings thrown across the backs of chairs; carved ebony stools and tables and statuettes; brass and copper trays and ewers; canoe paddles and masks. I saw South America and India and Africa and the Pacific Islands, the casual collection of a widely traveled man.

Maddox sat in a wheelchair beside an open window, his legs covered with a light blanket. His scanty hair was neatly combed, his hands carefully manicured. He regarded me without emotion or curiosity from eyes of a colorless, watery gray.

"Mr. Wirtz? Amelia sent me."

" 'Melia? How is she?" He spoke with no inflection, like a mechanical voice.

"She's fine."

"She's a lawyer, you know that? Quite something, 'Melia."

"Yes. She's a very fine lawyer."

This seemed to end the conversation so far as he was concerned. He turned his head to the window and went back to watching the traffic.

"Mr. Wirtz? Maddox?"

"What? What?" he said querulously.

"Your brother Hector left you some furniture."

"Didn't want it." He moved fretfully, lower lip quivering.

"He left you a note in the furniture."

His eyes widened, his hand came up, warding me off. "Don't want it."

"You don't have to have it," I said, shaking my head, putting out a hand to take his trembling one. "I just need you to tell me something about it, that's all."

"Always rotten," he mumbled. "Hector. Made everything rotten. Spoiled people's lives."

"Does St. Francis of Assisi mean anything to you, Mr. Wirtz?"

"Now see," he mumbled through quivering lips, "that's what I mean. Always saying things like that. My brother the ass," he says. "The ass my brother. Me, he was talking about. Me. He read about that, and he put it onto me. Ma would say stop hitting your little brother, and he'd say he'd sinned against his brother the ass. That's all I was, brother ass."

"Shhh," I soothed as he looked away once more, out at the traffic, stopped at the corner by a red light. His eyes went over the cars caressingly, a familiar sight, something he understood, a scene with no power to hurt him.

"Did you ever read Shakespeare's play *The Tempest*?"

"Went to it," he murmured, not taking his eyes from the cars. "Janet was in it. It was for charity."

"What does it mean, 'Of his bones are coral made.' "

"Means he drowned in the sea. Drowned deep. Turned into something else, down there. A sea change."

No help there. "Mr. Wirtz, what does ice mean to you?"

"Ice?" He turned on me furiously. "Ice! Godamighty, boy, don't you know what ice is? Didn't you ever go skating?"

My face must have fallen, for he suddenly looked concerned. And concentrated, his face losing twenty years in the effort at thought. "You don't mean just frozen water, do you? What's ice? Let's see. We used to say we put something on ice when we got rid of it. We used to say icing on a cake. Some women, they liked ice, the sparkly kind. I knew one or two. Never married, though. Had no prospects when I was young. Father, he left it all to Hector. Just left me enough to get by on.

Time I made my way, I was too old. . . ." The effort had tired him. His words were slurred.

"Why do you think Hector left you that furniture?"

"Because he was dying!" The old man's voice quavered. "Dying of cancer. And he hated it. Couldn't hurt people anymore. Couldn't yell and hit and ruin people's lives. Couldn't gloat. Called me on the phone, told me he was leaving me the answer to all his mysteries. I said no. I wanted no part. Not before he died, not after. He laughed. He said I had to take it if he left it, couldn't pick and choose, if I wanted the money, had to take the rest." His lips quivered. He patted them, gulped.

"Hector didn't know me. He never did. He thought I was like him, but I wasn't. I wouldn't take the money he left me. Wouldn't take the furniture, not anything. Not the land. Amelia wanted it, so I sold it to her, gave the money to charity."

"Why did he want you to know his mysteries? What did he mean by mysteries?"

"Things he'd done. Secret things. He wanted me to know so's I'd tell people. He'd be dead. Nobody could get at him, hurt him. Other people, though . . . They could still hurt. He wanted me to tell people, and I wouldn't. Bury the dead, that's what Janet used to say, Janet . . . oh, she used to say that. Bury the dead. Not Hector. He liked to dig 'em up, walk 'em around."

"Did you know Janet well?"

His eyes shut. He breathed deeply. When he opened his eyes, they were full of an old hurt, a pain that had nothing to do with his current situation. "Knew her. Loved her. Couldn't stand the way he treated her, so I moved out. She was . . . a lovely woman, Janet. Always wished I'd seen her first."

"Did you argue with Hector about her?"

"Told me to shut up or get out. I got out. I thought he'd kill me, he was so mad. Red face. Neck all swollen. Looked like a bullfrog. Told him so." He fingered his cheek, where, for the first time, I noticed a lengthy scar. "Threw an onyx pen stand at me. Twenty stitches. I moved out."

I waited. He seemed to doze. The housekeeper stuck her head in; I shrugged.

"He does that," she whispered. "Little catnaps."

It was half an hour before he woke.

"I was sayin' . . ." he mumbled.

"You were telling me what you and Hector argued over. When you moved out."

"Her. Janet. He said she belonged to him, he could do what he pleased with her. He said he owned her. I . . ." He shook his head.

"You figured it would be safer for her if you were somewhere else."

"That's right." He drifted off again. This time I got up and left, following the sound of a vacuum cleaner to find the housekeeper.

"What did Mr. Wirtz do for a living?" I asked.

"Oh, he was a petroleum engineer," she said. "He worked with a firm in Denver until he was in his forties, then he moved here to Chicago, but he traveled all around the world until he was almost seventy. That's when he bought this house."

"He never married?"

She looked over her shoulder furtively. "I'll show you something." She led the way out of the living room, across the hall, into a small room that might once have been a front parlor, one of those stiff little rooms that are always just so, waiting for visitors not close enough to enter upon family space. It had a faded but lovely old

Chinese silk carpet in soft shades of blue and lavender, cobwebby curtains in the same shade, one chair, one table, one picture on the wall. A woman, a girl, nineteen or twenty, dressed in the style of the thirties, hair soft around her face. Something about the eyes held my attention, and after a moment I realized who the painting resembled. Amelia.

"That's his sister-in-law," I said. "Janet."

"Well, I've wondered," she said, putting her hands on her hips. "I thought maybe she was his fiancée and she'd died, or married someone else. When he could move around, he used to sit in here for hours and hours. Sometimes even now he'll have me wheel him in here. He says he wants to spend a little time with his friend."

I went over to the table, set out with a collection of faded flowers, ribbons, a theatrical program. *A performance of Shakespeare's* The Tempest, *for the benefit of Children's Hospital. January 1948.* "So he sits here and looks at her."

"He sits here and cries. Is she dead?"

"Long time," I said. "She died almost forty years ago. In Mexico." I opened the program. *Dramatis Personae.* Each character with a picture. I recognized two of the names. Ferdinand had been played by Admar Credable. The pictured face was very like Edward. Miranda had been played by Janet Wirtz. Her picture was the same as the one on the wall.

"Forty years. Think of that." The housekeeper shook her head wonderingly, a practical woman out of sync with romantic notions.

"I wonder if she loved him?" I said musingly.

"You know, I don't think she did," the woman said.

I gave her a curious look, surprised at this declaration. She nodded, seeing my thought in my face.

"I've cared for a lot of old folks," she said. "Old folks raised back when everybody went to church, when folks were godly, when they believed. Widowers. Widows. And I'll tell you, Mr. Lynx, people who love someone who's gone on before, the older they get, the more they look forward to meeting again, on the other side. This old man, he doesn't have that to look forward to. That's why he cries so. I'm not a betting woman, but if I was, I'd bet she didn't love him. You look at that face, you know she was lovely, lovesome, as my grandma used to say. She loved someone, just had to, but it wasn't him. It was someone else."

" 'Dear old boy, apropos the last words of St. Francis, may the equid enjoy the legacy. All the lovely ice shall cool his brow, and of his bones are coral made. Look deep, brother. What can no longer be mine may as well be—Yours.' "

Monday morning early, Grace sat across the coffee table from me, in my living room. On the coffee table was the pile of papers from the davenport, surmounted by the note I'd found in Ron's rucksack. It was clear where the note had come from.

"Amelia's father intended his brother to find it, if anyone found it," I told Grace. "Old Hector used to call Maddox an ass, his brother the ass; the ass, his brother. The legacy referred to was the furniture and the land and a sum of money."

Grace frowned. "I don't get it, Jason."

"I'm not sure I do either," I confessed. "The one additional fact I can add to the puzzle is that Maddox was, still is, hopelessly in love with Janet Wirtz, Amelia's mother." I described the shrinelike parlor of Maddox's house. "He must have had the portrait painted from the photograph. It's a beautiful job, incidentally. It looks alive, charming. I can see why he loved her."

Grace squirmed in her chair. "I don't get what this has to do with Ron?"

"You'll have to tell me," I said. "I found that note and the envelope in his rucksack. He got it out of the furniture he was working on. What would it have meant to him?"

She picked it up, read through it, pursed her lips, frowned. "He'd have recognized the reference to bones and coral. His English class did a reading of *The Tempest*, and he read the part of Ariel. Unfortunately."

My eyebrows went up.

"Ariel was a fairy," said Grace. "A fact which his classmates picked up on."

"Why did he agree to play the part?"

"It was assigned," Grace said. "By Mr. Wentworth, a teacher who had more education than sense. I'm being charitable when I say that. He could have had a nastier reason than heedlessness."

I brought us back to the problem at hand. "What else would it have meant to Ron?"

"I suppose ice meant drugs, to him. That's what it would mean to me."

"Not what it would have meant to Hector, however," I commented. "If we assume he knew Maddox loved Janet, the cooling he had in mind might have been ardor."

Grace got up and walked around, her forehead furrowed in concentration. "If Hector knew Maddox loved his wife, maybe he thought Janet returned that love. Maybe Janet was frigid toward Hector. Back in the forties or fifties, that was way before the sexual revolution, before everybody talked about sex. Female frigidity was a big complaint, wasn't it?"

"That's possible."

"So Hector is telling his brother, go ahead, adore her, she's dead, I'm dying, her memory can't be mine, so let it be yours?"

It didn't satisfy me, though it didn't matter whether I was satisfied or not, since all we needed to know was what Ron had made of this, if anything. "If Ron read this to mean ice, drugs, he might have convinced someone he either knew or could find out where the drugs were. There's no year date on this note."

"But he knew the furniture was old," Grace objected. "You said the drawer was painted shut. He couldn't have thought it was recent."

"What I'm saying is, despite what Ron *knew*, he might have convinced someone else that it referred to a cache, to something valuable. He told Will Chappy that he'd come into money. He told Margaret Pace that ice got him in, ice got him out. The people who were holding him, who wanted their money, let him go, presumably because he'd convinced them he knew where something valuable was. More valuable, by the way, than what he owed them. That's what he told Chappy."

"They thought he had it at my place?" Grace asked. "That's why my place was searched?"

"They may have thought that. Or that he cached it during our Sunday picnic. Or that he gave it to me or cached it here at Jason Lynx Interiors. Or at Margaret Pace's place."

"None of which explains why he was killed," said Grace between her teeth. "I need to know why he was killed!"

I took a deep breath. "What if his death was an accident?"

Grace spun around, openmouthed.

I said, "Look, on a Friday, Ron learned about the Wirtz land, from me. I was looking at maps. I pointed out the Wirtz land. I told him about it, including the potty shaft. I told him it had been owned by Hector Wirtz, that he'd left it to his brother, but Amelia had bought it back. So Ron knew all about the land.

"Roughly concurrent with learning about the land, Ron found this note in the drawer of the davenport. By the time Saturday night came, he had the map and this note. On Saturday night he was picked up and threatened by X. To save his neck, Ron came up with this story about the treasure, buried on the mountain land, probably in the potty shaft. He managed to convince X it existed. They let him go. The next day we go up there, we're followed there, while we're away from the place the charge is set, and Ron accidently gets in the way of it."

"Why was it set?" Grace demanded.

"The only reason I can think of for the explosion would be to seal the shaft against accidental discovery by me, by Amelia, by some contractor or worker. Whoever set it believed there was a treasure there. They wanted to close the shaft until there was an uninterrupted opportunity to retrieve whatever might be there. The last thing they wanted to do was kill someone, which would only draw attention to the place. So, the charge was set, probably the detonator was on a timer."

"But there was no treasure!" Grace cried.

"X thought there was."

"Why was Margaret Pace killed?" Grace wanted to know.

"Because the explosion did the opposite of what was intended: it caused people to actually go down the shaft, and the results were reported in newspapers and on TV. By Monday, it was clear there hadn't been anything down the shaft except Ron's body and a skeleton. Now the bomb setters must look to cut their losses. My guess is, they started looking for the drugs, which were still missing."

"At my place. At Margaret's."

"And following me," I offered. "In case I could lead them to it."

"I hope you're not planning to leave it like this?" Grace snarled at me.

"Like what?"

"Like this. Half theory, half supposition. No proof. No sureness. We'll have to do better than this, Jason."

"If no one intended to kill Ron—"

"That doesn't matter! Someone did kill Ron. I want to know who."

I felt like a scrubby Christian confronted by a hungry lioness, a set of glazing eyes, a stern face set in adamant. I'd been rather pleased with myself. I thought I'd come close to solving the thing, but Grace was not satisfied. She wasn't going to let me off the hook until the matter was resolved.

On Wednesday, Grace told me what she'd learned from the forensics people at the state lab. The skeletal remains of the woman had been given a thorough going-over. She had probably died of massive head injuries. Other broken bones had happened at the same time. She had fallen or been dropped into the shaft and simply left there, but it was unlikely she had suffered long. The skull had been so badly damaged that total unconsciousness was most likely.

"What about Margaret Pace?" I asked.

She shook her head. "Her blood alcohol was way up, Jason. About two and a half times what we'd call drunk if she'd been driving. There's always a tendency, when somebody's that drunk, to assume they've fallen, you know? There's no evidence she didn't. There's no evidence she did. Nobody heard a struggle, nobody heard a scream. Her father, Ben Pace, is keeping the pressure on, but nothing much is developing out of it."

"What about the man we saw going upstairs?"

"I've reported it. I've given them what description we could come up with. What else can we do? What are you going to do?"

I shook my head. I'd been asking myself the same question. "I don't have many roads left to try. The car. I guess. The blue car with the JZN plate. Is the Clear Creek Sheriff's Office checking that?"

She snorted. "The Clear Creek Sheriff's Office doesn't consider it relevant. We didn't see the car in Clear Creek County. We saw it in Denver County. No crime occurred in Denver County."

"Well then, can you get me some computer help?"

She could. She would get a motor-vehicle-registration printout, which she did, dropping it by the house that evening. There were over a hundred cars on the list; owners, addresses, makes and models of vehicles, but no color. I thanked her, trying not to sound depressed. I invited her to stay to supper. She declined. She sounded very moody, half-angry, half-sad. I didn't push.

Sitting over my lonely supper, I tried shortening the list by removing all trucks, vans, sports vehicles, and the like. There were over fifty left when I'd finished. I glanced down the column of owners, not expecting to recognize anyone. I didn't. Schnitz jumped up on the table and sat on the list. Cats do that. They always seek the "feli-center," that exact place that is most troublesome, most likely to result in their being fed, petted, or played with—or, I suppose, being booted out the window. They like to live dangerously. I gave him a bite of my spaghetti, which he rejected. I pulled him into my lap, which he accepted, revving up the purr. Now there was spaghetti sauce on the paper, so I wiped it off, leaving a smear under the name of Ronald Helvad, who owned a 1994-model Oldsmobile, license JZN 459.

Hel-vad, not Halved. Vaddy. Whom Jeremy had not seen in thirteen or fourteen years. His address was on the list.

Cats are prescient, so I'm told. Schnitz had been sent as a psychic facilitator, obviously. Now that I'd seen what I was supposed to see, he jumped down from my lap and wandered out into the back hall, from which I heard the sound of litter being scratched. Mental note. Change the upstairs litter box. Mental note, buy litter so I could change the upstairs litter box. Mostly Schnitz used the one down by the back door, which was larger and handier to the trash barrel. Grace claimed it was possible to teach cats to use the toilet. She'd promised to buy me a book about it. . . .

Helvad. Helvad, so said Jeremy, had been involved in drugs even back in high school. The fact that he was still alive argued cleverness, slyness, ability to look after himself. Not someone I should blithely go off visiting to accuse him of setting a bomb. He might take umbrage. He might knock my teeth down my throat. He might, in matter of fact, severely injure me.

I could turn the name over to Grace. She could get

some of her cop friends to help her, maybe. The way she was steamed up about all this, likely she'd go after him herself, alone. Which was not a good idea, either.

On the other hand, one might try civilized behavior and see how far one got.

Halved hadn't been listed, obviously, but information had a number for R. Helvad. I called. There was a clicking, clacking, transfer here, there, reringing.

"Yeah?"

"Is this Vaddy Helvad?"

"So?"

"My name is Jason Lynx."

Silence at the other end.

"I wanted to talk to you about Ron Willis."

"What about him?"

"I'm going to marry his sister. She and I are trying to find out why he died."

"You find out, you tell me."

"Do you care?"

"Not much. But the damn fool owed me. That's what you get when you try to do favors for people. I'm like a small businessman, here, you unnerstand? I can't, what you'd say, absorb losses like that."

I thought frantically. "I thought he'd made arrangements to pay you."

"Monday morning, we'da been square. Trouble is, he didn' make it to Monday. With him dead, who can collect, right?"

My mind went numb. "Collect what?" I asked.

"He had a check, bank draft. Made out to him. Monday morning he was going to cash it, give me the money."

"You saw it?"

"You think I'd take his word for it? You think I'm nuts?"

"Who ... who gave him a check?"

"Damn if I know. He didn' say."

"Did you ... did you search his sister's apartment?"

"Hell no. We want cop problems? Why'd we do that?"

"I thought ... maybe you'd want whatever you sold him back."

"Sure I want it. Do I want it enough to get tied up in some murder rap, the answer is no. You find it, you call me, I'll give you, what you call, a commission."

"You didn't look for it at Margaret Pace's place? The Polo Club?"

Long silence. Then: "She's dead, right."

"Yes. She is."

"You think the ... property is there? In her place?"

"I haven't heard that anyone's found it. We talked to her the night she died. She said not."

"She's a junkie. You can't trust a junkie. They'll tell you the sky's green they feel like it."

I fell back on plaintive sincerity. "Vaddy, help me here. Ron's sister is really grieving. Give me something."

"Whadda you think, I got a crystal ball? Old Ron calls me from California. He orders stuff from me, picks it up on credit—you believe that?—which I give him because we are old friends, right? So he takes it away, then tells me his customer can't pay. I say you pay me anyhow, he says he can't pay me, he'll get me the stuff back, I say I don't buy, I sell, I say you either get the money or I'll break your legs—which is only a figure of speech, you know, like we use in my business.

So, Saturday night he has me take him here, take him there, midnight he comes up with this piece paper."

"You took him out to Englewood?"

"Right."

"You took him to the Polo Club Apartments."

"Nah. He called her. But we took him three, four other places where he says he has old friends. Took him to another place out south, and to the Downstairs. Took him to a after-hours place in Five Points. The Jet Stream. Had to drag him out of there."

"And somewhere along the line an old friend gave him a bank draft."

"Maybe he had it all along, who knows? That night I figured that woman gave it to him."

"Margaret."

"The one that got punted off her penthouse roof, yeah."

"You're being very . . . cooperative," I murmured.

"All I did was drive the guy around, listen to him talk. I didn't kill him. Way I see it, you're gonna marry this cop, right? So chances are you got some influence. And she could be a pain in the ass, raising hell because her baby brother's dead. So I give what I got, which is not, what you'd say, anything incriminating, you calm her down, we all get along."

Which was sensible of him. It could have been a story, of course, pure fiction, but I was inclined to believe him. He had that slightly outraged innocence that any small businessman might have who'd been ripped off. Never mind that the drug trade was totally illegal, to him it was business. He was, in all likelihood, no worse than Hector Wirtz had been in his day. Certainly no worse than Grandpa Wirtz, who'd raided and raped his way to a fortune, breaking laws and bones with equal disregard.

And what he said fit my previous scenario well enough. The only change I'd have to make was to suppose it was one of Ron's old friends who had fallen for the buried-treasure story. Instead of Vaddy, it had been Brew, or Margaret, or Jeremy, or Chappy, or one of the other people he had seen that Saturday night. What others? I should have asked Vaddy if he had any other names.

The locations were enough to start with, at least as a hunch. Five Points was an almost totally black area. I dug out Ron's rucksack once more, once more dumped it out, this time focusing on the high-school annual. Kids wrote things in each other's annuals. In a large class, those who did so would likely be friends. If Vaddy had driven Ron to Five Points, it had been to see a black friend.

I went through the small photographs, which were arranged in alphabetical order. I found Chappy's picture, and Margaret's picture, and Jen's, and Brew Tyrell's, and Jeremy Wilkins, and Vaddy himself. I was glad I'd called him before I'd seen him. He was an absolute, cold-eyed villain, enough to scare you out of a year's growth. Margaret had written something about parting is such sweet sorrow. Brew, something about absent friends being friends still. There was nothing from Chappy, a sincere verbal handclasp from Jeremy. Vaddy had written, *I'll be seeing you. We got a lot in common.*

Of the black students, there were only two who had written anything. Zaralu Zeiss (how do parents come up with names like that?) had written *Our revels now are ended.* I'd bet anything she'd been in the drama club.

The other, Damon R. Whitmore, had been more prosaic. *It's been nice knowing you. Good luck.*

D. R. Whitmore was in the phone book, in Park Hill, the 2300 block on Cherry. I made a note of the address, seeing on the same sheet the shopping list I'd been accumulating for a week. Cat litter. Many things could be put off. Cat litter wasn't one of them. Tomorrow I would shop.

Thursday afternoon I did shop, extending the trip to Park Hill where I parked in front of the Whitmore house, a nice house, a big house, a well-kept house. As I was walking to the front porch a little guy in a pedal car came around the corner, stopped, stared at me. His mother answered the door. "Yes?"

I offered her my card. I told her I was making inquiries about a man named Ron Willis that her husband might have known in high school.

"We both did," she said. "He was in our class at East. Come in. Mikey, you come in, too. It's your nap time."

"Aw, Mom."

"Don't you 'aw Mom' me. I let you play for an extra half hour because you promised me you wouldn't fuss."

He hung his head, parked his car with a great deal of backing and forwarding, then came in, kicking at nothing, lower lip out a mile. Mrs. Whitmore caught me watching him and grinned, quickly hiding the expression as her son looked up at her, hoping she'd relent. Not a bit of it, off he went.

She returned in a minute. "Would you like some iced tea?"

I said I would. We went into the kitchen, shiny and new and bright. "This is nice," I said.

"It's the only room we really redid when we bought the house," she said. "It was awful. Dark and busy looking. They just finished it a month or so ago. I love it. Not that I get to spend much time in it."

"You work?"

"I'm a teacher. I'm taking a few days off because Mikey's day care is in crisis; they lost two people. Damon can't take off, he's in court all week."

"He's a lawyer?"

"That's right. What was it you wanted to know about Ron? I don't remember him all that well...."

"Would he have approached you or your husband, trying to borrow money?"

She laughed infectiously. "Ron wasn't that silly. Anytime Damon and I have two dimes to rattle, they go in Mikey's college fund."

I rubbed my forehead, sipped at my tea. "Do you remember someone named Vaddy Halved?"

She shivered. "The class dealer. Sure. Always putting his hands on you, offering free samples. Damon offered to break his arm for him once."

"Vaddy drove Ron all over town the Saturday before he died, looking up his old friends. One of the places was in Five Points. I thought that might mean a black friend. I looked in the annual...."

"It would have been George Franklin," she said firmly. "That's the only black friend Ron had. Damon and I, we were only what you'd call acquaintances. From the drama club."

"And who was George Franklin?"

"When we were in school, George Franklin's father owned a nightclub in Five Points. Now George owns it. George Franklin's father had a sideline; now George has that. George is one of those people who really don't care what color people are so long as their money's green."

"Green what?" asked a voice from the door.

I looked up to see a handsome, mustached man, his suit coat hung across his shoulder by one finger, his tie loosened, his eyebrows raised way up, giving him a look of arrogant surprise. He hadn't changed a lot since his senior year.

"Damon, this is Mr. Lynx," she said, offering the card I'd given her. "He's looking for people who used to know Ron Willis."

"I haven't seen Ron in years," he said. "Neither has Zara. He wasn't the kind of friend you try very hard to keep."

I nodded, agreeing. "His sister knows that, but she really wants to know who killed him."

Back up went the eyebrows. Mrs. Whitmore gasped. "Killed him?"

"Someone did. It may have been an accidental death. We really don't know. We believe someone lent him a good deal of money just before he died, and I'm trying to find out who."

Damon Whitmore laughed, more angrily than his wife had done, no less sincerely. "That'd be the day. No, Ron never borrowed from me. Even if he'd tried, I wouldn't have had it to lend."

"I told him maybe George Franklin," she said.

He nodded. "Could be George. He'd have money, that's for sure."

"He and Ron were close friends?" I asked.

He frowned. "It wasn't that kind of relationship. My guess would be Ron was an old customer."

"For?"

"Money. George lends money. He has the club, too, the Jet Stream, but mostly he lends money."

I began to see. "You mean he's a loan shark."

"Second generation. Maybe third. The family's been in business a long time, put it that way."

"And you're pretty sure Ron would have known that."

"George was into it in a minor way when we were in high school. He had a couple of friends for muscle— George isn't much on muscle, but he gives great mean. Everybody knew it. It wasn't any secret."

I flushed slightly as I asked, "Would it be safe for me to ask George about this?"

"You mean, will he beat on you for asking questions? I shouldn't think so. You don't think he killed Ron, do you?"

"I can't think of any reason why he should have." I couldn't think of any reason why a loan shark would have given someone a bank draft, either. Though I had no experience with loan sharks, common sense would indicate that usurers deal in cash. Still, George was someone to ask.

Damon flipped open the phone book, looked up an address and phone number, wrote it on a Post-It for me. "He's a night owl. Gets up around dinnertime. You wait much later, he'll be gone. Attending to business."

I thanked the Whitmores and departed, wondering as I went how Damon knew so much about George's personal habits. Maybe he had defended him. Or prosecuted him. Or had to borrow from him. As I went out the front door, a plaintive voice called from upstairs, "Ma, can I get up now?"

I went home and unloaded the groceries. Everyone was gone, the shop was closed up. Amelia had left a message, giving me the name of the nursing home where Wilson's aunt Carolyn lived. I didn't care about

Wilson, at the moment. I was much more concerned with other things.

I checked my watch. It was late enough. I called the man, told him what I wanted, and asked if I could buy him supper at the Hacienda, one of those anomalous enclaves most cities seem to have a few of: a Mexican restaurant owned by an Irishman and situated in the middle of an almost entirely black residential area. Grace and I had dinner there about once a month.

The voice on the other end sounded amused, if anything. We agreed to meet at six. I showered and shaved and left a little early to get there on time, going in past the take-out counter and settling for a table against the far wall. I'd had one drink and started on another before three men appeared at the arched entrance, two big ones and a small one. The big guys took a table beside the arch, the small one oozed across the room and slid into the chair opposite me. A round man. A round man no one in his right mind would call jolly. He ordered a drink. We ordered dinner. We talked about nothing much until the food came.

"So what's the story, man?" he asked.

I told him the story, keeping it succinct, staying away from any mention of treasure or drugs. According to this version, Ron owed money, he went to old friends, someone helped him out, but then he got killed. I just wanted to know who'd helped him out.

George had lizard eyes. Maybe they were contacts, but I'd swear he had vertical pupils. Snaky. "So, what's your angle?" he asked.

I became aware for the first time that I was on rather dangerous ground. "Presumably, someone will want to be repaid."

"'Spose I say it was me," he said with an evil grin.

I swallowed, conscious of a very dry throat. "Then you'd know what form the money took. And he'd have given you a note or something."

"What's it to you?"

"I'm engaged to Ron's sister."

"The cop?"

"The cop."

His manner changed. He shrugged, as though to set temptation aside. "Nah," he said, around a mouthful of tamale. "I saw him the night before he got it. He came to the club. He used to hang around when he was a kid, so I figured it was just hanging around again. There's people like that, color-blind, like they say. It's not he doesn't know we're black, it's like he doesn't much think he's white. So, one Saturday night he comes in with a couple guys, very uptight white guys, they don't like bein' there, I can tell. Where they come from, you don't go in the other guy's turf. Ron came over, told me hi, sat down, had a drink, we rapped. One of my people needed me for something; while I was gone, the two white guys, they dragged Ron out of there. Uptight, like I say."

"He never mentioned needing money."

"He didn't say anything about anything, just hey, how's it goin'? 'Course, I was gone from the table a good while. Maybe he'd been plannin' to ask and just hadn't gotten 'round to it."

I had a bite of posole, a bit of enchilada. The waitress came by to see if we needed anything. George had another drink.

"Since you're buyin'," he said with an evil grin. "You into this because of the sister, right?"

"That's it."

"You got no personal stake."

"Nothing at all. She's just grieving over Ron."

"Way I hear, he was a dead man anyhow."

I grimaced. "How'd you hear that?"

"The word gets around."

"Well, in this case, the word was right. That's why h
came home. He was sick."

"Yeah. Got a nephew went the same way. With hin
it was drugs. He was no good from the day he wa
born, but to hear my sister talk, he was one of God'
angels called home early."

That seemed to wrap up most of what we had to say
to each other. I asked about his business—the club, no
the loan sharking—and he asked about mine—interiors
not murder investigations. We parted at the door, me t
my car, he to a stretched-out Lincoln with a uniforme
driver. Status.

six

W HEN I GOT back to the house Thursday night, I
called Grace and asked her if she had searched
er place for anything Ron might have left there. She
sked me what she was looking for. I told her a cache
f drugs and a bank draft.

"He showed the bank draft to Vaddy Halved about
nidnight the Saturday night before he died," I said. "He
ad it with him when Vaddy let him out of the car Sun-
ay morning. He went into your house, came out again,
vent with us to the mountains, and it wasn't found on
is body or down that hole. He must have put it some-
vhere in your house, and he wasn't in there long
nough to have hidden it in any very complicated
lace."

She wondered who'd given Ron money. I said I
lidn't know. She said she'd look. I, meantime, had a
lace of my own to search. If the drugs weren't at
Grace's place, they might be in the basement of Jason
Lynx Interiors, where Ron had wandered around pretty
nuch unsupervised for several days. Assuming he
iadn't given them to Margaret, which was only an as-
sumption. She'd said he hadn't, but she could have lied.

I looked first in the workroom downstairs where he'd
een stripping the furniture. The drawers from the dav-

enport were still spread around as we'd left them, th
chalky-blue one still holding the tangle of string. Wi
some vague idea of neatening up, I put the two halve
of the chalk container together and began winding th
string into it. Someone had tied a knot in the string ev
ery few feet, but each knot was small and wound u
without tangling. Surprisingly, the whole thing came u
neatly. It had not been thrown in as a mass. The lin
had been unwound into the drawer, the two halves o
the container placed on top. A rather puzzling small de
tail. Was it symbolic? Was the color blue meaningful

I could always call Maddox's housekeeper and as
her to ask him, but finding Ron's cache was more im
portant at the moment. I looked through the secretar
he'd been working on, every pigeonhole, every drawe
The davenport drawers yielded nothing, nor did th
slots from which they'd been removed. I stacked them
up again, only then noticing that one of them, the to
one, was shallower by six inches than the others. Aha
There at the rear of the drawer slot was a false back
And there on the top edge of the davenport was
carved bit of decoration. Turn the one, the back flippe
down, revealing a neat little compartment for those in
discreet letters Victorian novelists were so fond of wri
ing about. Fun, but no help. The compartment wa
empty.

There was other furniture in the workroom, and
searched every piece of it, top, bottom, and sideway
Nothing at all. There were cupboards for the storage o
supplies, and I looked through those, too. Nada. Zip
This took me to the door leading to the cavernous base
ment, piled with odds and ends of good stuff and junk
at the moment—since we were vastly overdue for
thorough clean-out—rather indiscriminately mixed

earching it would be a monstrous task, one that would ke a very long time.

I called Grace back and asked her if the department .d drug-sniffing dogs. She said yes. I suggested she rrow one. In a remote, cool voice, she said she'd alady considered that. She'd let me know.

I went upstairs to put my head in my hands. Somew the whole question of Grace's relationship with me d become entangled with Ron's death. When she oke to me, her voice was remote, her manner distant. ne was watching me, like an experimenter watches a t running through a maze, taking notes, seeing if I did ell, measuring how much I cared for her by how soon reached the goal. If I cared, I'd find out who killed m. If I didn't find out, it meant I didn't care for her all. The rational, sensible Grace I knew was out the indow. If she were less grieved, she'd know how deructive this was. Maybe she did know, but was too any to care.

To make the problem worse, I was beginning to feel gry at her. I hadn't killed him, but I was the one she as angry with. I've never claimed to be infallible, but was the one she expected to be. The little interior oices kept telling me it wasn't her fault, she'd get over , but the voices had begun to sound tinny and false. Vorst of all, suppose I did figure it out and we stayed gether? Would I go through the rest of my life believg Grace had married me out of some twisted gratiide? What kind of relationship would that be? I'd nown people who married for reasons like that. He as so kind. She was so understanding. He got me rough a bad time. She nursed me back to health. Then ey married and stayed trapped in those same roles, beign, nurturing, understanding. . . .

The internal voice said stop, look both ways, don'
behave like a two-year-old. The voice said, take a de
breath and relax. The voice said quit playing emotion
games with yourself, Jason. Lately I seemed to have
penchant for these internal dialogues. Technically,
suppose they're monologues, though there always see
to be at least two entities talking! On the one hand, m
and on the other, me prime.

Too much thinking. Not enough action. Take the de
for a walk or something. As I rose I brushed against tl
stack of maps Ron had returned to me. They went fl
ing from the corner of the desk to the floor, where the
spread out like a deck of cards. As I gathered them u
I noticed that one of them was missing: the Forest Se
vice map, the one I'd marked the location of Amelia
land on. The one I'd specifically shown to Ron whe
I'd told him where the land was.

Well, yes, of course, it should be missing. If Ron ha
convinced someone there was a treasure trove there, th
map would have provided evidence. See, here, l
would have said: Jason Lynx marked where the land i
And this guy who wrote this letter, he owned this lan
and that's what he was talking about.

But I'd found the letter in Ron's rucksack. Either h
replaced it there on the Sunday he was killed, or it ha
been there all along. If it had been there all along, the
he hadn't had it with him on Saturday night, as ev
dence. Unless . . .

I went into the closet behind Mark's office, where th
copying machine lives. When the cleaners are in
hurry, they sometimes miss the copier room, and th
wastebasket in the corner hadn't been emptied for som
time. I dumped its contents on the floor and started gc
ing through it. There were some notes of Mark's on th

Credable furnishings plus what appeared to be a partial inventory of the jewelry Eugenia and I had seen at Credable Castle—Wilson must have told Mark he had decided to sell the jewelry rather than put it in the bank. The pages had been run on letterhead by mistake, so the entries at the top of the page weren't legible.

Under the letterheads were some copies of invoices we had provided to cost-plus customers, too dim to read easily, and at the very bottom, three bad copies of a section of the map, either too pale or too dark to see anything much. The copier hadn't picked up on the colors or the tiny print, and the result was not readable.

Ron must have made a copy of the letter, which was plain black on white and would have copied very well. He'd tried to copy the map, but it wouldn't copy, so he'd taken the original. The map and the letter were his evidence of a treasure, in return for which, Mr X had given him a bank draft and had later blown up the shaft to protect the site from discovery. Somewhere out there was a Mr. X who had the map and a copy of the letter.

Now all we needed was a search warrant for Margaret Pace's apartment, for Will Chappy's office and house, for Brew Tyrell's office and house, and Jeremy's and Damon's etc., etc. If we found the map, we'd find our Mr. X. Assuming Vaddy had told me the truth, which he might not have. Assuming I knew all the players, which I probably didn't.

I fell back into the chair, growling. There was nothing solid that Grace could use. Everything needed to be confirmed, one way or another. Perhaps Will Chappy's wife would confirm his account of the evening Ron had come to their home. Perhaps Brew Tyrell's wife could be questioned. At the moment, however, I could not imagine that doing so would produce anything significant.

It was another damned Thursday, as frustrating as all Thursdays. Too much to do, nothing accomplished. I sat there, glaring at the desktop, my eyes finally interpreting what I saw. The message from Amelia, giving me the address and phone number for Wilson's aunt Carolyn.

Maybe what I needed was a break. On Friday, instead of worrying about Ron's death, I'd concentrate on our clients. Valerie French needed our attention. Wilson Credäble needed our attention. Maybe I could find out from his aunt what was motivating Edward to be so hateful.

So determined, I took Bela out for a long walk; then took a long bath; then read a long, lazy novel for however long it took to fall asleep.

First thing Friday, I called Valerie and asked her if she could take some time off to meet with me. About an hour, I said, around ten. Fine, fine; she was bubbly and pleased.

"Before I go consult with our client," I said to Mark, "suppose you tell me the real reason you detest Espy Gryphon."

"I detest Espy Gryphon because he is a moneyed snob and a sadomasochistic son of a bitch. He will end up ruining that girl's life."

"A sadomasochistic . . . ?"

"He has put at least two women into the hospital that I know of."

My jaw dropped. "You don't think Valerie knows?"

"Of course she doesn't know. And neither do his parents. He gets his kicks out of beating up on his girlfriends."

"But he hasn't done it with Valerie?"

"No. He's keeping her happy. He's under pressure to get married, probably for the same reason my erstwhile friend from California married, because his father tells him he'll either get married and settle down or he'll get cut off at the pockets."

"Why did he pick on her?"

"Because she's attractive. She is attractive, Jason. Because she has no family or money, and he feels he can dominate her. He doesn't want someone from a family his parents know, someone to whom they would be sympathetic. He wants someone they vaguely disapprove of, so she'll be isolated. He has had his own way during his entire life, and he takes any evidence of female independence as a direct challenge."

"How come you know so much about him?"

"Paul Antier, a friend of mine, told me all about him. His sister Rebecca was one of Espy's girlfriends, and she ended up with a broken jaw and a cracked collarbone. She spent a week in the hospital as a result. Paul started asking around, and he found at least one other girlfriend of Espy's who'd also ended up there."

"You didn't say anything about that at first, before we took the job."

"Jason, I didn't know. I didn't know who she was marrying. You never mentioned who she was marrying. I didn't find out until we were involved."

"If he's as you say, why the check for twenty thousand?"

"So he throws money around. He threw money around with the others, too. He likes being thought of as generous. Then when the woman tells him no, he screams at her that he's been damned generous and she owes him. Look, he wants his female friends to be dependent and on the defensive. Can you think of any better way to put Valerie on the defensive than telling her she's on trial? No matter what she does, he'll pick it to pieces. And if he doesn't, his mother probably will."

In no very happy frame of mind, I kept my date with Valerie. She met me at the door, blooming. The slipcovers had come. The curtains had come. The chairs were back; the paintings had been hung. She loved the way it looked. It looked great, even without the furniture we'd bring after the carpets were cleaned.

"When is the big event?" I asked.

"Next Friday. A week."

"What are you serving?"

Her face went blank. Absolutely blank. "Oh, God," she said. "I was so excited, I forgot I'll have to feed them."

I couldn't help laughing, and after a moment she laughed, too. We sat on the newly slipcovered sofa; she brought coffee; we talked. Because of Grace, I have eaten well and often at some of the best restaurants in town. I have also, because of my profession, been invited to many homes for meals. I have been impressed by the apparently effortless ease with which some hostesses manage these things. I told Valerie about some of them, and we arrived at a menu she thought she could manage, keeping it simple.

"Oh, God," she moaned again as we finished writing down her shopping list. "I never even thought about this. I'll have to talk with them! What do I say?"

"It would be easier if you invited another couple," I told her. "Someone to carry the conversation."

"Who?" she blurted. "All my friends are scientists.

They can't talk about anything normal people care about. Besides, I have to work with them every day. I'm not sure I want any of them to know about this. What if it's awful? Oh, Jason, it could be awful. They might hate me!"

"How about me?" I offered. "And my fiancée, Grace Willis?" I had the tiniest seed of an idea, one totally dependent upon her answer. I held my breath.

She looked doubtful, casting a glance around her at the refurbished room.

I crossed my heart. "Not a word about doing the decorating, but I would retain the right to mention buying some of your finds."

"I guess that would be all right. Would your girl-friend, would Grace enjoy it?"

"She would enjoy it very much. She knows a little something about furniture, and it will make a good topic for dinner-table conversation."

I told her I'd check on her again before Friday, then went on to my next agenda item.

Wilson's aunt Carolyn was at an "assisted living" home run by St. Elizabeth's Church, a not unpleasant place with small, individual apartments, a common kitchen and dining room, and health-care people on the premises. So much I was told by the sturdy young woman who escorted me to Aunt Carolyn's door. When I had called early that morning Carolyn had seemed somewhat vague, but she answered the door herself, fully sensible and kempt, though relying heavily on her cane.

The apartment had a bedroom, which I could see through an open door, and a living room with a tiny kitchenette at one side. There were several good pieces of furniture, including a lovely little Queen Anne drop-leaf breakfast table by the window, where we sat in matching armchairs across from one another.

"I'd offer you coffee or tea," she said with an annoyed curl to her lip. "The refrigerator works, but the stove is disconnected."

"Disconnected?"

"They've shut off the gas. Accidents. Old biddies putting on the teakeattle and then going off and forgetting it. I don't know why they bothered to put stoves in if they were just going to shut them off. Not all of us forget. Sometimes I wish I did, but I never forget anything."

I could believe it. She had dark eyes that belied her white hair, a keen nose, a firm jaw, and even with the cane, she was as solidly erect as a doorpost.

"Have you heard about the fuss between Wilson Credable and Edward Credable?" I asked.

She shook her head, conveying disapproval. "Crispin the Third mentioned it, last time he was here. I don't approve of his calling himself Wilson. He is Crispin the Third and should be proud of that fact, though dear Emmeline always called him Threesy."

"Would you have any idea why Edward should be harassing him just now?"

She snorted. "One could not have lived in that house for the better part of a century without understanding what was going on. One didn't let on, of course. I always felt it was better to cultivate an attitude of vague uncertainty, even of forgetfulness. One did not wish to take sides, even if one had to appear 'vaporish' to avoid doing so."

Her tone had put the word in quotes. "Vaporish?"

"I believe that is what my brother called me, yes. Vaporish. His wife, Emmeline, knew better, of course. She and I were good friends."

"You avoided taking sides between whom?"

"Crispin Junior and Admar, of course. Admar, quite properly I thought, expected his brother to set him up a bit, share the family fortune. Crispin was determined not to do so. His animosity began when they were children. It was quite immature of Crispin, most ungentlemanly, but then, Crispin was not always gentlemanly. I am sure Edward resented this treatment of his father. Then there was the matter of the drowning."

I raised my eyebrows.

"Such a tempest in a teapot," she said. "My brother Crispin took Edward on a fishing trip when Edward was about twelve. Edward could not swim. The story, as Edward told it, was that my brother decided to teach him to swim by throwing him into the water and refusing to let him out, almost letting him drown."

"Was it true?"

"My brother was not sensitive to children, let us say that. I have no doubt Edward was terribly frightened. So far as I know, he never went near a beach or pool after that, so it must have been traumatic for him. His resentment of Crispin the Third is just part of that whole pattern."

"But why especially now, Miss Credable?"

She fondled the head of her cane, ivory, carved in the semblance of an eagle's head. "As to that, I truly cannot say. Edward is getting older, of course. Perhaps he feels he must do it now or not at all. Though both Admar and Edward did well for themselves, I always felt sorry for them. Such greedy men, both of them, though greedy for different things. Of course, it wasn't enviable to be the younger son of a man like Crispin Senior. To be the younger brother of Crispin Junior was no more so. And then, to be so hopelessly in love . . ."

"Edward? In love?"

"No, no. I was speaking of Admar. He was in love with Janet Wirtz. And I do not doubt she returned his affection. One could see it in their eyes, over the bridge table. I have always believed they ran away together."

"Janet Wirtz died," I said, somewhat at sea. "I know her daughter. She says her mother died. . . ."

"Well, that is what Hector Wirtz told the world, that his wife had died in Mexico, during a vacation. I never believed it. Hector told that story to protect his reputation. I have always believed they went away together, Janet and Admar."

My jaw dropped. Whatever I might have expected from Aunt Carolyn, it had not been this. "You really think she'd have gone like that? Leaving her daughter?"

"Amelia was almost grown, a strong, capable girl. I knew her. She came with her mother to our bridge afternoons. She amused Crispin the Third while we were at the table. They used to play dress-up. Even when Janet and Admar were no longer with us, Emmeline invited Amelia, almost, I used to think, as though Janet had asked her to do so, to keep an eye on the girl. It was one of the little things that led me to believe Janet and Admar had gone away together. Everyone else was quite upset when Admar didn't return, but Emmeline did not seem disturbed. It was that more than anything that made me quite sure Emmeline knew all about it."

"Why run away? Why not just get a divorce?"

She laughed, a high-pitched cackle. "You obviously never knew Hector Wirtz. One would not simply 'get a divorce' from Hector Wirtz. One might rather burn at the stake, I should think." She stood up and went to the phone. I heard her murmuring into it. In a moment she returned. "I've asked Gloria to bring us some coffee. I cannot bear to seem inhospitable, gas stove or no gas stove!"

Gloria, the same sturdy young woman who had brought me to Carolyn's door, turned up a few moments later with a thermal carafe, to which Carolyn added cups, silver spoons, sugar from the cupboard, cream from the refrigerator, a plate of gingersnaps.

"I always liked Janet," she said, when I had helped her arrange this assemblage on the table between us. "She was younger than I by a dozen years, and older than Emmeline by about the same span. She was very talented musically and dramatically. She used to do book reviews for our women's group, quite good ones, acting out the parts, and she played roles in several benefit performances the club put on. She played a sensible game of bridge as well, which I most enjoyed. One of the things that makes this place tolerable is the respectable number of bridge players."

"I'm surprised you didn't stay at Credable Castle?" I said in an inquiring tone.

She made a face. "I did, of course, until 1990, the year Emmeline died. She had survived my brother for eight years and was only sixty when she passed away. With her gone, the place was ... well, no longer hospitable for one of my generation. Crispin the Third is building what life he can. It wouldn't have been his father's life, or course, nor did Emmeline approve of his lifestyle. I should imagine he would like to tear Credable Castle down."

"Actually, I think he loves it," I said. "He feels very threatened by Edward. Amelia says he's a little hermit crab, rattling around in that big shell, but he needs the shell."

"Edward comes to see me every now and then. He plans to do so this weekend, as a matter of fact. When he comes, I'll find out what he's up to. As I've said, he has done well for himself. He has many admirable qualities. He's capable of hard work and decisive action. Once he decided upon a career, he worked at it from the ground up. Recently, he has made a fortune with his coal leases, so he doesn't need more money. If he's fussing with Crispin the Third, it may be the result of that greediness I spoke of."

We chatted a few moments more, about inconsequential things. I helped her wash the cups and saucers and put the spoons away.

"You will let me know, won't you?" she asked as I took my leave. "What happens?"

I said I'd let her know.

The sturdy young woman was at the reception desk as I went by. I stopped to thank her for fetching the coffee.

"Hey," she said. "I wish they were all as sharp as Miss Credable. We've got fifty-year-olds here who can't tie their own shoes. But her, she's right on top of things."

I got home before noon. Mark had left a note on my desk saying he was spending the afternoon with a customer. Eugenia was handling the phone. I went upstairs to my kitchen, thinking about lunch. Except for the few perishables that I'd tucked away yesterday, the sacks of groceries were on the kitchen table where I'd left them, including the large sack of cat litter. I spent the next quarter hour putting things away and changing the upstairs cat box. I left the litter by the stairs so when I went down I'd take it with me to do the downstairs box, the bigger one.

Schnitz materialized under the kitchen table. Bela came up the stairs and poked his head in the kitchen, assessing the likelihood of a snack. I'd bought a three-pound sack of vanilla wafers—Grace likes them with milk as a between-snack snack—and I offered one to Bela, which he crunched with obvious enjoyment. Schnitz doesn't care for cookies. He prefers buttered asparagus or artichoke hearts. At the moment I wasn't having either, so I gave him a bit of cream in a saucer while I brewed a pot of coffee and put together a sandwich for me.

It was when I stooped over to pick up the empty saucer that I noticed Schnitz's neat little cat prints on the floor, blue ones, one front foot only. I traced the footprints out into the hall, down the stairs to the large cat box in the old laundry room. I had obviously let it go too long! It smelled to high heaven, and much of the litter was thrown out on the floor. Schnitz had attempted an excavation and been thwarted by the fact that something foreign had been buried in the litter, a long, flat plastic-wrapped bundle. Schnitz had been frustrated enough to keep up the attempt until he shredded the plastic. I pulled the bundle out, the remains of a Ziploc bag that stank very badly.

Separated into its constituent parts, it yielded a blue-stained envelope and three separate pages. One was a copy, on plain white paper, of the letter I had already seen, the one Hector Wirtz had intended for Maddox. The next was the original of the typed jewelry inventory I'd found in the wastebasket upstairs. On this sheet, the heading was perfectly legible. The third was the original of another letter, one I hadn't seen before, which bore the salutation *My dear boy*. When folded, it fit the blue-stained envelope, the wettest of the papers and the source of the blue stain Schnitz had picked up on his front foot.

I blotted the papers with paper towels, drying them. They still smelled. I spread them on a large tray and covered them with cat litter to deodorize them. Then I cleaned up the mess Schnitz and I had made, sprayed the room with air freshener, and went upstairs to sit at my desk, staring into a distance of both time and space. What I was thinking was ridiculous. What I was thinking was impossible.

The stack of blue-stained papers was still in the envelope in my desk. I got them out and made a careful list. I made notes of various conversations I remembered. I went down to the basement and got the chalk line, unrolling it once more and running it in full spans between my outstretched arms. There were six knots in it, one of them at the very end.

I called Wilson Credable. I asked him to call Amelia and ask a certain question as a favor for me. His love of drama overcame his natural reluctance, and he agreed. Half an hour later he called me back to report the answer.

"Amelia says they were all stolen in Mexico. What's it all about, Jason?"

"I'll tell you all about it when I'm sure," I said vaguely, hoping the promise, however nonspecific, would keep him quiet until I knew what was what.

A large old trunk in the basement holds certain relics of my former lives, things left over from my navy days, from my college days. My diving gear is there. The last time I'd used it had been to explore a small mountain lake after my wife, Agatha, had disappeared, ten years r more ago. I'd put it away properly, however, so there vas no reason it shouldn't be serviceable. I ticked off ther needs. Tools. I had those. Explosives. Didn't have hem. Needed them, and didn't have them.

There was, however, one person who might have hem and give them to me. I talked to the person in question, going to ridiculous lengths in establishing my ona fides. The person at the other end finally agreed, eluctantly.

I went down to the workroom for a hammer, a cold hisel, a pry bar. They might do the job. They might ot. I might have to make several trips before I was ure. By two o'clock, I was ready. I took Bela with me, ust for company, telling Eugenia I'd be home later if nyone called. Going out the door, I briefly considered ;oing back, leaving a note, but decided against it. This vas just a reconnaissance. I wasn't going to need any elp.

Two stops en route. One to pick up the package from ny reluctant supplier, one to get my oxygen bottles illed. Then the drive, familiar by now, just ahead of the Friday-afternoon traffic, into the mountains, onto the side road, back toward the land that had been left by Hector to Maddox Wirtz.

After letting Bela have a very brief run, I put him back into the car. He didn't like this, but I couldn't risk his wandering about. I carried all the stuff up the hill, making three trips of it, piling everything neatly beside the teak cover that Amelia used to protect her spring. I fetched the tackle from her tin trunk in the cave, bolted it down, and threaded my lines through it. I put the tools and supplies on a small drop cloth, made a bundle of it, and lowered them into the shaft on another line bent around a handy rock, swinging them until they came to rest on a narrow ledge just above the surface of the water.

I got suited up. I'd already tested the equipment, but I did it again. Tanks and gauges were all right. Head lamp was all right. Suit was fine, a little shabby, but fine. When I'd gone over everything three times, being purposely finicky, I pushed the lid back to position the tackle over the opening and lowered myself awkwardly down into that dark throat. Light came through the vertical fissure in the cliff wall, a crack that started out about six inches across and narrowed as I went down. The shaft widened as I dropped. I know very little about geology, but the rock walls looked crystalline to me, tall, vertical crystals, vaguely hexagonal, very hard. Basalt. The word popped from nowhere, from something I'd read. And the shaft I was in must have been something softer once, something that had been washed away, leaving this vacancy.

About forty feet down, I came to the ledge just above the level of the water. It had looked narrow from above, but it was actually a niche that extended a foot or so under the shaft wall. Here the vertical fissure was about an inch and a half wide and about a foot deep. Only twelve inches of rock separated me from the open air, the view across the canyon at sunlit heights, at mountains covered with trees. As I turned, a blue splotch on the wall caught my attention. It was level with my eyes, but showed only by reflected glimmers from the surface of the water. I turned on my headlamp and saw a small hole, where a spike could have been driven in; below that, the splotch of blue; below that, the faintest line of blue, leading down parallel to the fissure, then along the edge of a foreign intrusion, not stone. Something else, blocking the fissure, damming it up.

The canvas-wrapped bundle of tools was at my feet, ell anchored behind the knob-shaped stone. When the pe was untied from the bundle, I tied it to the knob, pening the bundle up and spreading out the contents n the ledge, where they could be reached from the wa- r. I spent a moment or two arranging the tools so I ould get at each thing without tipping others into the aft below me—if they were needed at all. From this oint on, the climbing rope wasn't needed, and it, too, ot unhooked and tied to the same knobby protrusion.

Mask rinsed out and on. Mouthpiece in mouth. Head- mp on, and I lowered myself gingerly into the dark ater.

This was an unusual milieu for me. Navy demolition, y and large, concerns itself with bridges and ships and ther things either standing or floating free in quite rge bodies of water. Visible space may be limited by e lamp or by turbidity, but there is usually the sense f unlimited space beyond it. Some of my friends used enjoy diving in sunken ships, but I had never liked it. Valls underwater are entirely too reminiscent of rowned tombs and very wet graves. So, now, I was not elighted with what I could see of the shaft, which grew arrower farther down, feeling much like walls closing n. Also, the water was deadly cold. My hands were tiff and my cheekbones burned with the cold.

The rock was everywhere the same except beneath he fissure that had lighted the surface above. Below hat opening was an artificial roughness, clean-edged as ruler. I swam near to it, felt it, peered at it closely rom all angles, confirming that it was concrete over netal lath, the lath secured into the rock walls with an- hors that had been drilled in. The coating wasn't thick. Little more than an inch. It didn't need to be thick to

hold the water across a crack that narrow, but it wa
well and neatly done, nonetheless. The edges wer
straight. The material was evenly applied. It was
workmanlike job, done with finicky and totally unnec
essary attention. As though whoever had done it had er
joyed the work for its own sake.

I swam down the fissure, examining it for its entir
length, measuring it in multiples of my own height. A
about twenty-five or -six feet, just above a wide ledge, th
fissure had been constricted into a narrow throat throug
which the water spurted out. I could feel the rush of
along my cheek, between my icy fingers. This was wher
the water became visible on the cliff wall. It used to seep
Amelia had said. When she was a child, it used t
seep. Now it spurted. When she was a child, there ha
been no head of water to make it spurt, but now the pres
sure was high enough.

The ledge I was standing on extended three or fou
feet into the shaft from the front wall. Behind it th
shaft went downward again. Keeping my head leve
with the water hole, I lowered my feet and touched th
bottom. There was rubble there, about five feet down
rolling beneath my feet. Unwillingly, I turned an
pulled myself down, putting head where feet had been
putting lamplight where only darkness had lain fo
many years.

He looked back at me from vacant eyes behind a rop
of pearls. Emeralds set off with diamonds, glittering i
the light of my lamp, lay around his skull. His wrist
were bound with rubies. His waist was cinctured i
gold. Around his neck lay sapphires, like a dream o
summer skies.

Full fathom five, the note had said. *Full fathom fiv*
thy father lies.

Coming up the mountain, I had thought I might be sickened to find this, but it was too staged a setting to provoke horror. The horror lay elsewhere, not here. Not any longer.

Bubbles poured upward, a shuddering breath. I turned a somersault and kicked my way all the way up to the top ledge, where I spat out the mouthpiece and hung for a moment of quiet. There was something different about the place. For a moment I could not think what it was, but then I realized that during the ten or fifteen minutes I'd been below, the light from the hole above had gone. Only darkness up there. Daylight through the fissure beside me, but only darkness up there. Someone had covered the shaft.

I reached for the rope, knowing even before I touched it that it would not take me up again. It had been cut. Both of them had been cut. Their lengths trailed into the water beside me. I hung there, a little dazed, too suddenly aware to be thoroughly frightened yet, the terror creeping in as I realized where I was, how alone I was, that no one knew but me why I had come here. Bela was shut in the car. He would be no help.

I hung there for endless time, trying to hear something besides my own breathing, listening for any sound from outside, hearing none. I pressed my ear to the fissure. Nothing. Better to try something, anything, rather than hang there. I took the pry bar and tried to pry the metal lath away from the stone, keeping at it, with short rests, for a quarter hour by my watch. Half an inch, maybe. At this rate I would starve to death long before I worked the concrete and lath loose all the way to the bottom, emptying the shaft. Even then, I would have no way out.

I put the pry bar back and hung motionless once

more, listening again. This time there was a sound, a hammer-ringing sound, peck-pecking from the rock wall. I put my eye to the fissure, seeing nothing but sky. After a long time a line of darkness went across the fissure, then back again. A rope. Someone was hanging from a rope outside.

Someone who liked to use dynamite. What better way to get rid of me, to conceal all evidence of what lay in the shaft, than to blow it up. The peck-pecking from outside was quite purposeful and rhythmic: *clang, chuff, clang, chuff.* I'd used a cold chisel myself. Hit it and turn it, hit it and turn it, keep on hitting it and turning it while it drills deeper and deeper.

Everything went very cold and still inside me. Beside me on the ledge rested the tools from the shop and the items begged from Will Chappy. He hadn't wanted to let me have them. I'd convinced him it was a good idea, that I wouldn't hurt anybody with them, including myself, that we had to solve the mystery of Ron's death. I'd counted on his feeling guilty enough about Ron to help me out, and in the end, after I'd shown him my navy papers and told him something about my experience, he'd acquiesced.

I'd only been able to talk him out of one shaped charge, however, though he'd given me several detonators. A shaped charge is a specifically manufactured bomb that is designed to blow all its force in one direction when detonated. Shaped charges can be used to blow holes through things like walls and the sides of ships. Shaped charges can be used in manufacturing complex metal shapes, actually blowing a sheet of metal into a mold. They're also useful for loosening coal and ores of various kinds, for breaking up rock for highway construction, and to emit a known force through rock strata that can be tracked by high-resolution seismography for geological surveys. In short, they are a useful tool. Useful for me, I had thought, to drain the water out of this hole so I could see, so everyone could see what was here.

Now, however, there was someone outside who exploded things for other purposes, someone who had cut my ropes, who intended my destruction. The only question now was which of us could destroy first. Furiously, I gathered up the supplies I needed, gobbled my mouthpiece, and drove myself down to the drain hole where the water spurted out.

The charge would work just as well underwater as above it. I placed it at the bottom of the fissure, just below the jet of water, intending it to exert all its force outward. In order to do so, the charge had to be covered with something, closed in with something heavy. The only thing available to cover it with was stone. Most of the loose stones were down in the bottom of the shaft, where he lay, full fathom five. I turned over and kicked myself down. Most of the loose rocks looked impossibly huge. I grappled with a middle-sized one, shifted it loose, put my feet on the bottom, heaved it up, managed to roll it onto the shelf. The next one was smaller, easier. Three or four more smaller ones, easier yet. None of that size left. It had to be bigger ones.

I could get them to the level of my chest, but it took all my strength to heave them onto the shelf. My hands were frozen and stiff. Outside, the *clang, chuff, clang, chuff* slowed. I scrambled onto the shelf, rolled the stones into place, piled them around the charge. I needed another one or two. Each time I went down, the bones were there, staring at me, the bared teeth pleading. Don't. Please don't. Leave me in peace. Please.

"It's him or me," I told the bones. "Sorry about that."

The last two rocks seemed to weigh a ton each. I was surprised that I could move them at all, and as it was, I barely made it. There were no more. I was out of time, out of matériel. The rocks were placed as tightly together as I could get them. I'd attached the wire to the detonator before I'd fetched the stones. Now I swam upward, unreeling it behind me, stringing it out to the upper ledge. Decision time. Did I stand on the outer lip of the ledge where I might be hit by anything that fell? Or did I wedge myself under the solid stone and pray that the whole thing did not come down on top of me? Neither alternative seemed likely to improve my chance of survival, which wasn't great. Shaped charges are useful but not foolproof. Any explosion can set off a kind of chain reaction, one balanced force against another, an avalanche like a house of cards, a pile of jackstraws, everything coming down at once. I hadn't intended to be in this shaft when the charge went off. I had intended to be outside, in the fresh air and sunshine, pleased with my own cleverness.

The immediate problem was simply to get onto the shelf. My hands wouldn't grip and all the holds sloped down. I tried, heaving and heaving, slipping back each time. Finally, I looped one of the rope ends across the ledge, from stony knob to stony knob, and used it to lift myself partway up. Then, as I hung next to the ledge, readying myself for the task of getting onto it, the fissure next to me darkened. I looked through it and saw an eye.

"There you are," he said.

I didn't answer. I couldn't rage and I wouldn't plead.

"Scared speechless, huh?" The eye crinkled to show the face was grinning, pleased with itself.

I was almost speechless, but I managed, "How did you know Ron didn't have the letter and the bank draft with him?"

I had the tiny satisfaction of watching the eye go blank.

"Because I offered him cash for 'em that afternoon."

"The day he died?"

"Right. Just like now. Shoulda minded your own business," he said, sliding out of view downward.

I heaved on the rope, without thought, without plan, just hauled myself up and onto the ledge, getting one foot against the knob to hold me there. The wire was in my hand, the plunger gimmick was among the tools beside me. My hands were damned near frozen. I fumbled with the thing, almost dropped it. I shut my eyes, counted to ten slowly while I flexed fingers, then took a deep breath, opened my eyes, and tried again. This time the wire slid into a slot. Not the one I was aiming for, but who cared. I tightened the screw.

From below me, outside, came the *peck, peck, peck.*

I rammed the button down.

Nothing. I stared at the gimmick. Wrong screw. I had to tighten the other one. The thing was set up to handle a series of detonations. I didn't have a series. I only had one.

Peck peck crash. The sound of the rope slapping the wall. He was coming up.

I jammed the button down.

Hell happened. Earthquake and typhoon and tidal wave, all at once. Water erupted and fell. It was like being drowned under a waterfall. Rock trembled, pieces fell past me like missiles, a noise like a bathtub emptying with one vast sucking sound. Was there a sound outside, any sound at all? A scream? A voice?

Above me, darkness; below me, light. A sizable window blown in the side of the cliff, and all the water poured out in one mighty cataract. Only a small pool remained down there, behind the lower ledge. It looked like a long way down. I kicked off my fins and shrugged out of the tanks, leaving them on the ledge. I was shaking, so I sat down for a while until it stopped. The walls had little steplike fractures here and there, but as I'd already found out, they all sloped outward, and were slimed with some kind of mineral gunk. I wouldn't have made it without the rope. The two pieces knotted together, with a loose loop over the rock knob, were, I hoped, long enough to get me down the outside wall as well.

I let myself down. The rock slime coated me, and my feet and hands slipped and slid. Only the rope kept me from plunging. As it was, I dropped the last few feet. The opening in the cliff was about four feet on a side, roughly triangular. Plenty large enough to crawl into and look down. Perhaps fifty feet below, there was a scree slope. Down that slope a considerable way was a new fall of stone with what might have been an arm protruding from it.

It took a great many tries to flip the loop in my rope free of the rock above. It was barely long enough to reach the slope below, which meant the scree was farther than I'd estimated. I sat in the triangular hole a long time, deciding how and what. Before I went out of it, I did a little free diving in the pool behind me.

Things, even simple things, can take a dreadfully long time: getting down a rock wall, when one doesn't really know how and doesn't have the right equipment; hanging there, staring at the neat holes bored in that wall with the red casings visible inside; finding and gathering up the dynamite scattered below, half a dozen sticks of it, lying about like firecrackers.

I carried the explosives with me down the scree to the tumble of larger rocks. All that showed was an arm. The arm was dead. I didn't know whether it was connected to a person or not. Even if the rest of the person was elsewhere, he was no doubt dead as well. I stood there, trying to decide what to do about him. Finally I dropped the dynamite through holes in the pile, hiding it, then put more rocks over it, covering the arm so that nothing could be seen at all.

Bela and my car were back up that cliff, behind it. The journey there felt like a ten-mile hike in bare feet. It wasn't actually that far. The cliff didn't extend that far south, but petered out in a series of little canyons. I came up one of them, then northward up to the other side, to the road, the last few hundred yards hearing a muffled baying that had to be Bela. I freed him and fell onto the car seat, too weary to move. It took a long time before I could make myself function, time and darkness coming down around me.

Bela went with me back to the shaft, and I went down it to retrieve all evidence that anyone had been there. My tools. His tools. Supplies. Air tanks. Flippers. His rope. What was left of my rope. I removed the tackle from the teak cover and replaced it in Amelia's cave.

Before pulling the cover back into place, I dropped stones down the shaft, finding the proper angle to pitch them so they ricocheted off the bottom ledge and went into that remaining pocket of water at the bottom. Even when it was quite dark, I went on pitching stone after stone after stone, filling the pool, hiding what was in it. He'd wanted peace. I thought he should have peace.

I put everything of mine in my car. I had to search for the other car, even though I knew it had to be there somewhere. Bela found it and barked. My flashlight caught the metallic blue and Bela with his leg raised against a rear tire. It was well hidden and might stay hidden for a very long time. The trunk wasn't locked. It held a large case neatly fitted out with tools, fuses, dynamite, detonators, a handgun. Loaded. He should have shot me. One little miscalculation that ruined the whole plan. I wiped his tools and put them into his trunk, along with his rope. I unloaded the gun, but left it there. I locked the trunk.

His wallet was in the glove compartment. In the wallet was a copy of Hector Wirtz's letter and a copy of the jewelry inventory. I took them both and burned them on the spot, crushing the black pages into powder. When I had finished, it was very dark on the side of that mountain. No stars that night. No moon. And down the other side of the cliff, carrion hunters, no doubt, burrowing among the stones.

The drive home took forever. Nobody home at my house except an aggrieved Schnitz. The diving equipment went back in the trunk in the basement. The rope was wound into coils on the garage wall. My feet and hands were considerably the worse for wear. I soaked both, then put the feet into soft socks and the hands to work fixing supper. I was cold all the way through. I thought food might help.

It didn't greatly, though it gave me enough energy to make a neat package of the jewels I had brought from the shaft. I took them downstairs and put them in the secret compartment of the davenport, where, no doubt, someone would discover them within the next few days.

Mark didn't, I would. They had belonged to Janet Virtz; they now belonged to Amelia.

On my return through the backroom, I uncovered the letters that had been drying in kitty litter. They still smelled. Upstairs, I put them in a Ziploc bag inside a sealed envelope, and locked them in my top desk drawer. No smell, no tell. Then I collapsed into bed and slept forever.

Saturday morning I called Mark and told him to take the day off. Eugenia wasn't scheduled to work anyhow. I left a note on the front door that we were closed, then called Grace and told her I was coming over. She made some excuse, which I refused to listen to. Twenty minutes later I was on her back porch, knocking on the door, through which I could see her moving around in the kitchen.

"Hi," she said flatly, not meeting my eyes. "I was going to have a do-nothing day, Jason. I figure I need one."

"Sure you do," I told her cheerfully. "I won't interfere with your do-nothing day. It's just that my day is not complete without you in it. So even if you send me away immediately, I've still had my daily dose of Grace."

She blinked rapidly, tears threatening. "Jason, I've told you. I just can't think of anything but . . ."

"I know." I put my arms around her and hugged her. "You're completely tied up in Ron. In his living, and in his dying. You have no sense or emotion for anything else. You never asked me how the thing down in Santa Fe came out. You don't seem to care what I'm doing or feeling. I understand that."

"Well, if you do, then why are you bothering me?" she cried petulantly, utterly unlike herself.

I took her through to the living room and sat her down, sitting beside her to look into that rebellious face, those reddened eyelids, all that aggrieved anger surging around inside her.

"I'm bothering you because something you said bothers me. You said you couldn't think about us until you knew about Ron. You asked me to find out for you. Suppose, just for the sake of argument, that we never know about Ron."

"You're not trying!" she cried.

"Suppose I'm not," I said. "Does your loving me depend on my finding Ron's killer?"

She drew away, staring across my shoulder at nothing. "That wasn't . . . that wasn't exactly what I meant."

"Remember when you were sixteen," I said. "Remember the guys you went out with who told you if you really loved them you'd let them."

"Bastards," she said in a cracked voice. "It's not the same."

"It's the same. You seem to be saying to me, Jason, if you really love me, you'll do this. And if you can't do this, it must mean you don't really love me."

"That's not . . . I don't think—"

"Hey," I said. "It's all right. I just need to know. Before . . ."

"Before?"

"Before anything."

"I don't know!" she raged. "I just don't know!"

"Will you figure it out? And when you do, will you let me know?"

I kissed her chastely on the cheek and left her there. I hadn't told her we had a date for Friday. Maybe we id, and maybe we didn't. It more or less depended on hat she told me.

When I got back to the shop, I left the note on the oor and went upstairs. I called Carolyn Credable and hatted with her for a few moments, asking one or two ttle questions. Then I thought for a while. I wanted to rite it all down, pull all the pieces together. It was orthy of a document. One I'd give to Grace sooner or tter, no matter what she told me.

I sat down at my desk with a pen and sheets of plain aper. This document was not suited to a keyboard. his was something that needed to be handwritten. I as still cold inside. I wanted to get the coldness out, rite it out, onto the paper.

When Amelia Wirtz was a girl, I began.

Monday morning, Amelia called and asked if I would o with her to the state crime lab. Their reconstruction erson had finished the clay head she was building on he skull, and since she owned the land, Amelia was sked if she would come to the lab and see if she rec-gnized the person. She asked me if I would view this articular item with her and would I bring Grace.

I told her I would go with her, that Grace was busy—vhich I assumed she was, not having heard from her—hen spent the entire drive praying the head would be no ne Amelia had ever known. Unfortunately, the forensic erson was good at her work. The head was the image f that painting I had seen in Maddox's parlor. Even in he cold room with the hard blue light, there was some-hing warm and loving in that face.

Tears streaming down her face, Amelia said, "That is ny mother, Janet Wirtz. I was told by my father that he had died in Mexico in 1957." She said it in a voice that was utterly flat, unemotional. She said she woul answer no questions at the moment; later, if they like She staggered once as we were leaving. We sat in m car, she staring through the windshield at nothing.

"I knew," she whispered. "I always knew."

What had she known? How much, or how little?

"What did you know, Amelia?"

"I was seventeen. I was no fool, Jason. Even I coul see the way they looked at each other. Mother an Admar. I asked Emmeline once if my mother was reall dead. She put her arms around me and said she though Mother and Admar had gone off together. I alway hoped she had. I dreamed she had."

I was a little taken aback. "You hoped she had? Jus left you like that?"

"I could take care of myself better than she could. had some of Father's hardness. Toughness, maybe. Sh knew I was going away to school that fall, that wouldn't be living at home anymore. If she could onl have waited three years. But to do this to herself . . ."

A long silence while I absorbed this.

"You knew," she said.

"What makes you think that?"

"Wilson. That gnome! Calling me, wondering what ever happened to Mother's jewelry. You put him up t that."

"Only because I found it," I said desperately.

"Found it! Mother's jewelry?"

I nodded. "In that little davenport desk your fathe willed to your uncle. It was your mother's desk, yo know. There's a little secret compartment. I doubt you father knew the jewels were there. I imagine you mother hid them there before she left. For you."

"But I helped her pack. . . ."

"Then she unpacked them before she left, Amelia."

"Why did Father want Maddox to have that desk?"

"Because he knew how fond Maddox was of your other. He left it to Maddox as a kind of keepsake." Which was true. In a way.

"She must have refused to go to Mexico with Father. hat would have made him furious. He would have told r, get out of the car, he'd go alone. That was like Fa- er. Maybe she even said she was leaving him; that ould have put him into a rage. She never even came ome. She went up there, instead. And when Admar new she was gone, heard she was dead, he left. . . ."

"Why did your father say she'd died in Mexico?"

"Oh, well, Father. That's what he'd say. Once he lled home and Mother wasn't there, he knew she'd one. Not where, of course, but he didn't care where. le wouldn't let people gossip, not about him. Far better ly she died. . . ."

"Shall I take you home, Amelia?"

"Yes, Jason. Thank you. You'll understand, won't ou, if we just bury the institute idea. I don't think I ould bear . . ."

"Of course. But you needn't bury it. Just plan it for ome other place."

"Perhaps. I'll see."

The rest of Monday went by without a call from Grace. Tuesday there were things in the paper about the lentity of the skeleton. I figured Grace must have seen , but she didn't call. Wednesday went by without a call rom Grace. Thursday ditto. Friday morning early, while was shaving, the phone rang. Grace.

"Jason, we have to talk."

Her voice didn't tell me a thing. "That would [nice," I said, carefully neutral.

"How about tonight?"

"If you'll help me out by going to dinner with m first."

"Help you out?"

I described Valerie's situation, including Mark's rev[lations about Espy Gryphon.

"And you want to go to dinner with these people You want *me* to go to dinner with these people?"

"No. I don't even want to meet these people, but I d want to save Valerie French from making a terrible mis take that may ruin her life."

"How do you intend to do that?"

I told her.

"You want me to what!"

"Well, it boils down to being gushy and effusive an not saying you're a cop. Not at first, anyhow."

I could hear the wheels turning, even over the phone I expected a blast, but all I got was a sweet, "All right, Jason. If you think it's necessary."

Either she was going to let me down and didn't want to hurt my feelings, or she had decided she loved me and didn't want to hurt my feelings. Worrying about that, I went through such facial contortions that I cut my chin twice.

First thing was Valerie. I called, asked if she had time to see me. Yes. She'd taken the day off to get ready for the great event. I asked Mark to meet me there so he'd have his own car. I intended to stay a bit longer than he might wish to do.

The furniture had been delivered the day before. The place looked absolutely wonderful. Essentially, it was only a box without any architectural interest whatsoer, but within that limitation, we'd done wonders. Whenever I see a basically plain actress transformed in some romantic film or TV show into some raving beauty, I liken myself to the makeup artist who makes possible. This box had been transformed. It would be even better at night, when we could see it in lamplight. When Mark arrived, we shut the curtains and tried it, just to be sure.

"You know," Valerie said, staring around her like Judy Garland, just landed in Oz, "I could have done this."

"Of course you could," I said. "If you'd been trying."

"But why didn't I?"

"Because you didn't know you could," said Mark, plumping a green pillow. "Lots of us can do things if we think we can. It's only self-doubt holding us back."

"I think Espy needs to believe you did do it," I said.

"Oh." She shook her head doubtfully. "He's been here. He knows what it used to look like."

"Yes," said Mark. "But that's not the issue. The issue is, you did do it. You didn't use Espy's check. All the resources came from your own actions. Even consulting us was your own idea. I think it's terribly important for the Gryphons to understand that you aren't just some brainless little girl. You're a mature, sensible, intelligent woman with impeccable taste." He got out the envelope with the check in it and gave it back to her with a flourish.

"Really?" she said, staring first at the envelope, then giving him a glassy-eyed look, like someone who'd just been told she'd won several million in the lottery. "Do you really think so?"

I had urged Mark not to overdo it. So now, catching my eye, he merely nodded solemnly and assured her he did think so. He could not forbear adding, "I've said much to Jason. If you ever want to quit fooling arou with microscopes and slides and whatnot, you'd have marvelous career buying and selling treasures li these." He made a gesture that included everythi she'd found and collected.

She glowed. My only worry was that we'd have t little time to stoke her furnace, so to speak. On t other hand, she'd lived on her own for a number years, supported herself, made friends, gained some li experiences. She wasn't some kid, just out of scho She had eyes and a mind that worked well; if only s would take off the sentimental, romantic blinkers a use them.

Mark moved around the place, making a few not little things that would be needed that night. I patted t couch beside me, inviting her to sit.

"Grace and I would like to get here a little early, help you."

"Oh, would you? That would be marvelous. I'm ne vous. Like a bride, you know. Afraid I'll stutter something."

"You've never told me, how did you meet Espy?"

"Well actually, it was funny. Last year I went to Me Verde for my vacation, and as I was coming back stopped at a shop in Cortez, and some of the thin were beautiful but some just turned me off, you know I nodded. I did know. "So, when I got back, I went the art museum to look at the Indian collection, kind get some idea whether it was the things or whether was me. And Espy was there, with a group. They we being taken through by someone on the museum sta hoping they'd donate, you know."

I nodded again.

"Espy had sort of dropped out of the group, and we got to talking. That's how we met."

"What does he do?"

She looked puzzled for a moment. "You mean, a job?"

"Yes. How does he earn his living?"

"The family . . . they have a lot of money."

"I know they do, but even very wealthy people usually work at something."

Again that puzzlement. "Well, yes. Espy's in real estate. He manages his father's real estate. And he spends a lot of time with his horses. He rides."

I lifted my brow. Mark came in. "I think Espy Gryphon rides with the Arapahoe Hunt," he said. "He has quite a stable of hunters."

"That must cost a great deal," I said.

"Oh, twenty thousand a year per horse," he said offhandedly. "Vet bills. Feed. Farrier. Stable and training fees. Not counting the cost of the horse, of course. Horses like that sell for thirty thousand or more."

Valerie's face had gone blank. I was careful not to look at her. "He must be a really good real-estate manager to earn that amount of money."

"No," Mark said from around the corner. "The job's a sinecure. The family pretty much keeps him in horses because it's the only thing he's halfway good at."

"That's a terrible thing to say," I grated at Mark as he came back into the room. "I think you owe Valerie an apology."

He turned red, then pale. Even though we'd rehearsed the whole thing, I was surprised at this reaction. He actually stuttered as he said, "I'm s-s-sorry, Valerie. I wasn't thinking."

He bowed himself out, groveling. I patted Valerie's

hand. "Mark moves in the same circles as the Gryphons, and he hears the gossip. I'm sure that's all it is, just gossip. You couldn't care for the kind of man Mark was talking about. You're too intelligent."

She said, "It must be . . . like someone is jealous of him, or something. He's not like that. Everywhere we go, everyone is so . . . nice to him."

"Who?" I asked innocently.

"Oh, you know, waiters. And the maître d' at the restaurants. People we see when we're out together."

"He probably tips very well. What about his friends?"

"Well, we don't go out with his friends that much. He says they're dreadful bores."

"Your friends?"

"Well, he likes me to himself. You know."

"You must learn to ride, then," I said firmly. "So you'll have something to share."

She went blank again. "I've never . . . been that crazy about horses."

"I can certainly understand that, me neither, but you'll want to share his life as fully as possible, I'm sure. Look at poor Princess Di! How much better off she'd have been if she'd shared any interest at all with Charles." This had gone far enough. "Forgive me. I'm sounding fatherly, and I'm not old enough to be your father. Grace and I will be here at six tonight. They don't arrive until seven-thirty, right?"

She said yes, preoccupied with some other thought. I went on my way. When I was back at the office, Mark poked his head in and raised his eyebrows. I shrugged. Maybe.

"The wine for tonight is here," he said. "I picked it

up this morning. Be sure you take a corkscrew. She doesn't have one."

I had only one task that afternoon: to visit the stable where Espy Gryphon kept his horses.

I got back to the house about four, showered and changed, collected wine and corkscrew, and drove over to Grace's, arriving about five. She came scurrying in about ten minutes later: we had agreed we'd do our briefing while she was getting ready. While she showered I talked. While she dressed I talked. She nodded, asked questions, nodded again.

"Did you find a complaint?" I asked at last, when I'd run out of tactics to talk about.

"Oh, yes," she said. "Last year. Assault and rape. Her name was Lenore Stacy. The charges were dropped. I called her. We talked for about an hour. He threatened to kill her if she went on with the charge, and said he'd pay her thirty thousand if she dropped it."

"Did he pay?"

"He did. He treats money like it was Kleenex."

"It isn't his money," I commented. "He doesn't have to earn it."

"True." She came out of her bedroom looking like something out of an English garden. Grace, when she sets her mind to it, is gorgeous. The little match girl turns into a whole bouquet of orchids.

"You look lovely," I said, carefully temperate. If there was anything I did not want to hear, it was a dismissive, "Oh, Jason."

We went. We arrived. Grace was introduced and immediately taken to, which was good. I brought in the wine and the corkscrew, at which Valerie shrieked. "I didn't even think about that!"

"Mark did."

She turned to Grace. "With my friends, we order a pizza, and somebody brings a six-pack or the kind of wine you unscrew. Either that, or we all dress up and go out to a restaurant. We don't 'entertain.' I suppose the Gryphons do. I suppose I'll have to learn. . . ."

She and Grace disappeared around the corner into the kitchen, and I went around the table, straightening napkins, finding and removing a stick-on tag from the new tablecloth, going back to unfold the napkins and remove the tags from them, too. Valerie had just plopped them down without looking. Luckily, they were the kind that comes off easily, leaving no residual sticky patch. Grace came in with a tray of sherry glasses for the buffet. The decanters were already there.

"What are these glasses?" she whispered as she went past.

"Just plain old cut crystal with a little gilding," I whispered back. "Part of Wilson Credable's enormous inventory."

"Did you ever talk to his aunt Carolyn?"

"As a matter of fact, I did, yes."

She bustled back into the kitchen without pursuing the subject. I sat on the sofa and read the copy of *Scientific American* that was on the coffee table, an issue that fortuitously, had a cover that went with the decor.

At about a quarter after seven, the doorbell rang, and Valerie went to answer it. Him and her, Daddy and Mommy, dressed very casually indeed. Good! Advantage, our side. Both Valerie and Grace looked better than she did.

Introductions, how do you do, how nice to meet you, yes, we're old friends of Valerie's, blah, blah. Won't you sit down? Sherry? Yes, that is a lovely decanter, I wish I had Valerie's eye. I keep trying to hire her, but she is devoted to Science.

What do you do, Mr. Lynx?

Well, as to that, Mrs. Gryphon, blah, blah, drag in well-known names.

You really did the Van Zant penthouse? How marvelous. Don't you just love Zeebie.

I did not much love Zeebie, but I twinkled back.

And you really want to hire Valerie?

I do indeed, she would be invaluable. Rare to find that keenness of perception in someone that age.

Doorbell. Espy himself, also casual. Good. That told us what his perception of Valerie was. Not someone one dressed up for. I wondered if this was lost on her. It was a subtlety, but she might pick up on it.

Mushroom caps stuffed with crabmeat, puffed with cheese, thirty seconds in the microwave, onto a hot plate, onto the coffee table. Yes, aren't they delicious? Grace rising, going to buffet, running hand admiringly over the wood. "Valerie, where did you get this?"

"Yes, Val, I've been dying to ask," I said. "If you want to sell, I have a very, very wealthy buyer. Twenty thousand, maybe more?"

"I couldn't sell it," she cried. "It's one of my favorite things." And she went on, glowingly, to tell where she'd found it.

I shook my head, smiled confidingly into Mrs. Gryphon's narrowed eyes. "She's simply unerring. She could make a fortune if she wanted to work at it. She'll probably make a fortune just doing it as she is doing it."

"Doing what, Mr. Lynx?"

"Collecting," I said, wide-eyed, shaking my head in wonder, catching Espy's eye and dragging him into the conversation. "She collects the most marvelous pieces.

I just recently found some warehouse space for her so she could clear some of the things out of here."

His eyebrows drew together in a puzzled little scowl "I thought it looked different."

So much for him. Mark was right. He wouldn't know quality if it bit him on the ass.

Grace is talking with Daddy. I am talking with Mom and son. Valerie is putting the first course on the table. Dinner. How nice. Oh, how good this looks, cries Grace, hovering over the endive in fresh cucumber dressing.

We sit. Grace asks Valerie about her work. Valerie waxes eloquent about the search for a genetic marker. Daddy is interested; Mommy is not; Espy is bored stiff. When Espy is bored, he becomes whiny.

Grace switches attention to Espy and sparkles at him. He perks up slightly. Valerie and I clear salad plates and fetch entrée. Act-one curtain.

Act two. Everyone is seated, everyone has wine, everyone has a beautiful plate full of beautiful food, hot rolls on the side. Grace swallows a neat little mouthful, pats her lips with her napkin, and asks:

"Espy. That's such an unusual name. Didn't you used to know Lenore Stacy?"

He makes a production of chewing, swallowing, taking a sip of wine before answering. "The name is familiar. I think I knew her several years ago, yes. She was a friend of a friend."

"Poor thing." Grace sighs.

I am about to respond to this cue when Valerie steps on my line. "What happened to her?"

"The man she was going with beat her within an inch of her life," says Grace. "She was hospitalized for the longest time."

"Awful," I cry, obviously unbuttoned by wine. "We never used to hear about such things, and now we hear nothing else. I hope she prosecuted the man!"

"I hoped so, too," says Grace. "But he paid her off."

Daddy's fork stops halfway to his mouth, then slowly moves again. The phrase, paid her off, means something to Daddy.

"What was your involvement in all this?" asks good old Mom. "Are you a friend of hers?"

"Now I am. Before, I was a friend only in a manner of speaking," Grace replies, all innocence. "I'm a police officer, Mrs. Gryphon. Lenore's is one of those cases I take an interest in, crimes against women. We still hope Lenore will bring charges against the man who beat her. We're encouraging her to do so."

All unaware, Valerie steps into the trap. "I certainly would!" she cries, her cheeks quite pink with outrage. "If a person laid a hand on me, it would be the last time."

"Tough proving a criminal complaint like that," I say. "Women victims have a really rough time of it."

Valerie is undaunted. "If I couldn't win a criminal complaint, I'd sue him up one side and down the other."

"Let's change the subject," I say quickly. "It's too depressing. Tell me, Mrs. Gryphon, didn't I read just the other day that you're heading up the new fund-raising effort for the Botanic Gardens?"

We talk about that. Second-act curtain.

Third act. Dessert. Coffee. A liqueur. Chitchat. Grace rises, must go, such a lovely evening, hate to bring it to an end, but tomorrow's a workday. We'll be seeing you soon, Valerie. Hope to see you also, Espy. So nice to have met both of you, Mrs. Gryphon, Mr. Gryphon.

General uprising. General outgoing. Espy, departing

with parents, Valerie standing in door, troubled look on face. Something has happened. She hasn't picked up on what, yet. She'll go in the kitchen and wash the dishes and it will come to her.

"Your house or mine?" I asked Grace.

"Your house," she said. "We need to talk."

She settled onto my living-room couch while I brewed us some coffee. If Valerie had been nervous as a bride, I was certainly nervous as a bridegroom. I'd rehearsed this to myself, over and over. I knew what intellect said. Intellect said, if she doesn't love you enough, Jason, don't cling. But emotion said, cling like crazy. Be a limpet. Be a damned barnacle.

I heaved a breath and carried the cups into the living room. She was curled up at the foot of the couch, staring into the nonexistent fire. "All right, ma'am," I said. "Talk."

She didn't. She didn't even move for a moment.

"What?"

"Jason, I'm sorry."

I held my breath. "About what, love?"

"I . . . I shouldn't have said that to you. About if you loved me. I know you love me. The thing is . . . The thing is, right then I wasn't sure I loved you. Loved anybody. I thought . . . I thought if you found out, avenged, whatever, then I'd love you, just automatically, because I'd have to, you know. Like . . . the prince who saves the princess from the tower. Or the monster. More like that. It was like a monster, hating whoever killed him. You'd save me from that monster, and I'd be so grateful, I'd love you forever."

"But you don't," I said flatly.

"No, that's not . . . I mean, yes. Yes, I do. I should have known that. Even with what happened, I should have known that. The trouble was, there wasn't any background music."

I think my mouth dropped open. She gave me a hasty glance, a teary giggle.

"It's the background music that tells you how to feel, Jason! Scary, or romantic, or full of purpose, or marching off to battle. Lots of times, don't you think life would be easier if we had background music? First Ron was sick, and there wasn't any background music, then he was dead, and there still wasn't any background music. Was I supposed to cry, grieve, throw myself over a cliff, what? I didn't know what to feel."

Her words were a plea. I gave up my poised, neutral position and sat down beside her. Hell, I didn't know what to feel either.

"Some places, some cultures, I guess they have the background music all figured out. You hold a wake or a vigil or something, everybody cries or howls or beats drums, all the emotions sort of bear you up, like a river, carrying you along. And later on, when you wash up on shore, it's all right. You can go on, and you have to go on, Jason, you have to. We're such a long time dead."

"But you hadn't washed up on shore."

"I was stuck in midriver. Hating him. Whoever did it. Hating Ron for being that kind of person. And it didn't have anything to do with you. That's what I figured out, finally."

"Are we going to get married, Grace?"

"Yes. Music or no music. We're going to get married, Jason. Right away. Just as soon as we can."

I held her. She felt small, and dear, and strong. I could think of being there forty years hence, age eighty-something, still finding her small and dear and strong. "What about Ron?" I asked.

She shrugged in my arms. "If I find out, then I'll find
out. If I don't, then I'll live with that. It has nothing to
do with you."

The pages I had written were in my desk drawer. I
got them out and gave them to her.

seven

WHEN AMELIA WIRTZ was a girl, in the forties and fifties, she used to go with her mother and father picnicking on a piece of land high in the mountains above Dumont. The site had a high rock terrace looking out over thousands of miles. It also had a number of hollow shafts, one of which held a spring of water. Hector Wirtz owned the land. Amelia loved the picnics. Perhaps they were among the few occasions that all three members of the family enjoyed.

Amelia sometimes accompanied her mother, Janet, when she went to Credable Castle to play bridge. Playing bridge in the afternoons was a customary and acceptable activity for middle- and upper-class women, those who did not work outside the home. By all accounts, Janet's husband, Hector Wirtz, was a monster, possessive and violent, but even he abided by certain conventions and allowed his wife to take part in women's-club activities and play afternoon bridge with Emmeline Credable. It is possible he did not know that the usual foursome included not only Carolyn Credable but Admar Credable as well.

Though Admar had a reputation as a ladies' man, his sister Carolyn Credable believed him to be honestly in love with Janet Wirtz. Moreover, Carolyn believed Janet

returned that love. Janet's life with Hector lay some-
where between unloving and tortured. Certainly he was
psychologically abusive. He may have been physically
abusive. In any case, after seventeen or eighteen years
of marriage to Hector, Janet made plans to run away
with Admar Credable.

Admar had always wanted to go into business. Janet
had inherited from her mother a minor fortune in very
fine jewelry. Hector had no claim on it. Converted into
cash, it would capitalize the business that Admar would
run and she would perhaps help him with. Admar gave
Janet a ring to symbolize their plans. It featured tour-
malines, her birthstone, and bore the date of their
planned departure. August 9, 1957. On the inside it
said, Forever. A.

In some way Hector Wirtz became aware of these
plans. He may have overheard a phone call, opened a
letter, hired a private detective. He announced plans for
a two-week trip to Mexico for himself and Janet, leav-
ing in mid-July. Reluctantly, Janet made preparations to
go with him. Amelia helped her pack her clothing and
her jewels, which Hector insisted she take along be-
cause he intended to show her off.

In actuality, Hector had made plans of quite another
kind. He had gone to the land where the family had
often picnicked, put a ladder down into the spring shaft,
and closed off the fissure through which the water had
seeped. Until then, there had been only a shallow pool
in the shaft, a few feet of water that spilled out of a ver-
tical fissure and oozed down the cliff face. Hector
changed all this. He bought cement, metal lath, fasten-
ers, carbide bits. He may even have hired help. He went
to the mountain, let himself down inside the shaft, fas-
tened a chalk line along the fissure, and snapped it

*gainst the stone. The blue stain is still there. Like the
lue on the stones marking the land. Like the blue on
he stones, leading one to the shaft. Janet's favorite
olor was blue, so Carolyn says. Janet's favorite play
vas, The Tempest. She had acted in a charity produc-
ion of it in 1948, opposite Admar. Hector had, of
ourse, attended a performance.*

*Hector measured five fathoms of depth inside the
haft. Then he closed the fissure, letting the water rise
n that shaft to a level of five fathoms, thirty feet.*

*Carolyn remembers the events of that summer well.
On the sixteenth of July, 1957, Hector and Janet left
Denver by car. Their stated plan was to drive to
Albuquerque, where Hector said he had some brief
usiness to conduct, then fly to Mexico. Janet was never
een again. Hector called his home a week or so later
o say she had fallen ill in Mexico, then the word came
he had died and been cremated there after a short ill-
ess. Hector brought an urn back with him. He said it
ontained her ashes.*

*Almost concurrent with Janet's departure, Admar dis-
appeared. We can only speculate on how Hector tricked
Admar, ambushed him, immobilized him. Perhaps he
ook Janet and Admar to the mountain at different
imes, perhaps at the same time. Certainly, he stripped
hem and flung them into two, separate shafts, decking
Admar's corpse with the gems he was to have received
rom Janet. I can imagine Hector standing upon the
edge, raving, "You will never be together! You will stay
ere for eternity, separate and alone! Nobody steals
rom Hector Wirtz! Nobody!"*

*Later that summer Hector Wirtz was arrested for
hooting a man he said had broken into his house. A
witness said no, the man had worked for Hector. We*

may speculate that there had been an attempt at black mail. Perhaps Hector did not want anyone left alive who knew what he had done. This is mere supposition. We will never know.

No one knew where Admar was. Because Janet had supposedly died in Mexico, no one connected the double disappearance except Carolyn, and perhaps Emmeline, both of whom put a falsely optimistic interpretation upon the facts.

Three years later, in 1960, Hector knew he was dying. The murder of his wife and her lover had not satisfied him. His malice had not been quenched. In his last act of hideous spite, he wrote a letter to his brother, Maddox, and another to Admar's son, Edward, at that time a man in his early thirties.

We know what the letter addressed to Maddox said. We now have the contents of the letter written to Edward Credable:

My dear boy,

When your father left in 1957, he received over a million dollars' worth of expensive ice from my wife, jewelry her mother and grandmother had left her. He still has it, and I know where he is.

My brother, Maddox, can take you there—a place in the mountains near Alice, deep and still. Full fathom five thy father lies, Edward. He hath suffered a sea change, into something rich and strange. Him and Janet both.

Nobody steals from Hector Wirtz. Nobody.

In the envelope with the letter to Edward, Hector included an inventory list of Janet's jewelry. It is headed "Personal property of Janet Wirtz to be covered by Fed-

ral Trust Insurance policy #987-5537, sold to Hector Virtz. *It includes the 1957 valuations, over a million ollars.*

Hector told Amelia her mother's jewels had been sto-en in Mexico, but he never made a claim against the olicy. He wanted no investigation of Janet's ostensible death in Mexico.

Hector didn't want the letters found until after his death. He secreted them in a cherrywood davenport desk, one that Janet herself had used, together with the ales tickets for the materials he had used to seal the shaft. He then slapped a coat of paint onto the little desk, sealing the drawer in which the letters lay, and out it in an upstairs bedroom where it would be unlikely to be disturbed. He called his brother, saying enough to let Maddox know there were secrets, mysteries that he would inherit. Hector willed the desk to his brother, Maddox, along with several other items, coupling the gift with a sizable amount of money and the land on which the two corpses were entombed.

Hector knew that Maddox adored Janet. He and Maddox had come to blows over her. Hector knew that Maddox would recognize the little desk as one Janet had used and loved. He assumed Maddox would open every drawer looking for some keepsake, thus finding the letters, the proof of what Hector had done. He knew the letter would cause his brother much pain. That's why he wrote it. Hector wanted to torture both Maddox and Edward: Maddox because he had pre-sumed to love Janet; Edward because he was Admar's son.

The whole affair was botched, however. It was too complicated, too cumbersome, too much a product of Hector's conniving, twisty mind. Too much depended

upon Maddox being an avaricious man, which he w
not. Maddox rejected the legacy in its entirety. The fu
niture stayed with Amelia, who gave it to me. I put it
the workroom; Eugenia assigned Ron to strip the pain
Ron got the drawer open; he read the two letters an
examined the inventory list of gems. Though Ron ofte
behaved foolishly, he was no fool. He knew what he ha
before him, and he set about using the letters to bette
his own fortunes. He had no idea where Maddox Wir
was, but he found a Credable in the phone book, called
and asked where he could get in touch with Edwar
Credable. He was given a number in Wyoming. H
reached Edward Credable, read him parts of the lette
and proposed a split. Edward agreed.

Ron made the same mistake Hector had made. He di
not know his adversary. He believed he had a dea
Edward was not a man to honor any deal.

They met, probably on the Saturday afternoon, afte
the banks had closed. In return for a share of the pro
ceeds and enough money to get himself out of his imme
diate trouble, Ron gave Edward the map, and a copy o
the letter. The original of the letter was to go to Edwar
when the deal was completed. What Edward actuall
gave Ron was not cash, however, but a bank draft, no
cashable until Monday, when the banks opened. I hav
no doubt that during this meeting Edward also learne
everything Ron knew about the people who were inno
cently and tangentially involved: Grace, Amelia, Jaso
Lynx Interiors, the whole works. Ron may even hav
mentioned that he had already asked Margaret an
Brew Tyrell for money, that they were old friends. H
certainly said that we were going to the mountain lan
the following day. Perhaps Edward said he'd be there

too, that he and Ron should quietly look around, locate the shaft, see the lay of the land.

When they parted, Ron thought he had a deal that was going to yield a lot of money. He was so sure of it that when Vaddy Halved insisted on being paid that night, Ron didn't want to disclose the existence of the bank draft. He didn't want to give Vaddy even a hint of the deal he was working. Instead, he engaged in a long delaying action. He was taken to Chappy's house to ask for money, he was taken to a loan shark—where he would, no doubt, have received what he needed except that his escorts were edgy and dragged him off. Only when the threat became violent and imminent did he show the bank draft, make up some story about it, and get Vaddy to agree to wait until Monday, when Ron could cash the draft.

Throughout these peregrinations Ron and Vaddy were followed by Edward. Edward had no intention of letting Ron out of his sight.

On Sunday, Edward either followed us to the land or was there before we arrived. The three of us, Grace, Ron and I, were separated at various times during that afternoon as we wandered about, looking for mushrooms. Edward took the opportunity offered by one such separation to offer Ron cash for the bank draft and the letter, if Ron had it with him. Ron would have traded the bank draft for money in a minute, though he may not have been willing to sell the letter. He told the truth. He didn't have either document with him.

Edward didn't want the draft cashed. While the draft did not bear his name, it could be connected to him through bank records. He told Ron he'd left something for him back at the shaft, under the plank, maybe, or under the toilet-paper tin. Edward had worked around mines throughout his career; though he'd left the nitty-gritty behind him, he knew how to use explosives in a workmanlike manner. Workmanlike. Not expert. He had intended that the shaft be covered and Ron killed, not that Ron should be blown down into the shaft, which would then necessitate rescue workers going down after him.

Ron and Edward were focused on the wrong shaft, of course. I'd mentioned the potty shaft to Ron, but not the spring shaft. We didn't see the spring shaft that Sunday. Ron didn't know it was there, nor did Edward, though "full fathom five" certainly should have conveyed the idea of a watery grave, not a dry one. After that Sunday, Edward returned to the property, probably several times, on one occasion being run off by Bela. Sooner or later he found the right shaft. Both Carolyn and Wilson tell me that Edward is deathly afraid of water. He came close to drowning as a child, and water gives him the horrors, so he did not dive into the shaft. He decided to recover the treasure through the cliff wall, rather than from inside it.

Edward's more immediate concern was to find the bank draft and the original of Hector's letter to him. He didn't want either showing up later and involving him in Ron's murder. He thought Margaret might have the letter, and he may have killed her to prevent her talking about his being there. He wrecked your place, Grace, hunting for the letter. He followed me around, thinking I might lead him to the letter. He even worked himself up into a phony rage over Wilson and accused me of conspiracy, just to see if I'd fly into a fury and let something slip. I didn't; but Amelia did. She told him her plans for the institute had been canceled, which no *doubt delighted him. He could take all the time in the world.*

Edward either bought or rented another car for all this cruising around, since his own was so readily identifiable. It was probably not coincidence that it resembled Vaddy's car. By that first Sunday morning, Edward knew we had seen Vaddy's car, and it was to his advantage if we knew we were followed, to think it was Vaddy doing it.

All the time Edward was searching for the letter, the original was in Schnitz's cat box with the jewelry inventory, where Ron had put it after he made the copy. The letter to Maddox, which was not immediately useful, Ron had taken home with him, but the Edward letter and inventory he wanted to keep well hidden. He was bright enough to know they were the only hold he had over Edward.

We know Ron had the bank draft with him Saturday night and did not have it with him Sunday. He went into Grace's house only briefly on Sunday morning. The bank draft is in Grace's house, somewhere.

Also missing is a cache of drugs. No one knows where they are. I should not be surprised if Ron actually gave them to Margaret.

Edward Credable followed me to the mountains last Saturday afternoon. I went down the shaft in a wet suit, which must have surprised the hell out of him. He cut my ropes, let himself down the face of the cliff, and began drilling holes to receive enough dynamite to blow a hole in the shaft and kill me. I have wondered since why he simply didn't shoot me as he had Bela. I believe he didn't think he had to bother. He figured, no doubt, that with the shaft collapsed, I'd be out of the way and the fortune would be utterly safe until he came for it.

My plan had been to drain the shaft and find Admar's bones. Toward that end, I talked Chappy into giving me a shaped charge. Geologists sometimes use them for seismography. While Edward drilled holes in the rock of the cliff face, I set the shaped charge against the outer wall of the shaft. Just before Edward could bury me, I set off the charge. Edward was hanging on a rope just outside, in the full force of the blast. His remains lie under shattered stone on the slope below the rock terrace. Admar's skeleton remains in the shaft, buried under stone. I retrieved the jewels. They're in the little davenport desk, soon to be discovered. They are Amelia's, are they not?

Does she need to know the skeleton in the shaft was her mother? Does she need to know her father killed her mother? Does anyone need to know anything about all this?

Grace looked up from the pages, tears in her eyes. "She knows it's her mother, Jason."

"She thinks her mother committed suicide. She knows nothing about the Admar bit."

"But someone will find him."

"No. I don't think they ever will. It may be a very long time before anyone discovers Edward's body, either."

Her brow furrowed. I knew what she was thinking. Was she responsible for doing anything? After a time her face cleared. She had decided she wasn't.

I gave her the other envelope, the one with the jewelry inventory in it. She glanced at it, her mouth making a round *O*. It did read like something out of Ali Baba.

"What happened to the bank draft?" she asked. "What happened to the original letter to Edward?"

"Let's go over to your house," I suggested. "I have an idea."

We went in through her kitchen, into the little back hall, where Critter's box is kept. If the hiding place had worked for Ron at my place, why not here? I got some newspapers and partially emptied the litter box. Nothing. Then, as I was about to put it down, I decided to turn it over. There it was, taped to the bottom. The same-type Ziploc bag, and the original letter to Edward inside it. And the original of the inventory. And the bank draft. Which Ron had already endorsed.

Which Ron had already endorsed. With Grace trailing along, I took the documents, went through to Grace's desk, found a deposit slip in her checkbook, and made it out.

"I couldn't," she said, putting her hand on top of mine. "Besides, if you do that, I'll get into it with the IRS."

I shrugged. "It's endorsed. Where would you like it to go?"

"All the time I was reading that thing you wrote, I was thinking about those bones. I wondered where she could have gone, if she'd needed to. I wondered if she was running away with Admar because she loved him, or whether she loved him because he offered her a way out. I thought about that thing in Santa Fe, how those women had no one to turn to. Janet Wirtz was abused. Valerie will be if she marries that man. That other girl, the case I found, she was . . .

"Why don't we send it to the women's shelter?"

We sent it to the women's shelter.

A few last words.

Ron's drug cache never turned up. We have no idea

what he did with it. If Margaret ever had it, it has been quietly tidied away.

Amelia plans to sell the land, using the money she receives to buy a new site in Aspen for her institute. I begged off from any further involvement. Somehow I feel she needs something new and wonderful, without old memories hanging on.

Valerie French called me about a week after the dinner party at her house to say she'd broken up with Espy, and had I meant it that I'd like her to work for me? Just occasionally, she said, if she found something wonderful. I told her I had meant it, and I asked what the problem had been with Espy. She said she wasn't quite sure; he just wasn't what she'd thought he was.

Grace and I will be married the end of this week, by a judge, very quietly. We're taking a honeymoon in the Bahamas. I've never been there. Grace and I need something new and wonderful as well.

Jason Lynx
antiques dealer, interior decorator, and sleuth

A. J. ORDE

Published by Fawcett Books.
Available in your local bookstore.